Ca   **tion.**

So   machine
se   her, she was certain the message
wasn't good news.

She pressed Play, then listened as a voice said, "Carrie, it's me"—a voice so filled with distress she barely recognized it as her sister's.

"I'm just phoning to tell you I'm going to disappear for a while," Jenny's message went on. "I'm okay, but there's been some trouble and...well, I didn't want you to worry when you couldn't reach me. And...this is important. If anyone comes looking for me—and I mean *anyone*—just say you haven't heard from me in days. I'll call again when I've figured out what I'm doing. Bye."

Just as Carrie picked up the phone to try her sister's number, someone knocked on the front door. She hurried over and checked the peephole. Outside stood a stranger. Somewhere in his mid-thirties, he was the epitome of tall, dark and handsome. He knocked again.

She fought the temptation to pretend she wasn't home. By talking to him, she might find out what was going on. "Yes?" she said through the door.

"Carrie O'Reilly?"

"Yes?"

"Carrie, my name's Sam Evans. I'm looking for your sister."

Dear Reader,

Mixed Messages is the twenty-eighth novel I've written for Harlequin, and each has been special to me in its own way.

As I wrote this story, though, Sam Evans and Carrie O'Reilly were facing such a seemingly impossible task that I found myself racking my brain trying to figure out how they were going to make it through the book alive, let alone attain the happy ending they deserved.

Sam Evans is a man with a past that threatens to dog him for the rest of his life. When he falls in love with Carrie, he fears it will prevent her from loving him back.

Carrie O'Reilly isn't a woman who gives her heart easily. So when she falls in love with Sam, and then learns about his deep dark secret, she can't help wondering if she's made the mistake of her life.

But despite all odds, they do find their happy ending.

I sincerely hope you enjoy their story, and that you breathe the same sigh of relief when you finish reading it as I did when I finished writing it.

Warmest wishes,

Dawn Stewardson

MIXED MESSAGES
Dawn Stewardson

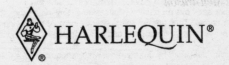

HARLEQUIN®

TORONTO • NEW YORK • LONDON
AMSTERDAM • PARIS • SYDNEY • HAMBURG
STOCKHOLM • ATHENS • TOKYO • MILAN • MADRID
PRAGUE • WARSAW • BUDAPEST • AUCKLAND

ISBN 0-373-70827-0

MIXED MESSAGES

This edition published by arrangement with Harlequin Books S.A.

® and TM are trademarks of the publisher. Trademarks indicated with ® are registered in the United States Patent and Trademark Office, the Canadian Trade Marks Office and in other countries.

Printed in U.S.A.

To John, always.

With special thanks to Superromance author and friend
Janice Carter, who helped fill the holes in my plot.

PROLOGUE

Twenty years earlier

"EARTH TO EARTH, ashes to ashes, dust to dust." As the minister spoke, Auntie Liz squeezed Carrie's hand.

She swallowed hard, then looked up. Uncle Ken gave her a sad smile, but it was Auntie Liz she focused on. Because that was almost like looking at her mother—before Mummy got sick.

Twins weren't the exact same people, though. And an aunt wasn't a mother, no matter how nice she was.

"Okay?" she whispered.

"Uh-huh," Carrie whispered back. But she wasn't. She was scared and her tummy felt as if there were knives in it. She didn't know what it would be like to live with her aunt and uncle. And her two cousins were awfully noisy, even worse than most boys.

Beside her, Jenny had started making the funny little sound she sometimes made before she began crying.

"Shhh," Carrie murmured. "Be good for just another minute, okay?"

"In sure and certain hope of the Resurrection unto eternal life," the minister concluded. "Amen."

"Amen," everyone repeated.

Jenny sniffed loudly.

"It's okay," Carrie whispered, wrapping her arm around her sister's shoulders. "Everything's gonna be okay."

Only a few days ago, Mummy had said, "Jenny's going to need a big sister who loves her a lot. And I'm counting on you to watch out for her."

"I will," she'd promised. And she always kept her promises.

Around them, the grown-ups began to move away from the grave, a few of them coming over to talk to her aunt and uncle.

"We can go back to the limo now," her cousin Tyler said.

Carrie nodded, but she didn't want to go just yet. Staring at the ground, she blinked her eyes fast so the tears stinging them couldn't leak out. She wasn't going to cry anymore. And she'd make sure Jenny didn't, either.

Mummy had said that Auntie Liz and Uncle Ken would look after them forever. But Carrie knew she'd better be the one to look after Jenny. That way neither of them would be a bother, and nobody would decide to stop loving them—the way people sometimes did. The way their father had.

When he left, Carrie had only been five. The same age Jenny was now. But she'd never forgotten why he'd gone. She was never in a million years going to tell Jenny, but she could still hear him yelling at their mother.

"I can't stand it!" he'd shouted. "That baby's been screaming every single night since we brought her home from the hospital. I told you I didn't want another kid, but did you care? No. And now I'm walking around like a zombie.

"I'm falling apart, Kate. And for what? So I can be a meal ticket for a wife who wouldn't even notice if I wasn't here? You're so wrapped up in those kids you don't have a second for me."

Swallowing hard again, Carrie thought about how Auntie Liz had sat them down and told them that Mummy hadn't died because of anything they'd done.

"And she didn't want to leave either of you," she'd said. "That's the last thing on earth she wanted. If she hadn't gotten sick, she'd have stayed and watched you both grow up. She'd have still been here when you had little girls of your own. It's just that sometimes things don't happen the way we want. No matter how much we want them to."

Carrie knew that wasn't true, though. If you wanted something bad enough, and tried hard enough, you could always get it.

That's what her favorite teacher in the whole world said. So she was going to be good as gold. And she'd make sure Jenny was, too. Then Auntie Liz would never go away. Or Uncle Ken, either.

"Carrie?" Jenny whined. "Carrie, I'm tired from standin'."

Auntie Liz stopped talking in the middle of a sentence and glanced down at Jenny.

Carrie looked up again and made herself smile. "It's okay. I'll take care of her." She gave her little sister a hug. "When we get back to Auntie Liz's," she whispered, "I'll draw some pictures and you can color them. You always like that."

CHAPTER ONE

SAM EVANS COULD FEEL the past breathing down his neck and it was scaring the hell out of him.

Glancing at Carrie O'Reilly's empty driveway once again, he ordered himself to relax. The town houses on her side of the cul-de-sac backed onto the west bank of Mimico Creek. By car, there was no access to them except from the street itself, so she couldn't possibly arrive home without his spotting her.

As anxious as he was to talk to her, though, he couldn't stop thinking it might be better if she didn't discover him lying in wait. Finally deciding there was no "might" about it, he drove off and found a doughnut shop on Lake Shore Boulevard. Coffee and a glazed chocolate doughnut didn't add up to much of a dinner, but he knew anything more wouldn't sit well. After drinking a refill of coffee, just to kill another ten minutes, he headed back to Carrie's. This time, when he turned onto the street, he breathed a sigh of relief. A blue Neon was just pulling into her driveway.

He parked, then watched while she got out of the car. She wasn't what he'd been expecting.

Jenny had told him her sister illustrated children's books. Given that, he'd imagined someone with

Jenny's red hair but without her flash. An artsy, but less dramatic version was what he'd pictured.

In reality, Carrie looked nothing like her sister. And even though he'd be hard pressed to define what he meant by "artsy," it wasn't Carrie O'Reilly.

She was wearing a simple white dress, short enough to make him notice she had great legs. And her long hair, tied smoothly back from her face, was so dark it was almost black.

After unloading a couple of bags from the trunk, she slammed it shut and went into the house. He sat in his car for a little longer, then climbed out into the muggy air—trying to convince himself, once again, that he'd be able to get out of this mess he was in.

All he needed was a little help.

DESPITE HER IRISH heritage, Carrie O'Reilly didn't believe that kissing the Blarney stone endowed people with the gift of eloquence. She also had serious doubts about the existence of leprechauns, although she'd be delighted to meet one who would lead her to a pot of gold.

But she did believe in intuition. So when the blinking light on her answering machine sent a tiny chill through her, she was certain the message wasn't good news.

She pressed Play, then listened as a voice said, "Carrie, it's me." A voice so filled with distress that she barely recognized it as her sister's. "I'm just phoning to tell you I'm going to disappear for a while."

Disappear? There was nothing tiny about the chill that shot through her this time.

"I'm okay, but there's been some trouble and...well, I didn't want you to worry when you couldn't reach me. And...this is important. If anyone comes looking for me, and I mean anyone, just say you haven't talked to me in days. I'll call again when I've figured out exactly what I'm doing. Bye."

Carrie grabbed the cordless and pressed the speed dial for Jenny's number, her heart pounding. Whatever was wrong, it had Jenny so frightened she didn't know what she should be doing—aside from disappearing.

Taking a deep breath as the call connected, she told herself to calm down. But worrying about her little sister came as naturally as breathing.

She'd taken responsibility for Jenny when they were children, and she was feeling the same panic now that she'd felt so many times since then. With any luck, though, Jenny hadn't left yet and—

A knock on the front door made her jump. Had the someone Jenny figured would be looking for her come calling?

Heading out of the kitchen, the phone to her ear, Carrie swore under her breath when Jenny's machine picked up.

"Jenny?" she said after the beep. "Jenny, are you home?"

There was only silence.

Clicking off the phone, she set it down on the hall table and checked the peephole.

Outside, in the still-bright sunshine of the July evening, stood a stranger. Somewhere in his mid-thirties, wearing a shirt the color of well-faded denim, he was the epitome of tall, dark and handsome. But if he was the someone, he had to be bad news.

He knocked again.

She fought the temptation to pretend she wasn't in. If he *was* looking for Jenny, then by talking to him she might find out what was going on.

"Yes?" she said through the door.

"Carrie O'Reilly?"

"Yes?"

"Carrie, my name's Sam Evans. I'm a friend of your sister's."

Yet another chill raced through her, almost making her wish she hadn't come within ten feet of the door. But listening to what he had to say was the only sensible thing to do.

When the door opened to the width of its chain, and cool air drifted out from inside, Sam smiled at Carrie.

She was even more attractive than he'd realized from a distance, with deep-gray eyes and a full mouth. And although it struck him as downright laughable, considering the circumstances, he could feel the slow heat of sexual awareness begin to curl lazily inside him.

Firmly, he told himself the only thing her appearance should be making him feel was grateful. It would give him a perfectly innocuous opening line, and if anything had ever needed easing into, it was his reason for being here.

"You don't look like Jenny," he said.

"No. I inherited the black Irish genes in the family."

He waited for her to say more.

She didn't. And she didn't take the door off the chain. She simply stood eyeing him, her expression both suspicious and apprehensive.

"Do you think I could come in?" he asked at last. "I've got to talk to you."

"I'm afraid I'm expecting company."

When she added "Any minute now," he decided she wasn't expecting a soul.

"But if you'd like to tell me what it's about...?"

So much for easing into things. "All right," he said. "Have you heard from Jenny in the past few hours?"

"No."

"Then you don't know what's happened, but..." He stopped speaking when a couple came out of the adjoining town house and glanced curiously over at him.

Once they started discussing something about their front yard, he quietly said, "Look, Jenny's taken off and I have to find her. And I know the two of you are close, so if anyone can help me figure out where she's gone..."

He hadn't been counting on Carrie's agreeing to help straight away, and sure enough, she said, "If Jenny's taken off, she probably doesn't want anyone figuring out where she's gone."

"No, she probably doesn't," he admitted. But if he didn't get to her first...

He could feel the fear that both of them were in

more trouble than they could handle growing
stronger. Doing his best to ignore it, he said, "I know
this is going to sound clichéd, but we could be talking
life or death."

Life or death. Carrie's throat went dry as the words
began echoing in her head. Jenny had gotten herself
into a few tight spots over the years, but they'd all
been typical teenage things—nothing nearly as serious as Sam Evans was painting this to be.

For a few seconds, she tried to convince herself he
was exaggerating. But if he was, then why had Jenny
sounded so panicky? And why was she running?

"Carrie?"

She focused on him again.

He'd produced a business card that identified him
as the president of Port Credit Custom Boats.

"This really isn't something we should be talking
about out here," he said as she looked at it. "Look,
I like your sister," he added when she still didn't
unlatch the chain. "I don't want anything awful happening to her. But if we don't find her..."

She hesitated for another second. Then, telling herself he knew her neighbors had gotten a good look at
him, she let him in.

The entrance hall was decorated with framed originals of her book illustrations, and as she closed the
door, she could see his gaze traveling over them.

"Are those yours?" he asked. "I mean, ones
you've done?"

She nodded, feeling a bit less anxious about his
being inside. If he knew what she did for a living,

then at least he and Jenny had to be more than nodding acquaintances.

"They're terrific," he said.

"I keep my favorites. The rest go to a gallery that specializes in illustrative work."

Sam nodded. "They're so bright and... I'll bet kids just love them."

"Fortunately, they seem to."

He wasn't here to admire her work, though. He was here to talk about her sister being in life-or-death danger, so she led the way into the living room. While he settled himself on the couch, she perched on one of the chairs—trying not to look half as worried as she felt.

She doubted she was succeeding, but he was no picture of equanimity, either. Not the way he was glancing everywhere except at her, as if he didn't have the foggiest idea how to begin.

Eventually meeting her gaze, he said, "This has to do with Leo Castanza."

"Oh?" Leo. She should have guessed. She waited for Sam to go on, certain he was about to give her yet another reason for wishing Jenny had never gotten involved with Leo. As if his reputation with women and the fact that he was more than twenty years older than Jenny weren't reasons enough.

"The thing is..." Sam paused, resting his hands on his knees and looking even more uncomfortable. "Leo killed someone," he said bluntly. "It happened at his house. Jenny was there. She called and told me about it before she took off."

Carrie felt as if someone had punched her. Hard. "Is she all right?" she managed to ask.

"As far as I know."

"And... Oh, Lord, she didn't have anything to do with it, did she?"

"No."

Thank heavens for that. But Leo? A murderer?

She might not be thrilled about Jenny going out with him, but he was one of Toronto's high-profile criminal lawyers. How could he possibly have killed anybody? And why had Jenny told this Sam Evans about it? Until a few minutes ago, Carrie had never even heard Sam's name.

Before she could ask anything aloud, he said, "Maybe I'd better start at the beginning."

"Yes. That's probably a good idea." Taking a deep breath that didn't calm her nearly enough, she made herself sit back in the chair. Before she could figure out how to help Jenny, she needed to know exactly what had happened.

"Okay. A few weeks ago, Leo approached me about building a boat for him. Since then, he and I have met at his house half a dozen times to customize the design specs. And Jenny's been sitting in on our discussions because he wanted her ideas. That's how I got to know her. At any rate, we wrapped up the remaining loose ends this afternoon. And it happened not long after I left."

"'It' being that Leo...murdered someone." Maybe by saying the words aloud she could make the reality of them sink in.

Sam nodded. "It was some guy named Bud. He

came by and the two of them went into the study. The next thing Jenny knew, Leo was telling her… Well, he said Bud had threatened him, and that he'd only been defending himself.''

''Threatened him how?''

''I don't know. But the bottom line is that Leo brained the guy with a cast-bronze sculpture.''

''Oh, Lord,'' Carrie whispered.

''And whether he meant to kill him or not, Bud's dead.'' Pushing himself up from the couch, Sam paced across to the window and stood staring out. When he finally turned and looked over at her, his mouth was set in a tight line.

''Here's the kicker,'' he said. ''Leo told Jenny the cops would have no choice but to charge him with murder. And that even if he got off, his reputation would be ruined. So he decided to pin it on me.''

''He what?''

Sam merely nodded.

''But that's absurd!''

''He didn't figure it was. And he wanted Jenny to help him.''

''You mean to tell the police you'd done it?''

''Not quite. He didn't ask her to say she'd actually seen the murder. But he wanted her to tell them I was still there when Bud arrived, and that she knew the three of us were in Leo's study when it happened.''

''She'd never lie about something like that. I know she sometimes comes across as a little flaky, but she'd never go along with anything so…immoral.''

''I didn't think she would. But she said she was

afraid of what Leo would do if he thought she wasn't going to.''

Staring at her shoes, Carrie did her best not to imagine exactly what Jenny had been afraid Leo would do. But imagining was only too easy.

''So she waited for a chance,'' Sam continued. ''Then she grabbed the keys to his Caddy and ran— headed for her apartment to pack a few things. That's when she called to warn me what he was up to. And after that... Well, I don't know where she went from there. That's why I need your help.''

Carrie hesitated, trying to decide whether helping Sam and helping Jenny would be one and the same. ''I take it you haven't gone to the police? Told them what really happened?'' she said to buy herself time.

Sam slowly shook his head. He'd known she was going to ask about that. After all, to the average law-abiding citizen it would seem the logical thing to do. But it didn't to him.

Been there, done that, he said silently. And he wasn't going there again.

''I didn't think it would be wise to go to the cops,'' he told her. ''I went straight home after I left Leo's. And since I live alone, there's nobody to back me up about when I got there. So if Leo says I was still at his place long after I'd actually left...

''Carrie, I'd have gone to the cops if Jenny'd agreed to go with me. When she phoned, I tried to make her see that's what she should do. But even while we were talking she was throwing things into a suitcase—in such a panic she just wasn't listening to reason.

"And I figured that going to the police on my own... Well, by then Leo would have already given them his version of things. So if they'd bought it, when I came strolling in they'd have—"

"But they wouldn't have simply bought it. They'd... No, wait, there probably isn't even anything for them to buy. Once the initial shock wore off, Leo would have realized he had to tell the truth. I mean, he's got to know all there is to know about crime scene investigations. He must have realized the evidence was pointing straight at him, and that he'd just make things worse for himself by lying."

"Only if the cops realized that's what he was doing, only if they could tell he'd rearranged things to make it look as if I'd done it. And as you said, he's got to know all there is to know about crime scenes, so—"

"But the idea that he could actually..."

When Carrie stopped midsentence, Sam's gut tensed. He held his breath until she began speaking again, then exhaled a silent sigh of relief when she merely said, "There's something you haven't told me, isn't there."

It hadn't occurred to her that he might be lying. Not yet. But unless he was awfully lucky, sooner or later it would.

"There's evidence Leo can use to back up his story," he made himself admit. "Not *real* evidence, but a couple of things... Look, why don't I just tell you exactly what Jenny said he was going to tell the cops, let you hear for yourself how neatly it hangs together."

Carrie nodded. Sam obviously needed to talk, and she wouldn't have stopped him even if she could. The more details she knew, the better.

"He was going to tell them Bud had asked me to build a boat for him, that we had a verbal contract. But that, this afternoon, he said he'd changed his mind. And when he did, I got angry and... Well, according to Leo's story, I was drunk. Drunk enough that I started a fight with Bud and ended up killing him."

"But...Sam, it doesn't really matter what Leo says. Or how believable it sounds. Not when Jenny knows you were gone before Bud even arrived."

"Right. And that's why I have to find her. Because, as I said, there are a couple of things... Carrie, I had a drink with Leo and Jenny after our meeting. Only one. But if he tells the cops it was half a dozen, how will they know he's lying? They'll only know there's a glass with remnants of Scotch in it and my prints on it.

"And worse yet, my prints are on that sculpture. Leo just bought it a couple of days ago—it's a bronze of a polar bear—and he was excited about its being number one of a limited edition. So when he was showing it to me, I acted suitably impressed—and picked it up to have a closer look."

"But his prints must be on it, too. If he—"

"Right, they must be. But that's not going to arouse any suspicions when he owns it. And...look, my first priority has to be finding Jenny. Once she's told the police I wasn't even there, it won't matter if they tie me up with questioning for a week. But right now it's critical that I find her. Fast.

"Hell, I don't want to terrify you, but taking off on her own the way she did... Well, she figures Leo's going to send someone looking for her. And considering the sort of people he must know..."

That just-been-punched feeling seized Carrie again. Leo often defended the scum of the earth; some of the city's most vicious criminals owed him their freedom. She didn't even want to think about who he could send after Jenny. Or about what they'd do when they caught up with her.

"Do you figure Leo *would* send someone looking for her?" she asked. At least, if Sam doubted that, things might not be so... He didn't doubt it, though. He was already nodding.

"If Leo's told the cops that I killed this guy, he'd want Jenny out of the picture. Otherwise, she could show up any minute and tell them the truth.

"But look," he added, "she'll be okay as long as we find her first. We'll convince her she has to give the police a statement, and once she's done that, it'll be too late for Leo to try anything."

"Yes, you're right. We have to..." The rest of the words caught in Carrie's throat. Something had been nagging away in the back of her mind, and she'd suddenly realized what it was.

"Are you okay?" Sam said.

"I...yes, I'm just feeling a little shaky. If I get some water I'll be fine." She turned and started for the kitchen, a bone-chilling fear creeping through her.

She'd been so caught off guard by what Sam had

been saying that she hadn't asked herself the obvious question. But now it was flashing inside her head like a bright neon sign.

How could she be sure that Leo's "story" wasn't actually the truth? That Sam hadn't killed this Bud person in a drunken fight? And that after he'd sobered up, he'd decided he'd better get rid of Jenny?

Maybe she *had* seen the murder. And maybe she wasn't running from Leo. Maybe she was running from Sam.

Her heart pounding, Carrie turned on the water and began mentally replaying their conversation. Had he said anything that was inconsistent? Anything that should have told her he was lying?

She couldn't think of a thing. Then, like a bolt from the blue, something else struck her.

If *Sam* had killed Bud, why would Jenny be running? Why wouldn't she have simply stayed with Leo while he called the police? Stayed and talked to them with him?

Of course. That would have been the only logical thing to do. If Leo's story was true, Jenny would have stayed right where she was. Which meant she must be running from *him*.

Weak with relief that she didn't have a murderer in her house, Carrie turned off the water and headed back out of the kitchen. Then, just as she walked into the living room, she realized she might have come to the wrong conclusion.

How could she be certain that Sam hadn't killed Bud, then murdered Leo, as well? And if that was the case, Jenny would have taken off before he could kill her.

"Feel all right now?" he asked.

She nodded, certain she'd never felt worse.

"Good. Then, if you don't have any better ideas, I think we should start by checking Jenny's apartment. See if there's any clue to where she's gone. Do you have a key to her place?"

"Yes," she admitted. There wasn't much point in saying no. She doubted the lack of a key would slow Sam down for even a second.

But what if they did turn up a clue? What if she helped him find Jenny and he was the killer?

The answer to that was painfully obvious. She'd be signing her sister's death warrant. And her own, too. She had no doubt about that.

On the other hand, if it was Leo who wanted Jenny dead and she didn't help Sam... Fleetingly, she searched his face for the truth.

All she saw was a darkly attractive man with a very worried look in his eyes. She had no idea, though, whether he was worried because he was being railroaded or because he was trying to get away with murder and knew he might not succeed.

"Carrie? You're sure you're not still feeling shaky?"

"No, I'm fine, thanks."

"Good, then let's get going."

"Right," she said, frantically trying to decide what to do. She glanced around the room, praying for inspiration. Then her gaze fell on the stereo and an idea came to her.

The news media had to be covering the story. Wouldn't listening to what they were reporting help her determine the truth? With any luck, it would.

"Sam?" she said as he started for the front door.

He looked back.

"I can't stop thinking that Leo must have realized he'd be crazy to try framing you—especially after Jenny was gone. And if he's told the police the truth, we're worrying for nothing. So why don't we see what they're saying on the radio before we do anything else."

ONE MOMENT THERE'D BEEN sympathy in Carrie's gray eyes, the next they'd darkened with fear.

That, Sam knew, was when it had dawned on her that *he* might have been the one who'd killed Bud. And that *he* might be the one her sister was running from. But he just hadn't been able to think of any magic words that would convince her he was telling the truth.

Now, watching her tune in to station after station, he was still desperately wishing he could. Because if she came across a report saying that Sam Evans was the prime suspect in the murder, and that anyone who knew his whereabouts should immediately contact the police, it might make her decide she'd better do exactly that.

By this point, though, she must have paused on at least half a dozen stations, and there still hadn't been a word about the murder. The obvious question was, why not?

Finally, she asked it.

"I don't know," he told her.

"Well, what frequency is that all-news station?"

"Ten-eighty," he said, figuring that even if he didn't tell her, she'd locate it sooner or later.

Besides, if the cops were looking for him, he'd be better off knowing it. He'd just have to hope that if they were, learning about it wouldn't spook her too badly.

"Here it is," she murmured as an announcer said, "Remember, if you see news in the making, call Toronto's news hotline at 555-NEWS."

"Where's your phone?" Sam asked. Whatever was going on, he might as well find out and get it over with.

Carrie wordlessly headed into the front hallway and returned with a cordless.

He punched in the number, and when a woman answered, he said, "There was something on another station about a man being murdered today."

"In Toronto?"

"Uh-huh, in Rosedale. Will you be updating the story soon?"

"Just a moment, please."

"What are they saying?" Carrie whispered.

"I'm on hold."

"Sir?" the woman said, coming back on the line. "Which station did you hear that story on?"

"I'm not sure."

"Well, we have nothing about a recent murder. And if there'd been one, we'd certainly know."

"Oh. Then I guess I heard wrong. Sorry to have bothered you."

"No bother, sir. And thank you for listening to 1080 News."

"She says there wasn't any murder," he told Carrie, clicking off.

"But how could they not know about it by now? Do you think the police are keeping it quiet?"

"No, there's not a chance. The first thing they'd have done was tape off the property as a crime scene. And when we're talking a neighborhood like Rosedale, the media would be on the story like white on rice."

"Then...?"

"Leo can't have called the cops."

"You mean he didn't report the murder?"

"He can't have."

"Then what's he doing?"

"He must have changed his mind. After Jenny took off, he must have decided it would be too risky to try framing me when she knew the truth. So he decided to try a cover-up instead."

"But... Sam, Jenny still knows what really happened. Regardless of what he tries."

"Right, she does. But by getting rid of Bud's body and destroying the evidence that there *was* a murder, he'd be setting things up so it would be her word against his. So that if she *did* go to the cops, he could say she was lying—maybe tell them she'd done some drugs and had been hallucinating or something. Even so, he'll still be hoping to catch up with her before she can decide to talk to them."

Sam's final words started a fresh ring of fear forming around Carrie's heart. If he had things figured right, Leo would do whatever it took to keep her sister quiet. She didn't doubt that for a second.

But Sam's theory wasn't the only feasible explanation for the lack of news coverage.

The other, every bit as plausible one, was that right this minute Leo was lying dead in his study next to Bud. And if that was true, she was standing here next to their killer.

CHAPTER TWO

EVER SINCE SHE AND SAM had left her place, Carrie had been making a concerted effort to think about anything and everything except the fact that he might be a murderer.

For the past few minutes she'd been focused on the horrendous traffic heading for the Blue Jays game. It had Sam's Mustang inching forward at crawl speed.

Once they made it past the SkyDome, though, and began picking up speed, she knew they'd soon be reaching their destination—which sent her mind zooming back to the question of whether Sam had been telling her the truth or lying through his teeth.

Glancing across at him, she tried assuring herself once more that he'd never have changed his mind and suggested going to Leo's place first, rather than Jenny's, if he'd killed two men there mere hours ago.

Unless he had a reason that hadn't occurred to her. And since that was entirely possible, she couldn't help fearing that she was completely insane to have teamed up with him.

She wasn't really teaming up with him, though. And even if he *was* a killer, she had to be fairly safe as long as he figured she could lead him to Jenny. Of course, if he decided she wasn't being any help...

She sat watching him anxiously as he drove. It scared her silly to think about what might happen if he decided she was expendable. But she couldn't just wait at home doing nothing when Jenny was in danger. And if she discovered Sam's story wasn't the true one, she'd disappear faster than a rabbit down its hole.

Just as she was telling herself that, he glanced over and caught her looking at him. She scrambled for something to say, but nothing came.

After a few awkward seconds, he said, "Have you ever been to Leo's?"

She shook her head. "He wasn't one of my favorite people even before today."

"I'd have been surprised to hear he was. I've got a kid sister, too, and if she'd ever gotten mixed up with someone like him, our father would have locked her in her room until she came to her senses—even if it had taken years."

"I guess that's what I should have done with Jenny."

Sam shot her a wry look. "It would have been a little tricky, considering she doesn't live with you."

"Yes…well, you know what I mean." Leaving it at that, she sat trying to imagine, as she had a million times before, what growing up with a caring father would have been like.

Not that Uncle Ken hadn't been terrific. In fact, with both of his own children being boys, she'd always felt that he'd treated her and Jenny as if they were very special.

Still, Jenny hadn't had much male attention when

she was really little. And maybe, if their father hadn't abandoned them...

She mentally shook her head. Jenny might have gotten involved with Leo because she was searching for a father figure, or that might not have had anything to do with it at all. Either way, there was little point in wondering how differently life would have unfolded if their father hadn't walked out. That was ancient history.

When it came to the more recent past, though, even if she couldn't have locked Jenny in her room, she should have done *something*. But Jenny had told her about Leo in one breath and issued an ultimatum in the next—she didn't want to hear a single critical comment about her relationship with the man.

So, rather than risk causing a rift between them, for the past few months Carrie had been biting her tongue when it came to Leo. Now, of course, it looked as if she'd played things wrong. If she'd objected more strongly, Jenny might not be in this mess.

"How did Jenny and Leo meet?" Sam asked, glancing over once more.

"At some party."

When he didn't reply to that, she told herself not to spend any more time worrying about how she could have handled the "Leo situation" better, and turned her thoughts to the immediate future.

Assuming Leo was alive and well, what on earth were they going to do when they reached his place and had to face him?

Finally, she asked Sam.

"We'll just have to play things by ear," he told her.

"I guess," she agreed. But she'd feel a lot better if they had a more specific plan. Besides, she knew something that he might not be aware of.

"Sam?" she said.

He looked across at her again.

"Jenny once told me that Leo has a gun."

"We'll be okay."

"But…if he's already killed this Bud…"

"We'll be okay," he repeated. Reaching under his seat, he produced a small automatic, then quickly stuck it back out of sight.

Merely glimpsing it was enough to make her mouth go dry. Canada's tough gun laws meant that, for the most part, the only people who had guns were cops and criminals. And Sam was no cop.

Leo had a gun permit, Jenny had explained, because every so often there were threats against his life. Apparently, that was an occupational hazard criminal lawyers faced. But when it came to a man in the boat-building business…

Lord, given the situation, she wasn't sure whether Sam's having a gun made her feel better or worse.

"I had some trouble at my boatyard a while back," he said. "Enough to warrant a gun for protection. And even though I've only got a permit to possess, not to carry, after Jenny phoned, I figured bringing it along was a good idea."

"Yes, you're probably right." She added his explanation to her mental list of things she wasn't sure whether to believe or not, then sat gazing out the window as he drove up Sherbourne and into Rosedale.

The residential neighborhood was one of Toronto's oldest and wealthiest, its tree-lined streets sedate and tranquil. A woman was out walking her Labrador and a couple of teenagers stood talking at the end of a driveway, but no one was whiling away the evening by washing a car or mowing a lawn. The residents of Rosedale paid other people to take care of life's mundane tasks.

The homes themselves were mostly brick and stone mansions. Built between the late 1800s and early 1900s, they sat on lots so large a modern builder would have stuck half a dozen houses on each of them.

Sam turned onto South Drive, then said, "Leo's is that stone one up ahead. And I was right—there's no way he reported the murder. If he had, the place would still be swarming with cops. And Bud's car would probably still be in the driveway. But if Leo *is* trying a cover-up, he'd have gotten rid of it."

Carrie gazed through the gathering twilight at the house. It stood in darkness against the faded light— no yellow police tape indicating a crime scene and no lamps on to suggest that anyone was inside. At least not anyone alive, she reflected uneasily.

"It doesn't look as if Leo's home," she said.

"We'll see." Sam pulled into the driveway as if he owned the place.

"I gather we aren't going for the element of surprise?"

"Not in this neighborhood. If we parked down the

block and started skulking around, someone would
call the cops in two seconds flat. We'll be smarter to
just walk up to the door and knock.''

''And then?''

He shrugged. ''That's where the playing-it-by-ear
part comes in.'' He reached under the seat for his gun
once more, this time tucking it into his waistband and
tugging the bottom of his shirt loose enough to conceal it.

''Ready?'' he asked, looking at her.

''That's hardly the first word that comes to mind.''

He almost smiled. The corners of his mouth turned
up just a tiny bit and amusement flickered in his dark
eyes. At that precise moment, her intuition whispered
that he wasn't a killer.

Reminding herself her intuition didn't have a perfect track record, she climbed out of the car.

They walked up the front steps and rang the bell.
She could hear it chiming through the heavy oak door,
but there was no other sound from inside.

Nervously, she licked her lips. Leo could be any
one of a thousand different places, yet she couldn't
stop imagining both him and his friend lying dead on
a study floor.

After ringing the bell a second time, Sam glanced
slowly around, looking puzzled, as if they'd been expected and he was trying to figure out where their
host could be.

''Maybe he's in the yard someplace,'' he said, so
loudly that his voice had to be carrying halfway down
the block. ''Let's have a look.''

Her heart beating rapidly, she trailed him back down the steps and around the side of the house.

"That's the study," he whispered as they neared a set of French doors leading out onto a ground-level patio.

Carrie was too frightened to even peek inside, but Sam looked through the glass doors, then quietly said, "The body's gone. If we needed proof that he's trying a cover-up, we've got it."

She edged closer and peered into the large room. To one side of the doors sat a desk with a computer on it. To the other was a conversation area with two pairs of wing chairs on either side of a coffee table.

The computer had been left on, and between the dim glow from its screen and the remaining light of evening, she could see the interior of the room fairly well. But her untrained eyes picked up no sign that there'd been a dead body in it this afternoon. No bloodstains on the floor, nothing that indicated a struggle.

"The sculpture's gone too," Sam said quietly. "It was sitting on the credenza behind the desk. And there was an area rug on the floor that's not there now. He must have used it to get the body out. Or maybe he got rid of it because it had bloodstains on it."

"Maybe." Or maybe not, she silently added. With his broad shoulders and lean, muscular build, Sam looked strong enough to have dragged any number of bodies out of that room.

Or he might have killed Bud and Leo in another part of the house. The reality of what had happened and his version of it could be miles apart. So while she'd act as if she believed everything he told her, she'd never for one minute forget that actually trusting him could prove deadly.

"What do you think he'd have done with the body?" she asked.

"Probably took it to some secluded place in the country. In this kind of weather, between the insects and the wild animals, it wouldn't be more than a week or two before…"

When he stopped midsentence, she realized her expression must be saying she didn't really want to hear any more.

"Sorry," he said. "But I read a lot of murder mysteries. You know," he added, glancing into the study again, "I think we should have a look inside. There might be something that would tell us—"

"No!" She grabbed his arm as he reached for the door handle, then pointed at the security company decal on one of the panes of glass.

That made him hesitate, but only for a moment. "The system might not be on," he said. "And if it is, we could say that Jenny asked us to pick her up but nobody answered the front door." With that, he tried the handle. The doors were locked.

When he looked at Carrie again, she knew he was thinking about breaking one of those panes.

"Let's just get out of here," she said. She didn't want to go inside. She didn't want to chance stumbling over a dead body. Or, worse yet, two of them.

She took a couple of backward steps, then stopped when he didn't follow. "Sam, we should go to the police now, right? Now that we know Leo can't have talked to them?''

Sam swore to himself. There was still no way he was doing that. ''I think we'd be a lot smarter to try to find Jenny,'' he said. ''Why don't we get back to the idea of checking out her apartment. Where is it?''

''But if we went to the police they'd put an APB out on her, wouldn't they? And—''

''No, I doubt it.''

''Not when she's practically a witness to the murder? And when she's in danger?''

''Not when all we have at this point is hearsay. We only know what she told me,'' he elaborated when Carrie looked uncertain. ''We don't know anything firsthand. And there isn't even a body where Jenny said it was, so the cops—''

''But that's because Leo moved it. Sam, they couldn't just ignore us. They'd have to investigate. And—''

''You're right, they would. But the first thing they'd want to do is talk to Leo. And if he's decided to drop out of sight for a few days, they wouldn't do anything till he showed up.''

''They wouldn't search the house?''

''Uh-uh. No judge is going to authorize a search warrant without a good reason.''

''You're saying the fact he murdered someone isn't a good reason?''

''Of course it is. Only not when all we have is hearsay. Look, the point is that they wouldn't put out an APB for Jenny just because we said we *think* someone wants her dead. They'd need more than that. And it's too early to consider her a missing person.

"Besides, if we went to them now, we'd be there half the night. Which means that if Leo *does* have someone looking for her, that would give him a better chance of finding her before we even got started. So I *really* think we should keep on worrying about finding her first and talking to the cops second."

Carrie simply studied him, her expression unreadable.

"What?" he finally said. "You're wondering why I still care so much about finding her? When it looks as if Leo's changed his mind about trying to make me the fall guy?"

"I... Yes, I guess I am. If you don't even know her that well, then why..."

He shook his head. "As I said before, I'd hate to see anything awful happen to her. But aside from that, Leo might still be planning to frame me."

"How?"

"I don't know. But he's smart and he's devious, so if Jenny isn't around to tell the police I left Leo's before Bud arrived, I could still find myself up the creek without a paddle."

"Yes...I guess you could."

When Carrie said nothing more, he found himself toying with the idea of telling her the rest of it, of explaining why he had even more reason to be worried.

There were times, though, when only a fool would tell the whole truth, so all he said was, "Should we get going, then? Head for Jenny's apartment and see what we can find there?''

Heart hammering, Carrie told herself she had to decide on her next move.

She'd already ruled out going to the police, because what Sam had said rang true. As things stood, it would mean getting tied up for hours without doing Jenny any good. And if Leo *was* the killer, there was no time to waste.

But if Sam was the killer... If he was, what would he do if she said she didn't think they should go to Jenny's?

She was pretty sure he'd simply go to the apartment on his own. And with only a few J. O'Reillys in the book, it would take him no time at all to determine which address was hers.

So if he was going there one way or the other, didn't it make more sense to go with him? See whether there were any clues or not?

''Jenny lives on Lake Shore Boulevard West,'' she said, praying she was making the right choice.

TO THE LOCALS, the main street that stretched along Lake Ontario's north shore was simply known as ''the Lake Shore.'' And even though Sam figured it had to be about thirty miles in length, he still found it highly coincidental that he, Carrie and Jenny all lived near it.

Jenny, though, won the prize for proximity. You couldn't get any closer than being right on the street itself.

He doubted that her apartment building, a three-story, nondescript brick structure of 1940s vintage, had many modern amenities. And with the streetcar line right out front, it couldn't be a quiet place. But as soon as he turned down the block that ran beside it, he saw where its appeal lay.

A narrow stretch of parkland sat directly between the small tenants' parking lot and the lake.

"It's beautiful, isn't it?" Carrie murmured as he pulled up beside the curb.

When he glanced at her, she was gazing out over the wash of moonlight on the water.

"Uh-huh," he said. "I live by the lake, too, but not this close."

"Oh?" She looked across the car at him, a stray moonbeam highlighting her hair and transforming her face into an ethereal silver portrait.

For the briefest moment he almost forgot they were only together because they had to find her sister. Almost, yet not quite.

Still, it left him with an unsettled feeling. There was something about Carrie O'Reilly that made him far more aware of her than he'd prefer to be. He didn't need a female distraction in his life.

Forcing his gaze from hers, he gestured toward the parking lot. "Jenny doesn't have a car, does she?"

"No."

"And I don't see Leo's Caddy. You think she's still got it?"

"I don't know. I found it hard to believe she'd taken off with it in the first place, but she sounded so terrified that I guess—"

"She sounded terrified *when?*" Earlier, Carrie had

said she hadn't heard from her sister recently. Apparently he wasn't the only one keeping secrets.

He sat eyeing her until she finally said, "I knew Jenny was in trouble before you showed up. She left a message on my machine."

"I see."

For a moment he considered telling her that she should at least have the good grace to be blushing. Instead he just asked, "Are there any *other* relevant facts you haven't mentioned? Like, for example, that she told you where she was taking off to?"

"Sam...her message said almost nothing. I didn't even know what the problem was until you filled me in. All she said was that there'd been some trouble and she was going to disappear for a while. That was it."

"I see," he repeated, not sure whether he should believe her or not. "Well, let's go have a look at her apartment."

Climbing out of the car, he told himself the only thing he needed less than a female distraction was a partner he couldn't trust. And that meant the sooner he and Carrie went their separate ways, the better. But first he had to see if she could help point him in the right direction.

By the time they reached the front door of the building, she'd dug a set of keys out of her purse. Rapidly, she let them inside and led the way up the stairs to a third-floor front apartment.

"Jenny doesn't have a lake view," he said as she unlocked the door.

"Not yet, but she's on the waiting list."

Once Carrie had opened the door and switched on the overhead light, Sam followed her inside and glanced around. A window air-conditioning unit was humming away, but its efforts were no match for a third-floor apartment on a muggy July night.

The living room was sparsely furnished, which wasn't much of a surprise. Jenny was only twenty-five, and although she'd told him she'd been modeling for years, she'd also confided that her assignments were sometimes so few and far between that she worked part-time as a waitress.

"Where do we start?" Carrie asked, drawing him back to the moment.

"Does Jenny have an answering machine?"

"It's in the bedroom." She turned and started across the living room.

He followed along, wondering whether they were the first to come looking for clues or if one of Leo's lackeys had beaten them to it. There were no obvious signs anyone had been here, but he doubted that meant a thing.

A second air conditioner was running in the bedroom, this one able to do its job more effectively because the room was so small that Jenny's double bed almost filled it.

As Carrie walked over to the bedside table, Sam paused in the doorway. There was enough light spilling in from the living room that he could see there was an open, but empty, suitcase on the floor and that clothes were lying all over the bottom of the bed— as if Jenny had tossed everything from the closet onto it and then decided she'd pack only one case.

When Carrie switched on the bedside lamp, he looked around at the room itself. It was both feminine and intimate, with a huge Oriental fan decorating the wall above the headboard and a tall vase filled with peacock feathers standing in the far corner.

A rose-colored scarf, wrapped around the lamp-shade, made the light so dusky-dim that it barely warmed the darkness with its glow.

All in all, the bedroom whispered of sex, and being alone in it with Carrie started his imagination wandering in a direction it had no business going.

Reminding himself they'd come into the room to check the answering machine, he focused on its blinking light—just as she glanced back at him and said, "I should check the messages, right?"

"Right."

She pressed a button. A moment later, her voice came on the tape, saying, "Jenny? Jenny, are you home?"

"I phoned after I got her message," she explained. "I was hoping she'd still be here."

The tape continued to run quietly for another couple of seconds, but there were no more messages.

"I'm going to call and check my own machine," Carrie said, picking up the receiver. "Maybe Jenny's tried to reach me."

"Wait. Don't do that just yet."

Moving forward quickly, he took the receiver from her and pushed the redial button. As he absently listened to the clicking of the numbers, he glanced down at the small pad of paper on the table. There was nothing written on it.

"Well, that's no help," he said once the call had connected. "I thought it might give us something to go on, but I was the last person she phoned. The redial just got my machine. Here—" he handed back the receiver "—go ahead and check for your messages."

Sam's words had started Carrie's mind racing so fast she suspected he could hear it whirring. She'd just learned what she'd been desperately wanting to know.

He hadn't been lying to her. His version of the story had to be true. There was no way in the world Jenny would have called him if he was the killer.

Relief tumbling through her, she began to punch in her phone number. Then, just as she finished, her sense of relief vanished.

Sam might have said the redial had gotten his machine, but how did she know it actually had? And now that she'd dialed a different number, there was no way she could check.

Wanting to kick herself for not thinking faster, she stood gazing at him as her phone began to ring— hoping against hope that his expression would tell her whether he'd just pulled a fast one.

It didn't, of course. But why hadn't he simply asked her to try the redial? She'd been standing with the receiver right in her hand, yet instead of saying, "Press Redial and see what you get," he'd taken over and done it himself.

At the other end of the line, her machine picked up. Numbly, she punched in the code to retrieve messages, listened, then put down the receiver.

"Nothing," she told him.

"We're not exactly batting a thousand, are we."

"No, we're not," she said. Then, when he began to look around the room, as if trying to figure out where they went from here, she took a long, deep breath.

It left her feeling a little less fragile, but not much. Her anxiety level was sky high, and she was so afraid for Jenny that she was on the verge of tears. On top of that, her uncertainty about Sam had her feeling as if she were coming apart at the seams. It wasn't easy to pretend she trusted him, while she was suspiciously analyzing everything he said.

But what else could she do? She couldn't let him know she *didn't* trust him.

She pushed her hair back from her face, hating to think how hot the apartment would be without the air conditioners. And then her anxiety level soared even higher.

"Sam?" she said. "There's something I should have thought of the minute we walked in here. Jenny pays her own electric bill. She never leaves the air conditioners on when she goes out."

His glance flickered to the one droning away in the bedroom window, then back to her. "She was awfully upset. She might have—"

"No, she wasn't upset when she *went* to Leo's, so she wouldn't have left them running then. And when she got home, she was in a major hurry to get going again. She wouldn't have turned them on knowing she'd only be in here a few minutes."

He stood gazing at her, not looking at all happy.

"I wondered earlier if someone else might have already been here."

"You mean Leo."

"More likely someone he sent. He'll be pretty careful about what he does himself."

"But given those air conditioners, there must have been *someone* here. And…"

"What?"

Her mind was racing again. She'd bet there wasn't a chance in a million that Jenny had left them running, so someone else *must* have been in the apartment. But how did she know the someone hadn't been Sam?

If he'd come here earlier, looking for Jenny, he'd have realized that she'd packed some things and run. And maybe at that point he'd decided to see if her sister knew where she'd gone. Or could figure it out.

"Carrie? You were going to say something more."

Telling herself to keep acting as if she trusted him, she said, "If whoever was in here thought to check the redial and got your machine… What does your message say?"

"This is Sam Evans, please leave… Yeah, I see what you're getting at."

She nodded. "If he checked the redial, he'll have told Leo that Jenny phoned you."

Sam's eyes darkened. "And Leo will assume she called to warn me."

"That's the way I was adding things up, all right."

"Dammit," he muttered.

"So if he knows Jenny told you about the murder, and he's hoping to cover it up…"

"Then I'm on his hit list right along with your sister."

She nodded once more. He certainly would be. If Leo actually did have a hit list. If Sam wasn't the killer.

CHAPTER THREE

SAM ABSENTLY RUBBED his jaw, thinking the odds he'd been added to Leo Castanza's hit list had to be pretty damned high. Then he began wishing he hadn't left his Beretta under the front seat of the car this time around.

It had occurred to him, later than it should have, that Leo might have somebody watching Jenny's apartment in the hope she'd come home. Somebody who, at the very minimum, would be curious about what he and Carrie were doing up here. And that stretch of dark night between the front door and where he'd parked would be an ideal place to intercept them.

He glanced toward the bedroom window, itching to take a look down at the street. But if Carrie realized what he was doing, she'd be more upset than she already was, so instead of checking, he simply looked over at her and said, "I guess we'd better figure out where we go from here."

"Yes. I guess we'd better."

Her voice didn't sound right, and even in the room's dusky light he could see that her eyes were filled with tears.

"Hey," he said quietly. "One way or another, we'll find Jenny. She's going to be okay."

"I hope so, Sam. But I'm just... Every time I let myself start imagining..."

Moving closer, he rested his hand on her bare arm—and breathed in the fragrance of her perfume. It was an intoxicating scent that reminded him of a lush spring night in the country, and each time he smelled it he couldn't keep from thinking of hot kisses and slow sex.

Since there were a hundred different reasons for not letting himself indulge in those sorts of fantasies, he'd been doing his darnedest to force them into the darkest recesses of his mind. But at the moment, the combination of her scent and the soft warmth of her skin had a very unsettling feeling tiptoeing around inside his chest.

Trying to ignore it, he said, "You know, we can't be certain Leo even has someone looking for Jenny."

"Oh, but he does. We both know he does."

Sam exhaled slowly. There wasn't much point in saying she might be wrong when he was sure she was right.

"Well...look," he finally said. "I guess our next step should be looking through the trash to see if we can turn up any clues. Why don't I check in here while you start in the bathroom."

She nodded again. Then, without another word, she headed out of the room.

Seizing his opportunity, he strode over to the window. A streetcar was rattling by, the metal-against-metal rumble of its wheels on the tracks almost drowning out the air conditioner's hum. Beyond the streetcar, idling next to the curb directly across the street from Jenny's building, sat a dark Ford Probe.

His heart began thudding loudly. Had he guessed right? Was someone watching the apartment?

All he could see inside the car was the glow of a cigarette. Then, as he watched, the driver's window slid down, someone tossed the lit butt out into the street and the window slid back up.

A moment later the car pulled away from the curb and drove off, leaving him with the distinct feeling that the driver had spotted him looking out—and that the car would only circle the block and be back.

IN THE BATHROOM, CARRIE splashed cold water on her face, hoping that would help her think more clearly. It seemed like a total contradiction to be positive Leo had someone looking for Jenny and at the same time be afraid that Sam was the villain of the piece.

The water didn't do any good at all. She still felt as if she were trying to put together a puzzle when half the pieces were missing. But was it really surprising that she was confused and frightened?

She didn't think so. Until she learned for sure what had happened this afternoon, or until she knew that her sister was no longer in danger, she'd be walking an emotional tightrope.

Her hands resting on the sides of the sink, she stood staring at her reflection in the mirror and thinking once again that she should have ignored Jenny's ultimatum. If she'd spoken her mind about Leo instead of biting her tongue, her sister might not have been at his place today.

A few tears made good their escape. If Jenny ended up dead because...

Ordering herself not to go there, she looked down at the garbage container. It was virtually empty. Still, she dumped what little there was in it onto the floor and checked through it—used tissues, an empty toothpaste box, a couple of manufacturer's coupons and the nub of an eyebrow pencil. Nothing that even resembled a clue.

Scooping the garbage back into the container, she headed out of the bathroom at the exact moment that Sam was emerging from the bedroom.

"Anything?" he asked.

"No."

"Nothing in the bedroom, either. Let's try the kitchen."

Like the container in the bathroom, the bag in the can under the sink was almost empty. Gingerly, she lifted out a filter full of coffee grinds and poked at the eggshells and vegetable scraps that had been concealed beneath it. When there was nothing under them, she gave Sam a shrug of defeat.

"It's always so damn easy on TV, isn't it?" he muttered. "But what about that stuff?" he added, looking over at the hodgepodge of magnets and scraps of paper on the fridge.

Pulling the notes free, she looked through them and tossed them onto the counter.

"Mostly just shopping reminders," she told him. Then she waited to see if he had any other ideas—

part of her hoping he would, part hoping he wouldn't. Even though she was desperate to find Jenny, the last thing she wanted was to do it with the wrong man along.

"Okay," he said at last. "I think what we do next is call everyone you figure she might conceivably have asked for help. Where does she keep her address book?"

"Sam, if she'd asked anyone for help it would have been me."

"Uh-uh. Not when she knew Leo would send someone after her. Your town house would be one of the first places he'd have gone looking."

She nodded slowly. Someone could easily have been snooping around her house while she'd been out this afternoon. And would he have been content to merely peer in the windows, or would he have gotten inside and had a good look around? And either way, was he likely to return?

Trying to force those questions from her mind, she said, "The address book's in the drawer of the bedside table."

They headed back into the bedroom, but the book wasn't where it normally lived.

Telling Sam that was strange, that her sister always kept it by the phone, she rummaged through the table's lower section. When she came up empty again, she checked under the clothes strewn across the bottom of the bed. The book wasn't there, either.

She slowly surveyed the room, thinking Jenny must have taken it with her, and then she spotted it—the corner of it at least—poking out from beneath the bed.

"Got it," she said, reaching down. As she did, her gaze flickered past the waste basket, then to Sam.

Catching his eye, she gestured toward the little notepad beside the phone. "Were there any pieces of paper from that in the garbage?"

"No, why?"

"Because Jenny always doodles the name of whoever she's phoning while she's waiting for them to answer. So why wouldn't she have doodled my name when she called this afternoon? Or yours when she called you?"

"She was probably too upset."

"Maybe. But it's such an ingrained habit that…"

Picking up the pad and the pencil lying beside it, Carrie sank onto the bed and began lightly rubbing the lead across the top piece of paper.

"I used to do that when I was a kid," Sam said. "I guess everyone did."

As she rubbed, two names became visible. When she was done, she sat gazing at them, telling herself not to panic.

"What have you got?" From where Sam was standing, the names were upside down.

"She wrote my name. The one beneath it is Linda."

"But mine's not there?"

"No."

He was silent for half a beat, then said, "I guess that wasn't from today, then. Or maybe when she called me, she was busy throwing things into a suitcase while my phone was ringing. I told you she was packing while we talked, remember?"

"Yes."

Those were two possible explanations. But the other one that came to mind, the terrifying one, was that Jenny *had* written those two names today and that she hadn't phoned Sam at all.

"What about this Linda?" he asked. "Who's she?"

Ordering herself to go along with him and see where it got her, Carrie said, "I'm not sure. Jenny knows more than one Linda. There's the woman who cuts her hair, and a woman she models with occasionally. And she has a friend named Linda Willenzik."

"And that's it?"

"Those are the only ones I can think of. But what about the bit of paper she actually wrote on? You're sure it wasn't in the garbage?"

"Positive."

"Then where did it go?" *Into your pocket?* she wanted to ask. *So that I wouldn't see she hadn't written your name on it?*

She kept quiet, though, waiting to hear what he'd come up with, and felt a stab of uneasiness when he simply shook his head, saying, "Let's check the book for those Lindas."

"The model's last name is Crocker," she said, flipping to the *C* page.

Her heart skipped a beat. The page had been ripped out.

"Try the others," Sam said when she told him.

The *W* page was missing, as well.

"I don't know the last name of the woman who

cuts her hair," she said, slowly flipping through. "But here. The *H* page is gone, too."

"And I'll bet that bit of paper she doodled on went the same place those pages did. Whoever beat us here ripped it off the pad and took both it and the pages with him, figuring he'd follow up on the Lindas until he found the one she called."

"Oh, Lord," Carrie whispered. Maybe that's what *had* happened.

"Does Jenny have both phone numbers and addresses for the names in her book?"

She glanced down at it and nodded.

"Then I'll bet he'd pay the Lindas personal visits rather than phoning them. But which one would Jenny have asked for help?"

"I think Linda Willenzik's the only one. I can't imagine it being her hair stylist, and she doesn't like the model."

"Then you'd better call Willenzik."

Carrie stashed the book in her purse, just in case whoever'd beaten them here came back, then reached down to the table's storage section again and dragged out the Toronto phone book. Her throat dry and her palms damp, she searched through it for Linda Willenzik's number.

"Thank heavens, there's only one L. Willenzik listed," she said, punching in the number. "And it's got to be her. Now that I see the address, I recall Jenny mentioning the street name. It's ringing," she announced a second later as the number connected.

It rang twice…three times…four…

After a dozen rings, she hung up. "No answer."

Sam didn't look as if he thought that was good news. As for Carrie, her imagination was busily painting another picture of dead bodies lying on a floor. This time, though, they weren't Leo's and Bud's. They were Jenny's and Linda's.

"Where does Linda live?" Sam asked.

"Elmhurst Avenue."

"That's way up by Yonge and Sheppard, but we'd better go check things out. If Jenny's with her, they might have just decided that answering the phone wouldn't be smart."

"Right," Carrie said slowly. She hadn't forgotten, not for a second, that the last thing she wanted was to find Jenny with the wrong man in tow. Which meant that she had to figure out some way...

"Sam, we're not far from my place," she said. "Maybe you should drop me off there and I can drive up to Linda's on my own. I mean, you must have someone waiting for you at home and—"

"No, I live alone. I thought I'd mentioned that."

"Oh...yes, I guess you did. It must have slipped my mind. I was thinking your wife would be wondering where you were."

He shook his head. "The closest I ever came to being married was getting engaged once. But it didn't last. At any rate, why don't you tell me what you know about Linda Willenzik."

Carrie hesitated. There had to be some way of getting rid of this man, but she wasn't coming up with any ideas at the moment.

"Does she live alone?" he pressed.

"As far as I know. I remember Jenny saying she

rented the basement apartment of a house, and that she felt really safe in it because there was usually someone home upstairs.''

''Well, jot down the house number and let's get going.''

Carrie scribbled down the address while Sam switched off the bedroom air conditioner. Then he followed her out into the living room and turned off the one in there. ''I wouldn't want your sister to have a fit when she gets her Hydro bill,'' he said.

She tried to smile, hoping with all her might that *when* was the right word, trying not to think that her sister might not be alive by the time the next bill arrived.

They headed into the outside hall, and she was just about to close the door when an idea popped into her head. It started her heart hammering a mile a minute.

''Wait here one second, okay?'' she said, trying to keep her voice normal. ''I'm dying of thirst. I'm going to get a couple of cans of pop from the fridge.''

Stepping back into the apartment, she practically ran to the kitchen and grabbed the cans. Then, as the refrigerator door swung shut, she pulled open one of the drawers beneath the counter.

When the mood struck, Jenny loved to cook. And a few months ago, she'd splurged on a nine-inch boning knife. Now it lay in the drawer, its gleaming sharpness almost mesmerizing.

It wasn't a gun, but it would be better than nothing. Her hand trembling, Carrie reached for it—half horrified at herself, half wondering whether she'd actually be able to use it if she needed to.

Until a few hours ago, she'd never have imagined herself wielding a knife. But this wasn't a few hours ago.

Emptying her purse onto the counter, she stashed the knife in the bottom, then shoved everything else, including the address book and the pop, on top of it.

CARRIE HURRIED DOWN THE stairs of Jenny's building ahead of Sam, but when they reached the front door, he said, "Wait here for a minute," and stepped outside into the night without her.

While he slowly scanned the street, her pulse began to race. He must be worried that someone was out there—unless this was just another part of an act.

Shaking her head, she told herself that if she kept second-guessing him, she'd drive herself crazy before this was over.

Finally, he turned back toward the door and pushed it open.

"What were you looking for?" she asked as they began walking quickly down the sidewalk.

"A dark Ford Probe. I think somebody sitting in one was watching the apartment while we were upstairs. I'm not sure, though. While I was looking out at him he drove off, but that could have been coincidence."

"And you didn't see him now?"

He shook his head. "Maybe my imagination just got carried away."

She glanced in both directions at the cars parked along the street, even though it was an exercise in futility when Sam had already checked them out.

But the fact that they couldn't see anyone watching them didn't mean there wasn't someone. It could simply mean he was being more careful.

As they headed down the street beside the apartment building, the noise of the traffic gradually faded behind them and they could hear the waves lapping the shoreline, their rhythmic sound punctuated by the occasional honking of a goose on the water. When they reached Sam's Mustang, they both turned to look back the way they'd come.

Carrie saw nothing alarming, but that made her no less anxious. Neither did the way Sam reached under his seat once they'd climbed into the car, checking that his gun was still there.

"If someone was watching us," she said as he started the engine, "he'd follow us to Linda's, wouldn't he?"

"We'll both keep a sharp eye out."

She nodded. Between the two of them, surely they'd spot a car trailing them.

"I thought you were dying of thirst," he said, making a U-turn and starting back up to Lake Shore Boulevard.

"Oh, right. You made me so nervous that I forgot all about it."

She dug out the cans of pop and handed him one, then zipped her purse shut again—very aware of the knife buried at the bottom, and very frightened that before the night was done, she might be glad of it. Trying not to think about that, she concentrated on checking the traffic for a dark Probe.

She didn't see one. Maybe Sam was right and his

imagination had simply gotten carried away. Still, she kept a careful watch through the rear window as he drove. But even though her eyes were focused on the cars behind them, she couldn't stop thinking that if someone was paying visits to the Lindas in Jenny's book, and if Jenny *was* hiding out at her friend's...

"Don't worry about something that probably won't happen," Sam said quietly.

"You do mind reading on the side?" she asked, managing to smile as his glance flicked toward her.

Something in the way he smiled back made her suspect that, under normal circumstances, he viewed the world with just the appropriate degrees of humor and skepticism. Then, for a second before he turned his attention to his driving again, his gaze locked with hers.

As it did, she felt a totally unexpected rush of warmth. And for the second time since they'd met, her intuition whispered, *This man isn't a killer.*

"Not only can I read minds," he told her as the whisper died, "I can predict the future."

He glanced at her again, his expression saying that yes, of course he was teasing. "And right now," he continued, "I've got a feeling we're going to find Jenny at Linda's."

"But if somebody's beaten us there..."

"Willenzik's got to have been the last Linda in the book. So logic says that—"

"Sam, we can't count on Leo's guy trying them alphabetically."

"No. But he was starting from Jenny's apartment.

And Linda's place is such a long way from it that she's probably the last one he'd check, anyway."

Carrie closed her eyes and told herself Sam was right. It *was* logical that Linda Willenzik's would be the last place someone would try. Then she let his words about being able to predict the future echo in her mind.

She wished he hadn't just been teasing, wished he really knew, with absolute certainty, that they were going to find Jenny soon.

It wasn't until after they were almost to Yonge and Sheppard that she realized she hadn't qualified her wish: she hadn't wished they'd find her sister Jenny soon, but only if Sam meant her no harm.

She'd forgotten all about being on her guard, and that realization scared her half to death. She didn't dare forget, no more than she dared forget that she still didn't know for sure which side Sam was on. And that she didn't, she couldn't risk letting him get anywhere near Jenny. So what was she going to do when they reached Linda's?

His going to the door with her was out of the question, because if Jenny was there…

"As I recall, Elmhurst's only two or three blocks north of Sheppard," he said. "And what's the number?"

Locating the piece of paper she'd scribbled it on, she read out the address.

When he flicked on his turn signal, her chest started feeling tight. There was almost no time left to figure out what she was going to do when they arrived.

As they pulled up in front of the house, she noticed

a car parked in the driveway, and through the living room window she could see a man watching television. But from the street, there was no way of telling whether any lights were on in the basement.

"You'd better wait here," she told Sam, reaching for the door handle.

"Oh?"

She nodded firmly. "The message Jenny left me said that if anyone came looking for her, I should pretend I hadn't heard from her. So if she called Linda, she'd have told her the same thing. Which means Linda might not say a word if you were standing there."

"Yeah, I guess that makes sense."

The tightness in her chest eased a little, but she was a long way from home free. Sam might decide, at any second, that as long as he was with Jenny's sister, there was no good reason Linda wouldn't talk in front of him.

Getting out of the car, she walked down the driveway to the side entrance. The mailbox, with L. Willenzik neatly printed on it, assured her she'd written down the right number. And there were lights on in the basement, which she took as a promising sign.

She raised her hand to knock—then glanced back to make sure Sam was still sitting in the car. He was. So far so good.

And if Jenny *was* here, she thought as she knocked, she didn't have to let him know that. She'd just say Linda hadn't heard from Jenny. Then it would simply be a matter of getting rid of Sam. After that, she and Jenny could...

Telling herself she'd figure out the rest later, she knocked a second time, feeling more anxious by the moment. Was Linda in there and just not answering the door? Or had someone beaten them here? And if that had happened…

Her thoughts racing off in all sorts of frightening directions, she knocked yet again. When there was still no answer she headed back along the driveway and up the front steps of the house.

Only seconds after she rang the bell, the man she'd seen through the window opened the door.

"Hi," she said, forcing a smile. "I'm sorry to bother you, but I'm looking for Linda Willenzik and she isn't answering her door. I thought you might know if she's home?"

"Sorry, I don't. My wife and I were out. We only got in a few minutes ago."

"Oh. Well…I'd hate to leave without seeing her if she's just in the shower or something."

"Why not wait a couple of minutes and give it another shot?"

"Yes…of course. The only thing is…I'm afraid my boyfriend's kind of impatient." She gestured toward the Mustang. "Is there an inside door to the basement that you could knock on and just check for me? I wouldn't ask except that I know she hasn't been feeling well and I'm kind of worried about her."

"Well…"

"If she *is* home, if you'd just tell her that Jenny's sister is here… I really am worried."

She held her breath until the man said, "Yeah, okay, I'll give her a shout."

When he headed off, she looked out to the street once more and gave Sam a little shrug, willing him to stay right where he was. Then she turned back to the door and waited.

The man was gone for a couple of minutes that seemed like hours. When he came back, he said, ''Yeah, she's home.''

Carrie exhaled slowly. At least she could stop worrying about Jenny and Linda lying dead down there.

''I think she must have gone to bed early or something,'' he added. '''Cuz you were right, she sounded sick. But she said for you to go around to her door.''

''Well, thanks a lot. And I'm really sorry to have bothered you.''

''No problem.''

As the man closed his door, she gave Sam a thumbs-up, then hurried back down the steps and along the driveway.

She was just reaching the side door when it opened—and her heart almost stopped.

Linda's eyes were puffy, her cheeks were tear-stained, and she looked positively petrified.

CHAPTER FOUR

"Oh, my God," Carrie whispered, fearing the worst. "What's wrong?"

Her expression still terrified, Linda glanced along the driveway to the street. When she spotted Sam's car, her body tensed.

"It's okay, he's with me," Carrie told her. "But where's Jenny?"

"Carrie, I..." Linda bit her lower lip and tears started trickling down her cheeks.

"Is she here?" Carrie demanded, practically pushing her way inside.

As she peered down the stairs from the landing, Linda said, "No. She was, but..."

"Well, where is she now? What's going on?"

"I...she was here when I got home from work. Sitting outside in Leo's Cadillac. And...did you know a bunch of us were up at my parents' cabin one weekend last summer?"

"Yes, she told me about it. Is that where she's gone?"

Linda nodded. "She asked if she could use it for a few days, and there's nobody up there just now, so I gave her my keys."

Carrie waited a couple of beats, then said, "Why are you so upset?"

"I…"

"What happened? Tell me."

"I can't. He told me not to."

"*Who* told you not to?"

When Linda didn't answer, Carrie felt like shaking her. "Listen to me," she said. "We're talking serious trouble here, so tell me what happened."

"A…a man came looking for her."

"Oh, my God," Carrie whispered again. "He came looking when?"

"Not right away. Not right after she was here, I mean. Just…it couldn't have been more than half an hour ago. I didn't want to tell him where she'd gone, but…he had a gun. He said he'd kill me if I didn't cooperate."

"So you told him she'd gone to your cabin," Carrie said, almost unable to force the words out.

"I had to. I'm sorry, but I… And he told me not to tell anyone he'd been here asking about her, so if anyone asks you, you can't—"

"Don't worry, I won't say a word. But did you call Jenny and warn her?"

"No, the cabin doesn't have a phone."

"Then did you at least call the police?"

"No."

"*Why not?*"

"He said he'd put a bug on my phone line. Somewhere outside. And that if I called anyone he'd know. And he'd come back and kill me."

"Then why didn't you go upstairs and call from there?"

"Because I thought if the bug was outside, it would be on their line, too."

"But you could have gone to a neighbor's! Or to a pay phone!"

"I... I guess I should have." Fresh tears began streaming down Linda's face.

"Look, I didn't mean to sound so angry," Carrie said as calmly as she could. "I know you were scared. But Jenny's obviously in danger, so tell me where the cabin is."

Linda took an infuriatingly long time to wipe her eyes, then said, "Near Peterborough."

"How long a drive?"

"You mean leaving from here?"

Carrie nodded.

"Well, in light traffic like tonight, you could easily make it in an hour and a half."

"Oh, Lord. And he's got half an hour's lead time."

"But I didn't give him a map."

"What?"

"The cabin's secluded, set off the road and in the middle of acres of forest, so it's hard to find. I've got photocopies of a map my mom drew, but I didn't give him one. I only gave him directions. And without a map, people usually have to ask around before they can find us."

Thank heavens for small mercies, Carrie silently murmured. Aloud, she said, "Then get me a map, okay?"

Linda started down the stairs, Carrie on her heels. If she and Sam drove at top speed and...

Sam. If someone had come here looking for Jenny, didn't that prove Sam's story was true?

Sweet relief began sweeping through her. Now that she was sure she could trust him, it would be safe to let him drive her to this cabin.

But was she sure? What if she was missing some crucial piece of the puzzle?

"Linda?" she said. "Did Jenny tell you why she needed a place to hide out?"

Linda stopped in the apartment doorway and looked back, while Carrie prayed she wouldn't say Jenny had been running from someone named Sam.

"She said she'd had a huge fight with Leo and didn't want him to find her."

"Leo," Carrie repeated.

"I...I knew he had a bad temper. She'd told me that before. But I never thought he'd send someone after her with a gun. And it scared me so much...." Linda gave a little shrug, then disappeared into her apartment, leaving Carrie to digest what she'd just learned.

Jenny was running from Leo. She hadn't told Linda the real reason why, but that wasn't important. The critical fact was that she hadn't said she was running from Sam.

That didn't make Carrie any less frightened about how things might play out, but at least she was finally sure she hadn't teamed up with a murderer.

She walked into the apartment and stood trying to

think of what else she should ask about while Linda rummaged through a drawer in her desk.

"What did this guy look like?" she finally said.

"Just...big," Linda told her without glancing around. "And mean-looking."

"What kind of car was he driving?"

Linda shook her head. "I didn't see it. I was so scared I didn't even think to look. But here's a copy of the map," she added, turning away from the desk with a sheet of paper in her hand.

SAM RAN EVERY YELLOW light he hit between Linda's place and the highway.

He wanted to get to that cabin just as soon as he could, because even though he'd stopped at a pay phone and called the provincial police detachment nearest Peterborough, neither he nor Carrie believed that was going to do much good.

He'd explained that there was a woman alone at the Willenziks' cabin, and that a man with a gun was on his way there. But even though the officer had said he'd have a patrol car check things out right away, he'd obviously figured he was sending his people on a wild-goose chase. And when they got there, that was probably what it would seem to be.

One glimpse of a car's headlights would likely send Jenny high-tailing it into the woods. And even if she stayed close enough to see that it was a cruiser, she'd probably keep out of sight.

After all, she hadn't wanted anything to do with the police earlier. And she wouldn't realize these particular officers had come to help her, because she had no way of knowing that one of Leo's men was so close on her trail.

No, the way he had things figured, all the officers were going to see was Leo's Caddy parked outside. There'd be no sign of people, so they'd have a look around, then leave. But it would only be a matter of time before Leo's guy showed up.

"Linda said it's *really* tough to locate this place without a map?" he asked, glancing at Carrie.

"She said people usually have to ask around if they don't have one."

"Good, then he's bound to have trouble finding it in the dark."

"But will he have *enough* trouble? Sam, if he gets there first…"

"Hey, we've already talked about that, remember? Even if he does, with a few acres of forest to hide in, Jenny will be okay until we get there." But not indefinitely, he thought, pressing down more firmly on the accelerator.

Carrie stared silently out into the darkness rushing by, telling herself Sam was right. Jenny would be okay until they got there. And with any luck at all, they'd have her safely away from the cabin before Leo's thug even found it.

If they didn't…well, then it would be another instance of having to play things by ear. So right now she should try not to worry about what was going to happen. That would only get her more upset than she already was.

Ordering herself to think about something else entirely, she glanced over at Sam again, looking at him through different eyes now that she knew her intuition had been right. Knew for sure he wasn't a killer.

She let her gaze linger on his even profile, sizing him up from her new perspective.

For starters, he was a very attractive man. Broad shoulders, lean muscles, dark hair with just a bit of curl to it, and warm dark eyes that she should have known from the start couldn't belong to a murderer.

When it came to more important things than appearance, she hadn't really known him long enough to be an accurate judge. Still, they'd been through a lot in the short time since they'd met, and he certainly held up well under fire.

He was honest, too. He hadn't tried to con her into thinking he was only concerned about Jenny's safety. He'd wanted help finding her so he could convince her to go to the police with him, and he'd been up front about it. But he hadn't *only* been concerned about saving his own skin.

She thought back to what he'd said after they'd discovered Bud's body was gone—that Leo might not have entirely given up on the idea of trying to frame him.

Even at the time, she'd figured that possibility was slim. He must have known it, too. Yet here he was, hours later, still helping her get to Jenny.

And she was very glad he was. Otherwise, she didn't know if she'd have had the nerve to be speeding through the night, hoping to keep a man with a gun from murdering her sister.

She slowly shook her head. Who was she trying to

kid? Without Sam, she wouldn't have a hope in the world of keeping Jenny safe.

She studied him for another minute, then finally said, "Sam?"

He glanced over at her.

"Thanks for what you're doing."

He looked uncertain for a moment, then gave her a smile.

As brief as it was, it did something funny to her insides. The sensation wasn't something she wanted to think about, though. Not here and now, at least. Not until she knew Jenny was going to be all right.

For the next couple of minutes, Sam forced himself to keep his gaze firmly on the road. Then he glanced over at Carrie once more.

She was a picture of vulnerability. Her lower lip was caught between her teeth and she was staring straight ahead into the darkness, her hands clenched together on her lap. And he'd lay odds that if she looked at him he'd see tears in her eyes.

Without even thinking about what he was doing, he reached across and rested his hand on hers. "She'll be okay," he said. "For a pair of amateurs, we've made a lot of progress."

"I just hope we've made it fast enough," she murmured.

This time he *did* think about what he was doing—and he left his hand right where it was.

He hadn't forgotten that he didn't want any female distractions in his life. Or that he'd been hoping to dissolve their little partnership just as soon as possible.

But by now it was obvious they were in this together till the end. And until then, Carrie needed whatever reassurance he could give her. As for him...

He stared at the moonlit countryside stretching out on either side of the highway, a dull hollowness in his chest. He'd give everything he owned if he could simply will away part of his past. The part that made it hazardous to even think about letting himself feel something for a woman like Carrie.

ONCE THEY'D TURNED OFF the highway, Carrie had to keep flicking on the little map light in Sam's car to check their bearings.

The gravel back roads curved frequently, and a lot of the intersections would be easy to miss. Even with a map, finding the Willenziks' cabin in the dark was decidedly tricky.

Too tricky, she hoped, for the man with the gun. But she wasn't counting on it. They'd passed a couple of late-night gas stations where he could have stopped to check his directions, and her stomach was tight with fear that he'd already beaten them to the cabin.

She forced her mind back to her navigating as they passed the final landmark indicated on the map. ''The driveway should be half a kilometer ahead on the right,'' she told Sam.

Moments later, he turned sharply down a narrow dirt driveway she hadn't even seen. Her heart began beating faster and she held her breath as they zigged and zagged along it. Whoever had put it in had taken the path of least resistance—going around major trees rather than cutting them down.

The driveway was far darker than the road had been, the trees totally blocking out the moonlight. But she doubted the growth was thick enough to prevent someone in the cabin from seeing their headlights.

They wound around a final curve and a ramshackle two-story log building stood before them, set in a small clearing that was faintly lit by moon shadows and surrounded by the dense darkness of an evergreen forest.

There were no lights on inside, no more sign of life than there'd been at Leo's house. But halfway down one side of the cabin sat his silver Cadillac.

Sam pulled his car onto the grass and parked about twenty feet from the front door. "There's nobody here except Jenny," he said. "We made it first."

Swallowing uneasily, Carrie tried not to think that wasn't necessarily true. Maybe the man who was looking for Jenny had already been and gone. And had accomplished what he'd come to do.

Praying that hadn't happened, she said, "Do you think she's someplace where she can see that it's us?"

"I don't know." Sam reached under the seat for his gun. "But call her as loudly as you can. Wherever she is, she should be near enough to hear you."

Carrie climbed out of the car and slung her purse over her shoulder. Her heart was pounding now, and the sound reverberated in her head like the rapid tattoo of a drum.

"Jenny?" she called. "Jenny, it's Carrie."

She waited a few seconds, straining her ears to hear her sister's voice. When she didn't, she tried again.

"Why isn't she answering?" she finally whispered, glancing at Sam.

He hadn't tucked his gun into his belt this time. He was standing with it in his hand, as if he expected he might need it at any moment. And even with only the pale moonlight to see by, his expression told her something she didn't want to know.

"You're not sure we beat him here, are you?" she made herself say.

"I'll have a look in the cabin," he said, starting forward without answering her question.

For a moment, she stood frozen to the spot. Then she started after him. When he realized she had, he reached for her hand and took it firmly in his.

They stepped up onto the porch and headed across it. Then, his gun at the ready, he let go of her hand and tried the door.

"Locked," he said. "But maybe we'll have better luck round the back."

As they walked along the side of the cabin, Carrie paused and peered nervously into Leo's car. Sam merely watched her in silence, but he obviously knew she was afraid she'd discover Jenny's dead body in it.

If she'd had a key, she'd have checked the trunk, but since she didn't, she simply followed him the rest of the way to the back door. It wasn't locked.

He glanced at her as he turned the handle. "Do you want to wait out here?"

Yes and no. She was afraid of what might be inside, but she had to find out.

"I'll come with you," she told him.

The hinges creaked ominously as he pushed the door open. In the kitchen, the moonlight filtering through the windows illuminated the room in a spooky, ghostly way.

Telling herself it was only her anxiety that was making the cabin seem menacing, Carrie called Jenny's name again. There was no reply this time, either.

After Sam found a light switch, they made their way through the ground floor of the cabin. Downstairs, there was the kitchen, a large main room and a bathroom with only a toilet and sink. On the second floor were three bedrooms.

Despite her fear, they didn't find Jenny lying dead up there. In fact, they didn't find any sign of her. No suitcase, no purse, and none of her clothes.

Turning off the last of the bedroom lights, they started down the stairs.

"If it weren't for Leo's car out there," Carrie said once they were back in the kitchen, "I'd think Jenny changed her mind about coming here."

"She's got to be outside someplace," Sam said. "She must have run when she saw the lights of my car, just like we figured she would."

Carrie nodded. But what if it wasn't *Sam's* car Jenny had run from? The man Leo had sent after her could already have been and gone, and when she'd seen *his* car coming, she'd have taken off into the woods. And if he'd followed her...

Sam switched off the kitchen light, plunging the cabin into total darkness once more, and they headed back out into the night.

There was a storage shed about twenty feet from the cabin, but when she silently pointed at it, Sam shook his head. He was right, she realized. It would be a far too obvious place for Jenny to try hiding.

They'd barely started toward the trees when the purr of a car engine became audible and Carrie saw a brief flash of light from the drive.

"Sam!" she whispered, but he already had hold of her hand and was hustling her back the way they'd come.

They stepped out of sight behind the cabin at the exact moment the wash of a car's headlights swept into the clearing. Then the sound of its engine died and the light vanished.

Carrie stood listening to the pounding of her heart until a car door opened and closed. A minute later, someone was knocking on the cabin's front door.

Sam edged closer to the corner and peered around. "It's not a patrol car," he whispered. "It's some kind of four-by-four, pulled up tight behind the Caddy. I guess it could be a neighbor, but my money's on Leo's guy."

"He'll know Jenny isn't alone," she whispered back. "He'll have seen your car."

"But he won't know who's here with her. Or exactly where any of us are. We'd better get away from the cabin, though."

Quietly, they hurried across the back of the clearing. Just as they reached the trees, a solid crashing noise shattered the silence of the night, followed by the creak of another set of hinges in desperate need of oiling.

"He's kicked open the front door," Sam said. "So much for the thought that it might be a neighbor."

They stood staring back at the cabin, a couple of watchers in the woods, until a light in the main room went on.

"Now what?" Carrie asked.

She'd barely uttered the words when, from behind them, Jenny whispered, "We're in big trouble!"

Carrie whirled around, her heart slamming against her ribs.

"You shouldn't have come here!" Jenny said. "That's got to be someone Leo sent looking for me, and you led him straight here."

For an instant, Carrie couldn't decide whether she wanted to hug her sister or shake her. Then she realized Jenny was close to tears, so she went with the hug while Sam said, "We didn't lead him here. Linda Willenzik told him where you were. We just managed to find the cabin before he did."

"What? She told?"

"She didn't have any choice. He threatened to kill her."

"But how did he even know about her?"

"Jenny, we'll explain everything later," Carrie said. "But why on earth were you hiding from us? Why didn't you answer when I called?"

"Because I thought I'd better wait until I was sure no one had followed you. The cops have already been here once and—"

"They've been and gone?" Sam interrupted.

Jenny nodded.

"What did they do?"

"Just what you did. Discovered the back door was open and went in to look around. Then they left."

"What about the Caddy? Did they check it out?"

"They had a look. But it's just a parked car. At any rate, when you showed up I figured someone might have followed you—either somebody Leo sent or more cops. I mean, I just know Leo's got someone after me, and the police will be looking for you, right?" she added to Sam.

"Actually, I don't think they are," he told her. "We're not sure what's going on, but it doesn't seem as if Leo's told anyone his friend is dead, let alone that I killed him."

"*What?*"

He shook his head. "There was nothing on the news about a murder, so Carrie and I went to his place to see what we could find. And there was no body in the study. And not the slightest sign that there'd been any struggle in the room."

"But...then what's he up to?"

"The only thing we could figure," Carrie said, "was that after you ran, Leo decided to try covering up the murder instead of trying to frame Sam."

"I...yes, maybe he did. But... Look, no matter what he's decided, we're all in big trouble." She gestured toward the cabin. "That guy's here to kill me. And if you and Sam get in his way, he'll kill you, too."

Carrie looked at Sam, her mouth dry with fear. "We've got to get out of here."

"He'd be on our tail in two seconds flat. Unless...

Okay, come on. We can get pretty close to my car and still stay out of sight.''

"Wait," Jenny said as he was turning away. "I've got my stuff out here."

Dashing over to a tree, she produced a suitcase and purse from behind it. "I had everything right at the back door," she explained. "I knew I might have to run for it."

"I think you'd better ditch the suitcase," Sam told her. "It'll only slow you down."

"No! I can't. Sam, even if we get out of here, this isn't going to be over. And I'll really need some of the stuff I packed."

Without another word, he took the suitcase and began heading through the woods. Carrie fell into step after him, with Jenny right behind her.

They circled around the perimeter of the clearing, not stopping until they were as close as they could get to the Mustang without losing the cover of the trees.

Inside the cabin, all the lights in the main room were on now, as well as the one in the kitchen.

Sam dug his keys out of his pocket and handed them to Carrie, quietly saying, "Okay, here's what we're going to do. As soon as a light goes on upstairs, the two of you run for the car and get out of here. Then find a phone and call the cops."

"What about you?"

"I'll keep him here. I've got my gun, remember."

"I'll bet he's got a bigger one," Carrie said, her heart in her throat.

Sam nodded. "That's exactly why all three of us can't leave and have him chasing after us."

"But…" Frantically, she tried to think of a better plan.

Given the way Jenny had sounded, Carrie figured the guy in the cabin was a professional killer. And if he was, Sam would be no match for him.

"Sam, I've got an idea," Jenny whispered. "If you shot out one of the tires on that four-by-four, he'd be stranded. You wouldn't have to stay behind."

That sounded like such an inspired idea it made Carrie weak with relief. Then she realized Sam was shaking his head.

"The keys for the Caddy are in my purse," Jenny pressed. "So if his car was out of commission, he—"

"The problem," Sam interrupted, "is that the second he hears a sound he'll race for a window—his gun drawn. Which means we can't let him hear anything until Carrie starts my car."

Jenny nervously rubbed her hands against her shorts. "But when he hears that, he'll shoot out *our* tires."

"That mostly only happens in the movies," Sam told her. "In real life, it's tough to hit a moving target. Trust me, I've done enough target practice to know. It's hard to even hit something stationary when you're trying to do it fast. You'll have to make a quick getaway, though," he added to Carrie. "The more time he's got, the more chance he'll have for a lucky shot."

"But I don't think you should stay…." Carrie's

words trailed off as Sam began shaking his head again.

"It's the only way. I'll keep him pinned down until you get the cops here."

"No! You'll only keep him pinned down until you run out of bullets!"

When he simply shrugged, tears began to sting her eyes. He knew as well as she did that if they left him behind, he'd probably end up dead.

There had to be something else they could do, but even though her thoughts were racing so fast they were tripping all over one another, she couldn't come up with an alternative.

Then, just as her tears were starting to escape, she remembered she had something that might help them. "What about slashing one of his tires? That wouldn't make much noise, would it?"

"No, but what would I slash it with?" Sam asked.

Kneeling on the ground, she opened her purse and turned it upside down. The map slid out, followed by her sister's address book.

"Take your book, Jenny," she whispered as her brush landed on top of it. Next came her makeup bag, an assortment of standard purse junk, and finally Jenny's boning knife.

"Could you slash it with this?" Gingerly picking it up, she held it out to him.

Sam stood gazing at the knife, almost afraid to believe it was for real. It looked long and sharp enough to kill a grizzly bear.

For half a second he thought about asking Carrie

what the hell it had been doing in her purse. But right this minute he couldn't care less.

"What do you think?" she asked.

"I think I should probably adopt you," he said.

CHAPTER FIVE

LEAVING CARRIE AND JENNY safely hidden in the woods, Sam crept across the clearing and dropped to his haunches beside the four-by-four.

Adrenaline pumping, he clutched the knife with both hands and drove it into the front tire. The blade pierced the rubber with a dull thud and disappeared practically up to its handle.

After wrenching it back out, he waited and listened, not sure if he could actually hear the hiss of air escaping or was only imagining it.

Either way, he watched until he was satisfied the tire was going flat, then fleetingly considered putting a second one out of commission.

He decided not to press his luck when Leo's hired help might head back downstairs any moment. Pushing himself up, he slipped the Beretta's barrel out from under his belt. He hoped he wouldn't have to use it, but if he did he didn't want to be fumbling for it at the last second.

He glanced across to the edge of the clearing, knowing the time had come to signal Carrie and Jenny but hesitating. The instant they stepped out into the open they'd be at serious risk, and the thought of someone having a clear shot at them was making his blood run cold.

Telling himself Carrie had a good view of things from where she was, and that she wouldn't make a move unless she thought it was safe, he gave an exaggerated thumbs-up and started for his car. A few seconds later, the two women came hurrying out of the woods—Jenny determinedly lugging her suitcase.

He made it to the car before they did and crouched beside it, able to check out the front of the cabin for himself now. He couldn't see any movement inside, but that didn't mean they hadn't been spotted.

"Okay," he whispered as the women reached the car. "So far so good."

When he and Carrie eased the doors open and the interior light flashed on, it seemed ten times brighter than usual. He looked over at the cabin again, his anxiety level soaring while Carrie flipped her seat forward and Jenny shoved her suitcase into the back and scrambled in after it.

As he slid into the driver's seat and tucked the Beretta beneath it, Carrie climbed in beside him. He glanced at her, silently reminding her to close her door as quietly as she could. Then he pulled his shut and reached forward to stick the key into the ignition.

And that was when the night exploded around them.

"Get down!" he hollered, the gunfire drowning his words.

"Yikes!" Jenny screamed. "Get us out of here!"

Crouching low behind the wheel, he managed to slide the key in and turn it. When the engine came alive, he tromped the accelerator so hard that the car lurched wildly forward.

By the time they reached the driveway he had it under control. Switching on the headlights, he roared out of the clearing, slowing down as soon as the shooting stopped. The last thing he needed was to try taking one of the sharp curves so fast that he slammed into a tree.

"Oh, wow," Jenny said. "You think the shooting will bring the cops back here?"

"I doubt it," he told her. "Linda's map didn't show any neighbors very close by. And unless somebody heard the shots and called to report them..."

He stopped at the end of the drive and looked over at Carrie, his heart still racing furiously.

"Are we all okay?" she asked, her voice catching a little on the words.

"We all look just fine from where I'm sitting," Jenny told her.

"Good." She gave Sam a nervous smile. "I can't believe we really did it."

He grinned at her, relief flooding him. They *had* done it, but they wouldn't have without her knife.

Sometime, he was going to ask her what the story was about that. But not at the moment.

Right now, the only thing he was interested in was talking to the police. Regardless of what Leo was trying to pull off, he wouldn't be able to get away with it once Jenny told the cops the truth.

Swinging out of the driveway and onto the road, he started to imagine Leo's guy standing beside his four-by-four and kicking the flat. The picture was still clearly in his mind's eye when a pinpoint of light flashed in the rearview mirror. Focusing on it, he saw a sweep of headlights swerving onto the road behind them. For a second, he didn't realize what had happened—but only for a second.

"What?" Carrie said when he swore at his own stupidity.

"The Caddy's on our tail," he told her. "Either we were up against the hot-wiring king of the world or Leo gave him a set of keys."

"Oh, that's exactly what Leo would have done," Jenny wailed. "I should have known. He thinks of everything. But, Sam, you've got to lose that guy."

"Tell me something I don't know," he muttered under his breath.

He sped up rapidly, until he was going as fast as he dared on the winding gravel road. Even so, he doubted he'd gained an inch on the Cadillac. With each curve he hit, it vanished from sight. But each time it did, the beam of its headlights reappeared within seconds.

"Those two gas stations we passed on our way to the cabin," he said to Carrie. "How far are we from the closest one?"

She pulled Linda's map from her purse and turned on the map light. "Have we gone by the Nineteenth Line yet?" she asked anxiously.

"Right there!" Jenny said. "We zipped by it while you were asking!"

"Then the station's only a kilometer farther."

After she switched the light back off, Sam kept his

gaze half on the road and half on the odometer, hoping the distance on the map was accurate.

As they raced past a warning sign for the next curve, he flicked off the headlights, plunging the road before them into darkness.

Carrie made a strangled little noise in her throat. Jenny whispered, "Yikes!"

With only the moonlight to see by, he could make out little more than shapes and shadows. Praying he wouldn't screw up, he negotiated the curve. And there on the left was the dark, hulking form of a building.

Wheeling off the road, he pulled behind it and hit the brakes. He didn't breathe after the car had shuddered to a stop, and he was certain Carrie and Jenny were holding their breath as well.

A second passed. Another one. Then there was a sweep of headlights from the road. A few moments later, taillights were racing away into the night on the far side of the gas station.

"He's gone," Carrie murmured as they faded from sight.

"I just hope he's gone for good," he told her. "Now let's check the real map and figure out how we get from here to the police."

"Sam?" Jenny said. "Could we talk about all this before we do anything else?"

He looked back at her, not quite able to believe what he'd heard. If what they'd just been through hadn't convinced her she had to go to the cops, what the hell would?

Anger simmering inside him, he said, "Jenny, somebody just tried to kill us. Which wouldn't have happened if you'd gone to the police with me in the first place. And as soon as you tell them what happened at Leo's, they'll—''

''But that's what we need to talk about.'' Because…when I told you what happened, I kind of…changed a couple of details.''

As her words sank in, Sam could feel himself getting hotter, even though her little revelation didn't totally surprise him. Jenny was the sort of woman you couldn't help liking. Still, you knew you couldn't trust her to always tell the whole truth and nothing but.

He ordered himself not to say anything until he'd counted to ten. Exploding at her wouldn't help the situation. In fact, never mind just counting to ten. He'd be far smarter to keep quiet and let Carrie do the talking.

Just as he came to that decision, she said, ''What details did you change? Did you actually *see* the murder?''

''No. I was nowhere near the study when it happened. But…look, if Leo didn't call the cops, and there was no body when you went to check on things, then I can't be any more sure of what he's up to than you are. But I'm absolutely certain that if I go to the police, I'll end up dead. So can we *please* find a place to sit and talk?''

''What's wrong with right here?'' Carrie said.

''It could be a long conversation. You and Sam would probably end up with stiff necks if you were sitting turned half-backward the way you are.''

Sam shifted around and put the car into Drive.

"I'm not very worried about getting a stiff neck," he said when Carrie glanced at him. "But if Leo's pal realizes how we gave him the slip, he might backtrack to look for us."

FIGURING THE WISEST THING to do was get out of the area entirely, Sam decided he'd drive all the way down to Highway 401 before he even started looking for a place they could talk.

On the way, Carrie turned around in her seat and told Jenny how they knew Leo's guy had been in her apartment. And that the bit of paper with Linda Willenzik's name scribbled on it was what had led him to her.

"I couldn't help wondering why you didn't write down *my* name," Sam put in, glancing into the rearview mirror.

"Didn't I?" Jenny said.

When he shook his head, she shrugged. "Normally I would have—without even being aware I was doing it. But you were the last one I called, and I was really scared by then. So I guess while your phone was ringing, I must have been too busy sorting through the stuff I was packing to be doodling a name."

"Sam figured that had to be it," Carrie said. "Oh, and we weren't sure, but we think somebody might have been watching your apartment. Sam spotted someone sitting outside the building in a dark Probe."

"I know who that would have been. A guy who sometimes does *favors* for Leo."

With at least a couple of the blanks filled in, albeit small ones, Sam went back to concentrating on his driving, only absently listening while Carrie elaborated to Jenny about what they'd seen at Leo's.

After she told her that both the area rug and the sculpture had been gone from the study, Jenny said, "I think you're right. Leo must have decided to just try covering up the murder. A blow to the head doesn't always cause a lot of bleeding, so maybe getting the study squeaky clean wasn't a big deal. Not that the forensic types wouldn't find something if they tried, but…"

When Jenny paused, Sam glanced at Carrie. She was giving her sister a how-do-you-know-all-that? look.

He checked the rearview just in time to see Jenny shrug.

"Hanging out with Leo, I've learned a lot about murders and stuff," she said. "And if he was lucky, the only blood would have been on the rug and the sculpture. And maybe some on his clothes. I didn't notice any, but there could have been some.

"But if he got rid of the body one way or another, and took the rug and clothes out to the country someplace and burned them…and dumped the sculpture into the middle of a lake or something… Well, I think he could maybe get away with it."

On that cheery note, Sam pulled onto the 401. Then, knowing a conversation about why Jenny didn't want to go to the police wouldn't be the sort they'd want to have in an all-night fast-food restaurant, he pulled off the highway again at the first motel he spotted with a lit vacancy sign.

"You'd better stay in the car," he told the women

once he'd parked out of view of the office. "In case our friend decides to stop at a few places along the way back to Toronto and ask if anyone's seen us."

Inside, he registered as Robert Beckwith, wrote down a phony license plate number and paid cash for the room. That done, he drove along the entire row of units and parked around the end, where the car couldn't be seen from the highway.

After climbing out, they stashed Jenny's suitcase in the trunk, then headed back along the building. As they walked, the two women a couple of steps in front of him, Sam began absently thinking it seemed strange that, of the two, Jenny was the model.

Oh, with her red hair and even features there was no denying she was a striking woman. And she was rail thin, which he guessed counted for a lot.

But for his money, Carrie was far more beautiful. She had the sort of slender curves he liked. And there was something so warm and appealing about her that...

He stopped himself right there. If Carrie knew the truth about him, she'd do exactly what any sensible woman would—run as fast as she could in the opposite direction. Which was precisely why he should be repressing those sorts of thoughts.

It was tough to do, though. And the longer they were together, the tougher it was getting.

Glancing at the number on the unit they were passing, he said, "Ours is the next one."

When he opened the door of number twenty-seven, the digital display on the clock radio read three minutes after 2:00 a.m. Bone weary, he sank onto one of the two double beds and waited while first Jenny, then Carrie used the bathroom. Finally, they were both sitting on the other bed, facing him.

"Well?" he said to Jenny.

He interpreted the glance she gave Carrie as a request to cut her some slack.

"Jenny, we're all beat," she said. "So let's just hear exactly what happened. And don't change any details this time. Or leave any out."

Sam almost smiled at her no-nonsense approach. As much as she loved her sister, and he had no doubt that was a lot, Carrie was a sensible woman. He'd already seen her demonstrate that over and over again. And she knew it would be far smarter to learn whatever it was they didn't know than to waste time mollycoddling Jenny.

"Well," she began tentatively, "it's like I told Sam when I phoned him. Half an hour or so after he left, this Bud arrived."

"Do you know his last name?" Carrie asked.

Jenny shook her head. "I don't even know his real first name. I mean, Bud's always just a nickname, right? But that's all Leo said when he introduced him."

"Did Bud say what he wanted?" Sam asked.

"Not in front of me. But I could tell he and Leo knew each other pretty well. And they were about the same age, so I assumed they were friends. They might just have been business acquaintances, though. All I know for sure is that Leo wasn't expecting him, that he was surprised to see him.

"Anyway, Leo told me they were going to talk in

the study, so I figured I'd take the *Globe* out to the patio and read it. You know, that little patio outside the study?''

Sam nodded.

''But I was just following them into the room when Leo said why didn't I go read on the back deck, instead of the patio. I knew from that he didn't want me overhearing whatever it was they were going to talk about.

''At any rate, I went and sat out back. Then, after a while, Leo came out, so upset it scared me. And he said to come into the house because there was something he had to tell me. And it was that Bud had threatened him and they'd gotten into a fight and...Bud was dead.''

''And Leo said he'd hit him over the head with the sculpture?'' Sam asked. ''That detail was true?''

The sculpture that had my fingerprints on it was how he'd wanted to phrase it, but he hadn't let himself.

''Of course it was true,'' Jenny said. ''And it's totally bizarre, eh? I mean, one day he's bragging to everyone who'll listen about this wonderful limited-edition piece of art he's just bought, and the next day he's killing someone with it.

''But, Sam, I really did tell you pretty much what happened. The only thing I... You know, I think it would be easier if I just keep going in sequence, okay?''

When he nodded, she pushed her hair back from her face, then continued.

''Well, like I explained before, after he said that

Bud was dead, he started in about how if the cops charged him his career would be ruined—so he was going to frame you. But he needed me to say you were still there when Bud arrived, and that when I went out to the deck, all three of you were in the study.''

"And you agreed to go along with that?" Carrie asked.

"Yes. I mean, I *told* him I would. I never really would have, but if you'd seen the state he was in, you'd have said you would, too. You'd have been afraid not to.

"So I said, okay, I'd tell the police exactly what he wanted me to. And it didn't seem to even occur to him that I might not. I think that must have been because he was pretty unhinged, 'cuz he's normally suspicious. But this time it was like, when I said okay, he figured he could totally trust me.''

Sam nodded again, thinking Leo *must* have been "pretty unhinged." Under normal circumstances, he'd have realized Jenny was smart enough to know that lying about a murder was very serious stuff.

"Then he started saying he had to call the cops soon," she continued, "or else they'd wonder why he'd waited so long. But he figured he could buy a little time to 'straighten around the study'—that's how he put it—if he turned off the air-conditioning and opened the house up. He said that way the body wouldn't cool off much, because it was so hot out. And that would affect the time-of-death estimate.''

"He wasn't missing a trick," Sam muttered.

"Well, he wasn't and yet he was. I mean, like I

said, for him to believe that I'd lie to the police about a murder... Usually, he'd never buy something like that at all, let alone so easily. But his mind was ticking away just fine when it came to other details. The entire thing was pretty surreal.

"Anyway, he said he had to get started setting things up so it would look like you'd killed Bud. He knew that when the cops arrived they'd be going over every inch of the house, not just the study. And he said there was something he didn't want them to find, so I'd have to get it out of there for him and hide it in my apartment. He said that by the time I got back, he'd be ready to phone the police.

"And... Well, that's really the only part I changed when I was telling you before. I didn't grab his car keys and run. He gave them to me."

"Why didn't you just say that?"

She hesitated. "Because I didn't want to tell you he'd given me something to hide."

"Why not?" Carrie asked.

"Because... It just didn't strike me as a good idea. I hadn't had enough time to think things through and... Let's leave that part for the moment, okay?"

"All right," Carrie said slowly.

"Okay. So I left his place, and the whole time I was driving home I was trying to figure out what I should do."

Although she'd been making it clear she didn't appreciate them interrupting, Sam couldn't stop himself from asking, "Why didn't you just go back to Leo's, then tell the police the truth when they questioned you?"

She shot him a look that said she'd been giving him credit for more brains than he had. "I told you, Leo wasn't thinking quite straight when it came to the idea of my lying for him. But I knew that, sooner or later, it would dawn on him that I might tell the cops you'd left before Bud arrived. Which meant that if I'd gone back, he might have killed me so I wouldn't be able to."

"Oh, Lord," Carrie whispered. "But you could have gone to the police with Sam—without going near Leo again."

"No, I…" A tear trickled down Jenny's face. She quickly wiped it away. "Just let me finish, okay? Then maybe you'll understand."

"All right," Carrie told her. "We'll try to keep quiet."

"Okay. I knew that once he realized I'd taken off, he'd send someone looking for me. But since he thought I was coming back, I figured I had time to pack and make a few phone calls. And after that…well, you pretty much know the rest. I went to Linda's, and when she got home from work, she gave me the keys to the cabin."

With that, Jenny lapsed into silence.

Carrie waited a couple of seconds, then said, "What about this thing Leo gave you to hide? And you haven't explained why you refused to go to the police with Sam."

"Carrie, I've said a dozen times why I can't talk to the police—either with Sam or without him. If I told them that I know Leo murdered Bud, he'd have me killed."

"Dammit, he's *already* trying to have you killed. And if you don't talk to them, he might get away with murdering Bud. And probably you, too."

"But if I *do* talk to them I'll end up dead for sure! There won't be any 'probably' about it."

"No, that just doesn't compute. If you gave them a statement, what good would it do Leo to kill you after that? It would be too late. And if anything happened to you, they'd know he'd had something to do with it."

"Oh, puh-leeze," Jenny muttered. "As I said, hanging around with him, I've learned a lot. And I know exactly how that would play out. I'd die accidentally. Maybe, at most, under suspicious circumstances. And it wouldn't be too late at all.

"If I was dead, I wouldn't be able to testify at a trial. So all the prosecution would have was my statement. Period. And just think about where things would go from there.

"Leo's one of the top criminal lawyers in the country. If he was charged with Bud's murder, he'd obviously orchestrate his own defense. And can you seriously imagine the Crown getting a conviction against Leo Castanza on the basis of a statement made by a dead woman?"

"But—"

Jenny shook her head, cutting Carrie off. "There's no way the prosecutor would have a prayer. Especially not when you tell me Leo got rid of Bud's body.

"If he's trying to cover up that murder, he'll do a darned good job of it. And without a body, it's always tough to prove there ever was a murder. So he might end up never being tried at all. And even if he was, it would take him about thirty seconds to convince a jury that...

"Oh, I don't know. Maybe he'd say he'd broken up with me. And that I accused him of murder as a way of getting revenge. He's always talking about cases where he broke the Crown's key witness in cross examination—made people admit they were lying just to get revenge."

"But..." Carrie paused. The scenario her sister was painting seemed preposterous, yet somehow she could imagine it happening—and that was scaring her half to death.

"Believe me," Jenny continued, "if Leo claimed he'd dumped me, he'd have people to back that up. He'd have witnesses who'd back up whatever story he decided to go with. And the fact that I died before he came to trial would be just one of those unfortunate things."

Carrie's stomach had begun to churn, and she felt so upset she couldn't think of what to say next.

The motel room was silent until Sam said, "What about this thing Leo gave you to hide?"

Jenny looked across the space between the beds at him. "I think that's my only chance. *Our* only chance. I mean, when Leo's guy tells him you were at the cabin—"

"He won't know who we were," Carrie interrupted.

"Oh, Carrie, they'll find out. There's no doubt

about that. And Leo will be certain I've told you everything, which means…''

''Which means he'll want *all* of us dead,'' Carrie said, almost able to feel the color drain from her face. ''But if *three* of us went to the police…''

She looked at Sam. Surely she wasn't the only one who realized how insane this was. Leo couldn't just get away with murder because the people who knew what he'd done were afraid to speak up.

But Sam was shaking his head.

''I think Jenny's probably right,'' he said. ''If she goes to the cops, Leo will kill her. And if we went without her, he'd want her dead even more than he already does—so she could never back up what we'd told them.

''Besides, our going to them on our own wouldn't be any real help. We've talked about this before. We have nothing but hearsay. And that makes us worthless as witnesses.

''Not that I'm saying Leo wouldn't be a lot happier if we were dead. I'm sure he would. He isn't the sort of man who likes loose ends. But that's all we represent to him.''

''We're only loose ends? Even though his guy tried to kill us tonight?'' Carrie demanded. ''That certainly wasn't hearsay.''

''No, but knowing Leo, I'll bet there's nothing that could tie what happened at the cabin to Bud's murder.''

''Sam?'' Jenny said. ''I think I can get us all out of this mess. I think I can cut a deal with Leo.''

Carrie stared at her sister, waiting for her to go on.

If there was a viable way out, she dearly wanted to know what it was.

"I can offer to give Leo back what he gave me in exchange for our safety," Jenny elaborated.

"Exactly what did he give you?" Sam asked.

"I'm not really sure. It was a padded envelope with two computer disks in it, but I have no idea what's on them. Or why they're so important to him. I only know they are."

"Because he was worried about the police finding them," Sam said.

"Well, yeah, partly. But when he handed me the envelope, I asked what was in it. And he gave me the funniest look and said, 'The keys to the vault.' Like whatever's on the disks has to be *really* important."

"But only two little disks?" Carrie said.

Jenny nodded.

"Then why didn't he just stick them in his pocket? Why send you off with them?"

"I don't know. I didn't ask."

"He was wearing shorts and a T-shirt," Sam said. "Maybe there wasn't a pocket in his shorts. Or maybe he was afraid of wrecking the disks.

"But wait a minute," he added to Jenny. "I just thought of something. You said that you followed Leo and Bud into the study before Leo told you to take your paper out back."

"Right."

"Was Leo's computer on then? When you walked into the room? Did you notice?"

She hesitated a moment, then said, "No, I didn't, but it couldn't have been. Because it wasn't on during our meeting with you. And after you left, Leo and I were just sitting in the living room talking. He hadn't gone back into the study at all before Bud arrived. Why?''

''Because when Carrie and I went to have a look around at his place, it was on. Remember, Carrie?''

She nodded. It had been easier to see the room because of the glow from the screen.

''So he must have been using it while Bud was there,'' Sam said. ''Either that or he was using it afterward, which isn't nearly as likely. Not if he was as upset as Jenny says.

''And that means we should check out those disks. Maybe something on them would tell us what he and Bud were arguing about. And that might tell us...well, who knows, but it's got to be worth a look.''

''Where are they?'' Carrie asked Jenny. ''In your suitcase?''

''No.''

''Then where? Oh, Lord, you didn't leave them in your apartment, did you? Leo's guy might have—''

''No, of course I didn't leave them in my apartment. If I had, I'd have had a fit when you told me somebody'd been in there.''

''Then where are they?''

Jenny stared at her sneakers. ''I can't tell you,'' she said at last.

''What do you mean you *can't?*''

''All right, I guess I should be saying I'm not going to.''

CHAPTER SIX

CARRIE SIMPLY LOOKED at Jenny, the pulse in her temple throbbing so hard she could hear it inside her head.

"Jenny, Leo wants you dead," she said at last. "And he'd be only too happy if Sam and I were dead right along with you. But despite that, you figure it's a good idea to be keeping secrets from us?"

"Yes, because if you knew where those disks are, Leo could make you tell him. Then we'd all be completely screwed."

"Dammit, Jenny, if we knew where they were, we could see what's on them. And like Sam said, they might tell us something very worthwhile. Don't you think—"

"No! I don't. Carrie, I've been thinking and thinking about all this. And as long as I'm the only one who knows where they are, and Leo can't find me, it'll—"

"He can't find you?" Sam said. "Let's get real here. We've already seen how easily he found you once."

She shook her head. "I need to go someplace a whole lot farther away. Out of the country. I realized that as soon as I started thinking things through, and I've got my passport in my suitcase.

"But I was afraid that when it dawned on Leo that I wasn't coming back, he'd send people to check the airport departures. So I thought it would make sense to lie low in the cabin for a few days, *then* head for someplace where he can't possibly find me."

"And live the rest of your life afraid he eventually might?" Carrie said.

"No, I've got no intention of hiding out forever. But… I'm trying to think the way Leo will. And for the first couple of days, he'll figure he can track me down in no time. So I'll wait three or four days before I contact him, until he's had time to sweat a little. Until he's realized there's a good chance he's *not* going to find me. Then he'll be more receptive to making a deal."

"And in the meantime?" Carrie demanded. "As you said yourself, he'll be certain you've told us everything, so he's going to pay us a visit and—"

"Carrie, I'm really, really sorry you got involved in this. I never meant you to, not for a minute! I mean, I had to tell Sam what was happening. Otherwise Leo would have been able to frame him. But there was no reason you had to get mixed up in it."

"That's my fault," Sam said.

Carrie glanced at him. His expression was so guilty she felt a pang of sympathy. Maybe she *wouldn't* be mixed up in this if it weren't for him, but he had no reason to feel badly that she was. Especially not when he was still with her, doing all he could to help.

"Look, I'm *glad* I'm involved," she said, realizing

glad was the wrong word the instant it came out. "You know what I'm saying," she added. "I wish this situation didn't exist, but since it does, I wouldn't want to *not* be involved. It's just that we seem to be in so deep I'm not sure how we're going to get out."

Jenny gave her a wan smile. "Don't look so worried. I think I made things sound worse for you and Sam than they really are, because he's right about the hearsay. Leo will know you two aren't a serious threat to him. If you started trying to tell people he was a murderer, he'd just turn around and slap you with a slander suit. And he'll realize that even though he might get away with killing me, he'd never get away with killing all three of us. Not even the great Leo Castanza would be able to convince a jury that we *all* died accidentally."

"You know what?" Sam said.

Jenny looked over at him. "What?"

"That's another good argument for telling us where those disks are. If we knew, not only could we check them out, but if anything happened to one of us, there'd still be two who—"

"No," Jenny said firmly. "I told you, I've given this a lot of thought. And I'm not telling *anyone* where they are, so there's no point in wasting time discussing it.

"So, where were we?" she continued, before either Carrie or Sam could argue further. "Oh, yeah, Leo's bound to pay you a visit. And when he does, just tell him that you don't know where I've gone, but—"

"Jenny, he wouldn't believe that for a second," Sam interrupted.

"But it won't matter. Not if you say that you've got a message for him from me—that I said to remind him I've got an envelope that belongs to him.

"Maybe you shouldn't let on that you know about the disks, though. I mean, he's going to be absolutely certain I told you about the murder, but for all he knows, I never even opened the envelope. And it would keep him more off balance if he can't be sure whether you really know everything or not.

"But tell him I said I left the envelope somewhere safe before I went to Linda's—with instructions that if anything bad happens, either to me or one of you two, it's to be turned over to the RCMP."

"The RCMP?" Carrie repeated.

Jenny nodded. "Leo has some friends high up in the Toronto police force. Well, actually, at all levels. I doubt most of them are friends who really like him, but money talks. And even in Toronto the Good, things can disappear from an evidence room, which makes the RCMP a better bet. He's never mentioned having any Mounties in his pocket.

"At any rate, he was worried enough about the police finding those disks that he's sure not going to want the RCMP getting hold of them. So as I said, I'll contact him in a few days. And I'll say that I *did* have a look at what was in the envelope. And that he can have the original disks back in exchange for our continued safety. But that before he gets them, I'm going to have copies made—to hang on to for protection."

Carrie glanced at Sam once more, surprised to realize just how much weight she was prepared to give what he had to say about this. Less than twenty-four hours ago he'd been a complete stranger to her. But in the short time since they'd met, she'd come to trust him implicitly.

When he noticed she was watching him expectantly, he shrugged, then focused on Jenny.

"You might not have to worry about getting copies made," he told her. "If the data's important, Leo would have it backed up. His concern's more likely just what you figure—that he doesn't want the authorities knowing what he's got. In which case, you're right. Threatening him with the RCMP would scare the hell out of him."

Carrie slowly shook her head. If both Sam and Jenny were reading things the same way, maybe the plan would work. But she didn't like it.

"Doesn't there have to be a better way of handling this?" she asked. "I mean, playing a blackmailing game with Leo Castanza has to be dangerous as hell."

"If you can figure out a better way, I'd love to hear it," Jenny said. "But if I didn't have something on him, I'd end up dead. I'm absolutely positive I would. Since I do, though..."

"Let's just not start thinking we're home free," Sam told her. "Your plan might carry us through the short term, but think about what Carrie said a few minutes ago. You'd end up living the rest of your life in fear of Leo—knowing that he'd be doing his damnedest to learn where those disks are, and that if he ever got his hands on them you'd be toast. And I'll bet Carrie and I would end up dead pretty damned fast, too.

"So even if he agreed to play let's make a deal, none of us would ever really be safe. Not until he's either pushing up daisies or he's been convicted of Bud's murder. And we obviously shouldn't hold our breath hoping one of those things will happen soon."

Carrie licked her lips uneasily. She might be crazy to suggest what she was thinking...

"What?" Sam asked her.

"What you just said. That none of us will really be safe until Leo's either dead or convicted."

He gave her a weary smile. "You want to kill him?"

Much to her surprise, she managed to smile back. "Well," she said, "I'll admit that option has a lot of appeal. But I was thinking more about helping to get him convicted."

BY THE TIME SAM, CARRIE and Jenny had finished talking, it was after four in the morning.

Faced with the choice of catching a little sleep or getting Jenny out of the country as quickly as possible, they voted to forgo sleep and hit the road again. And when they reached Toronto, Sam didn't even slow down.

He'd had the car radio on since they'd left the motel, and there was still nothing on the news about a murder. From that, they'd concluded the police still didn't know what Leo had done.

Obviously, he'd want to keep it that way, and they knew Jenny was right—he could easily have people watching the airline departures at Pearson International. Plus the trains at Union Station and the buses at the depot downtown. But they decided even Leo wouldn't have sent anyone the ninety-plus miles to the Buffalo airport.

With that in mind, they stayed on the highway and headed for the New York State border. As they sped through the dawning light, they filled in the time by trying to decide what Jenny's ultimate destination should be.

Since she was buying her ticket at the last minute, the airline would require ID. That meant she'd have to travel under her real name, so they'd just have to hope Leo wouldn't try to check the lists of Buffalo's departing passengers. Or that if he did, whichever airline she used actually kept its records confidential. But in case he did learn which flight she'd taken, they wanted her to end up someplace where she wouldn't be easy to find.

After they'd talked about a few potential destinations, she said, "You know, I think the farther I go, the better. Maybe I'm being paranoid, but I've seen people underestimate Leo and come to regret it awfully fast."

"I don't think you're being paranoid," Carrie told her. "Not when he knows he could be looking at a murder charge if he doesn't track you down."

Sam glanced into the rearview mirror at Jenny, wondering if Carrie's words had frightened her even more. It wasn't obvious, but he knew that none of them were feeling confident about how this would ultimately end up.

That started him wishing, yet again, that Jenny would tell them where those disks were. Knowing why they were so important to Leo might give them more leverage. And he'd like to be sure they were as safely out of Leo's grasp as Jenny seemed to think, because Leo would be doing all he could to find them.

Briefly, he considered asking her about them again. But she'd been adamant she wasn't going to tell, so he simply kept quiet and turned his thoughts to Carrie's idea about trying to help convict Leo of murder.

If Leo was behind bars they'd all be able to breathe easier because Jenny had made a valid point about the statement of a dead woman not being worth much in court. Whereas, if she actually testified before a jury, it would be too late for Leo to gain anything by having her killed.

Anything except revenge.

Realizing they were a long way from having to worry about that, Sam turned his thoughts back to the prospect of Carrie and him trying to find evidence.

He figured, at best, it would be a shot in the dark. Hell, at this point they didn't even know Bud's identity. All they had was Jenny's description of him, and an awful lot of men were in their late forties, average height, a little overweight, with graying brown hair and glasses.

"Jenny, try thinking like Leo again," Carrie said. "Would he assume you'd head for a big city?"

"Probably. So I was already figuring that might not be a good idea. If he learned more or less where I was, he might go the private detective route. And if we were talking a place with big law firms, he'd find someone who'd refer him to the best. He can get contacts in any major city."

"Then what about someplace in Mexico," Sam suggested. "It has a lot of small towns. And so many tourists you wouldn't seem out of place."

Carrie shot him a look that said he was dreaming. And she was right. A woman who looked like Jenny would be noticed wherever she went. That was one of their problems.

Nobody spoke for a minute or so, then Carrie said, "Costa Rica has a lot of small towns, too. I spent a couple of weeks there last year. And it might not be a place Leo would think of." She looked back at Jenny. "Remember I told you about that little town near where I was staying? Playas del Coco? And how there were some of the tiniest hotels in it? All the towns probably have places like that."

"Right," Jenny said thoughtfully. "And they wouldn't be part of any chain. I'll bet Leo could run a check on a hotel chain's registration pretty easily."

"Well, I doubt some of those hotels in Coco even had phones, let alone computerized registration."

There was another minute or two of silence, then Jenny said, "Okay, if I can get a flight there without waiting forever, let's make it Costa Rica. But…"

"But what?" Carrie prompted.

"Oh, it's just that when Leo talks about cases he's working on, I always think it's scary that he can find out things so easily."

"Well, once you're through customs you can use a phony name. That'll make it harder."

"In most countries, any hotel she checked into would ask for her passport," Sam pointed out. "Even small ones."

"Oh, right. Lord, I'm so tired I didn't even think about that."

She looked tired, he thought, glancing at her. There were dark circles under her eyes and he could see little lines he hadn't noticed before on either side.

Laugh lines, his mother used to call them. *I don't have wrinkles,* she'd say. *I have laugh lines.*

"What are you thinking about?" Carrie asked.

When he glanced over again, she was studying him closely.

"You had a strange expression on your face," she explained.

He shrugged. "Something made me think about my mother. I don't know why, though. She died when I was a kid, so it's not as if I think of her very often."

"Our mother died when we were kids, too," Jenny said. "When Carrie was ten and I was five."

"Oh?" He looked at her in the rearview once more. "My younger sister was five when it happened. It's not the greatest thing to have in common, is it?" he added to Carrie.

She merely shook her head.

"Sam?" Jenny said after a few seconds.

"Uh-huh?"

"Does your sister remember your mom very well?"

"I'm not sure. She says she does, but I think it might be more that my father was always talking about her. I guess yours did, too."

"Yeah, right. Our dad wasn't there to talk about anything. He took off practically the day I was born."

The bitterness in Jenny's voice made Sam cringe.

"I was too much for him, right, Carrie?" she added. "He took one look at me and packed his bags."

"Why do you always say things like that?" Carrie murmured. "Neither of us knows why he left."

Something in her voice told Sam that was a subject she'd rather Jenny didn't dwell on, so he said, "And after your mother died, who did you live with?"

"Mom's twin sister and her husband," Carrie told him. "Our Aunt Liz and Uncle Ken. They were great. They still are. And they had two boys, so it was like suddenly having brothers."

"Which had its good points and its bad," Jenny put in.

Sam nodded, a question forming in his mind. When Jenny had first told him she had a sister, she'd teased him that she should fix them up.

"Carrie's very picky when it comes to men," he remembered her saying. "But you're both too old to still be single."

Since he'd met Carrie, he'd wondered more than once why she *was* still single.

It had to be by choice. He couldn't be the only man in the world who'd realized she was something special. So now that he knew about her father taking a hike, the obvious question was whether that had scared her off men.

He stared at the road ahead, telling himself he shouldn't be trying to play psychologist. Especially when it didn't matter to him whether she was skittish of men or not. He had no intention of getting involved with her—no matter how much the desire to do exactly that kept nagging at him.

Forcing his mind from that track, he began thinking that things sure hadn't turned out the way he'd anticipated when he'd gone to Carrie's place. He'd simply been hoping that she'd help him find Jenny. And he'd assumed that, if they succeeded, he and Jenny would talk to the police and he'd never see Carrie again.

Life had thrown him a real doozy of a curve, though. Instead of dissolving their partnership, he and Carrie were going into the detective business together. A couple of amateurs trying to help put a high-powered criminal lawyer in jail for murder.

Hell, the idea would be downright laughable if it wasn't so frightening.

They had to do something, though. They couldn't just sit around and hope Leo would let things slide, because he wouldn't.

In fact, Sam wouldn't be surprised to find Mr. Castanza waiting on either his or Carrie's doorstep when they arrived home. And until it became clear how the good counselor intended to play things...

He looked at Carrie once more, knowing that after they got back home he was going to be afraid to let her out of his sight. Which was an awfully far cry from never seeing her again.

The problem was, the more time he spent with her, the stronger his attraction to her was growing. And he knew better than to play with fire.

Surreptitiously, he glanced at her yet again, admitting to himself that if he wasn't so damned sure he'd get burned, he'd have no objection to playing with this particular fire.

THEY REACHED THE Greater Buffalo International Airport so early that none of the smaller airlines were even open for business yet.

The major ones were, though, and within two minutes a male American Airlines' agent was falling all over himself trying to help Jenny get to Costa Rica.

While they were discussing possible flights, Carrie stood watching Sam, trying to sort out exactly what was happening between them. Or happening to her, at least.

She hadn't been aware of any sexual attraction to him at first, but it was definitely there now. And the longer they were together, the stronger it was getting. Or maybe it had been there from the beginning but she'd suppressed her awareness of it.

That would hardly have been surprising when she'd been terrified he was a murderer. But once she'd learned that Leo was definitely the killer...

Well, whatever was happening to her was highly unusual. Normally, she'd never be more than mildly interested in someone she'd only known for a short time. And she had to admit she was more than mildly interested in Sam.

Of course, the fact that he'd helped save her sister's life had to be influencing her feelings for him. Still, she couldn't make herself believe that was all there was to it. Something about Sam Evans that reached out and touched her deep inside.

Maybe it was simply that he cared, that he wasn't just passing through life as an observer. He didn't stand around passively waiting to see how things developed, he decided what had to be done and did it.

She liked that. And she liked him—aside from the sexual chemistry. In fact, she'd come to like him so quickly and so much that it was almost frightening.

Right this minute, though, he was making her very uneasy—furtively looking around the terminal as if he half expected Leo Castanza to pop up from behind one of the counters.

Telling herself she'd be better off not watching him, she forced her gaze away and tuned in to Jenny and the agent.

"You're in luck," he was telling her. "There are a couple of seats left on our next flight to Miami. It'll be boarding any minute now. Then you'll only have a two-hour wait for the flight to Costa Rica. How does that sound?"

"Terrific."

Carrie watched while her sister gave him some money and he began counting it. The three of them—Sam, Jenny and herself—had maxed their daily cash withdrawal limits at an ATM machine so there'd be no credit card record of Jenny buying the ticket. They knew Leo might try to check on items charged to her account.

The agent finished his counting and handed Jenny her change. As he was moving her suitcase from the scale to the conveyer belt, she looked over at Carrie. "You heard him say the plane will be boarding any minute now?"

When she nodded, Jenny flashed her a smile. "See? Costa Rica was meant to be my destination. I'll bet it was written in the stars."

Her tone didn't fool Carrie for a second. Even though she'd soon be thousands of miles away from Leo, she was still running scared.

"Here you are." The agent handed over the ticket. "It's Gate B, and you should head down there right away."

They'd barely started along the terminal, Sam falling into step beside them, when the boarding call for Jenny's flight came over the loudspeaker.

"Perfect timing," she said.

"That's a good omen," Sam told her.

"Must be," Carrie agreed, hoping it really was. Then, noting the way Jenny's red hair was already peeking out from beneath the scarf she'd bought in the gift shop, she said, "You *did* say you'd packed a wig, didn't you?"

They'd been going over so many details that she couldn't remember the answers to half the questions she'd already asked.

"Models always pack wigs," Jenny assured her. "I've got both a dark one and a blond one along."

"So if anyone *is* looking for you, it'll be like looking for a multiple personality," Sam teased.

Carrie tried to laugh but couldn't. Someone in Costa Rica looking for Jenny was their worst-case scenario.

"Just try to keep a low profile and blend in with the tourists," Sam told her for at least the third time.

"And you probably shouldn't stay in one place very long," Carrie added.

"Will you two stop? You're making me feel like the guy in *The Fugitive*."

"We only want you to be careful," Carrie said as the second boarding call was announced.

"I *will* be careful. Believe me, there's no way I'm underestimating Leo."

Jenny's brave expression vanished momentarily, then she manufactured another smile. "And I'll let you know exactly where I am just as soon as I can."

"Through one of your friends," Sam reminded her.

They'd decided that Leo might have both Carrie's and Sam's phone lines bugged. And possibly Aunt Liz and Uncle Ken's, as well. So it would be too risky for Jenny to call any of those numbers.

"Oh, one more thing." Jenny dug through her purse and produced a pair of keys.

"They're Linda's keys to the cabin," she explained, handing them to Carrie. "Could you get them back to her for me? I *really* think I'll be able to work out something with Leo pretty fast, but just in case..."

"Sure."

"And you won't forget to call the restaurant. Right away, because I'm supposed to be working tomorrow."

"No, I won't forget."

"And make sure you convince them it's something really serious. I might not be crazy about the job, but I don't want to lose it. By the time this is over I'm going to be in serious debt."

"Right," Carrie said, trying not to think that the possibility of losing her waitressing job was the least of Jenny's worries.

"And don't forget to call the agency, too. Tell them I'll check in with them the minute I'm available for assignments again."

They'd almost reached the security check by that point, and they stopped a few yards from it.

"Take care, huh?" Sam gave Jenny a brotherly hug, then backed away. "I'll just wait over by the wall," he told Carrie.

She nodded, her throat tight with emotion. She'd spent the past twenty years doing her best to look out for Jenny, and right now she felt as if there had to be something more she could be doing.

"Well...this is it," Jenny said.

Carrie hugged her sister tightly. "I wish you didn't have to go off on your own," she whispered.

"And I'm sorry you got involved in this," Jenny said. "I know I already told you that, but I really, really didn't mean it to happen."

"I know."

"We'll both be okay, though. You'll see."

"Sure. Nobody's ever managed to kill either of us before." She was only trying to lighten the mood, but the instant the words were out, her tears spilled over.

"Oh, Carrie, don't cry," Jenny whispered. "You'll get me started, too."

"This is the final boarding call for American Airlines flight 116 to Miami," the loudspeaker announced. "All passengers should now be at Gate B."

"Get going," Carrie murmured. She released Jenny from their hug, her vision blurred by the tears.

"Right. I've just got to warn you about something first. Whatever you do, don't go letting yourself fall for Sam."

"What?"

"I can tell he's really interested in you. He practically starts drooling whenever he looks at you. But there are things you don't know about him."

"What *things?* What are you saying? That he's a bigamist or something?"

"No, I don't think he's even been married once."

"Then what *things?*"

"Carrie, if I told you the bare bones and not the details I'd only scare you half to death. And there just isn't time to get into them now, so—"

"Dammit, then why didn't you start this conversation hours ago?"

"Because I haven't been alone with you for even half a second since we left the cabin! He's been right there with us the whole time. And that's the reason I couldn't tell you exactly what I did with the disks— the reason I didn't tell Sam that Leo had given me anything to hide when I phoned him.

"Carrie, Sam's a nice enough guy that I didn't want Leo railroading him, but he isn't exactly Mr. Straight and Narrow. So I can't be sure that if he got his hands on those disks he wouldn't decide to make a deal with Leo all on his own."

"But—"

"Just listen. The bottom line is that you shouldn't

get any more involved with him than you have to.
And—''

"Jenny?" Sam said, so close beside Carrie that she
jumped. "If you don't get going you'll miss the
plane."

She nodded, then caught Carrie's eye. "Remember
what I just said. It's *really* important."

With that, she turned and ran toward the security
check. A second later, she'd disappeared.

"Hey," Sam said, gently wiping tears from Carrie's cheek.

Her heart began beating furiously as he wrapped
his arms around her and drew her to him. She might
have been aware of her attraction to him before this,
but she was suddenly ten times *more* aware.

He smelled deliciously like a woods in autumn, and
it felt every bit as good in his arms as she'd known
it would. The two of them fit perfectly together. His
chest was firm and warm against her; his chin brushed
the top of her head, making her feel totally enveloped
by him.

But what *things* had Jenny been talking about?

"It's going to be okay," he murmured. "We'll
work it out. But what was Jenny telling you? What
did she say is so important?"

Carrie pressed her cheek against his chest, knowing
she should pull away but unable to.

"Nothing, really," she made herself whisper. "She
was just worried about Leo realizing what you and I
are up to."

CHAPTER SEVEN

IT WAS STILL EARLY morning when Carrie and Sam left the Buffalo airport behind and headed back toward Canada.

As he drove, she did her best not to let her gaze drift in his direction. But it was an exercise in futility.

Over and over again, she caught herself looking at him—wondering what the hell those things were she didn't know about him and trying to pretend that Jenny's warning hadn't come more than a little late.

But it had. The sexual pull between her and Sam was so strong that she could scarcely keep her eyes off him, despite what her sister had said.

She forced herself to stare out at the passing countryside, but forcing Jenny's words from her mind proved impossible. ''If I told you the bare bones and not the details,'' she'd said, ''I'd only scare you half to death.''

In retrospect, the statement seemed more than a little excessive.

Of course, Jenny was prone to exaggeration. And when you added that to her flair for the dramatic, maybe those ''things'' weren't nearly as bad as she'd implied.

Or maybe you're trying to kid yourself, an imaginary voice whispered.

No. If there was anything *terribly* bad about Sam, Jenny would have been specific about what it was.

Except that she hadn't had the chance. And if she hadn't been referring to something serious, why would she have bothered with the warning at all?

Carrie swore under her breath. How was she going to find out what her sister had been talking about? Come right out and say, "Sam, Jenny mentioned that you have some deep, dark secrets. Would you mind telling me what they are?"

Hardly. So what could she do? Get him talking? Ask a few leading questions?

Just as she was deciding that was worth a try, he glanced over at her.

"You're awfully quiet," he said, giving her such a warm smile she could feel its heat all the way down to her toes.

"I guess I'm talked out. But I wouldn't mind listening—as long as you promise not to talk about Leo. I think we really need a break from him, so why don't you tell me something about yourself?"

Sam smiled again. "Hasn't anyone ever told you it's dangerous to suggest that to a man?"

"I'll risk it. After all the time we've spent together, virtually the only things I know about you are that you live alone, have a younger sister and build boats."

"Then...let's see. I'm originally from the West Coast, and my father and sister—Dianne's her name—still live in Vancouver.

"She got married a couple of years ago. In fact, she's about to make me an uncle."

"Uncle Sam."

He laughed at that, his laugh so deep and rich it made Carrie tingle inside.

"Right. I guess I'll have to get a stars-and-stripes suit before I go see the baby."

"And you came to Toronto because...?" she prompted when he didn't continue. Maybe the "things" were in the long-ago past and he'd left them behind out West.

"Well, I originally intended to be an architect," he told her. "And I came east right after I'd finished the first year of the program.

"I hadn't been able to line up a summer job that would give me any relevant experience. Then a friend of my father's, a man named Slade Coburn, suggested I spend the summer working for him. He was the founder of Port Credit Custom Boats. Which is my company now," he added, glancing over.

She nodded. "I noticed the company's name when you showed me your card."

"You've got a good memory," he said, giving her yet another smile. "At any rate, there I was without a useful job. And since I was obviously going to learn a lot more about design and construction by working on boats than by flipping burgers, I took Slade up on his offer. And that, as they say, was history.

"It turned out I really liked the boat business. And I liked Slade, as well. So instead of going back to university, I kept on working for him. Then a few years back, when he decided to retire, I bought the company. I mean, I'm still paying him for it, but it's pretty much mine now.''

Sam looked across the car again. ''And that's the basic Sam Evans life story.''

''Minus a few details.''

''Yeah, but I'd get downright boring if I started in on the details.''

She forced a smile, resisting the urge to tell him the details were what she was after. ''And what do you do when you're not building boats?'' she said instead.

''Actually, I don't get to do as much of the building part as I'd like to anymore. I have to spend most of my time on the business side of things.''

''But your life can't be *all* work.''

''Boring as it sounds, since I bought the company it pretty well has been.''

''Oh.''

She wondered if that explained why his engagement hadn't worked out, but she wasn't going to ask. And she couldn't think of how to push any harder about his past without its being obvious she was digging for something specific.

When Sam glanced over at Carrie once more, heat started curling in his groin. He wasn't totally naive when it came to women. He knew what was happening here. She was curious about his life because she was attracted to him in exactly the same way he was to her.

It made him desperately wish things were different. If they were, the way she kept watching him would make him so damned happy he'd stop the car and take her in his arms right this second.

But nothing could change the past. And if Carrie knew…

He told himself there was at least a chance she'd be okay with it. That she and his ex-fiancée were two very different women. But if Valerie—who'd once claimed to love him enough to marry him—had dumped him when he'd confided in her, why would a woman he barely knew take a chance on him?

There was little likelihood that she would. Not a woman like Carrie, who could probably have just about any man she wanted.

Still, he couldn't keep his gaze from stealing in her direction again. Then, even though he was aware how foolish he was being, he allowed it to linger on her a moment longer.

When he focused on the road ahead once more, his thoughts remained on Carrie. The longer he spent with her, the closer he could feel himself being drawn to that emotional line he hadn't dared cross for years. Of course, since Valerie had walked out on him, he'd never met a woman who'd seriously tempted him.

Oh, there'd been the occasional bout of recreational sex, but never any serious expectations on either side.

He just knew that wasn't how things would be with Carrie, though, just knew she was the sort of woman who only played for keeps. He also knew, courtesy of her sister, that she was awfully picky when it came to the type of man she played with. And he had no illusions about fitting the bill, which meant that if he let himself cross that line with her, he'd end up hurting.

So he just wasn't going to—despite the fact that his desire for what he couldn't have was getting stronger by the minute.

NOT LONG AFTER THEY'D passed through Customs at Niagara Falls, Sam was able to pick up Toronto's all-news station. There still wasn't a word on it about Bud's murder, so the cops still couldn't be aware of it.

The more he thought about that, the more uneasy it made him. It had to mean he and Carrie might well find Leo Castanza lying in wait for them when they got back. Finally, he told her what he was worrying about.

"I know," she said. "And what's got me most frightened is the uncertainty. I mean, he's got to have realized that we know what he did. And what if he isn't planning on starting off by just talking to us? What if we don't have a chance to lay Jenny's threat on him before…"

"I think we'll be okay there. As she said, even the great Leo Castanza wouldn't be able to convince a jury that a whole bunch of us died accidentally. But…"

"But what?"

He was reluctant to continue because, in one respect, he was only begging for trouble. Yet what else could he do? The thought of Carrie having to confront Leo alone wasn't something he wanted to even contemplate.

"I think we'd be smart to stick together for the next little while," he said at last. "Until we're sure how Leo is going to play things. I mean, stick together twenty-four hours a day."

"Stay at either your place or mine," he added in the face of her silence. "And during the day, when I have to be at the boatyard, you could bring what you're working on down there. I've got more than enough space for you to set up an easel or whatever you need."

Carrie nervously caught her lower lip between her teeth and considered the suggestion. Since they were going to tell Leo the RCMP would get that envelope if any harm came to them, logic said he wouldn't try to kill them.

But the universe didn't always unfold logically. And for all they knew, he'd thought of a critical angle they'd missed. Or maybe he'd somehow learned where Jenny had left the disks and already had them back.

In that case, killing them would be his obvious next move. Then he'd search for Jenny until he found her.

"Hey," Sam said quietly. "Surely this can't be a tough decision. Not when we know Leo has friends with guns. I mean, I'm not the best shot in the world, but I'm not the worst, either."

Exhaling slowly, she tried to decide what she should do. The prospect of them living under one roof, even briefly, made her extremely nervous. But she had to admit it was probably the safest plan.

There was no way in the world she wanted to be on her own, terrified of every moving shadow that crossed her path and every creak her house made. And she couldn't come up with any other viable options.

If she went to stay with Aunt Liz and Uncle Ken, or with one of her friends, she'd be putting them in danger. Whereas Sam, she reflected unhappily, was already in danger.

Besides that, none of her friends or relatives owned guns. And as anxious as the thought of Sam actually having to use his Beretta made her, she was glad he had it.

The problem was that she had little trouble imagining what might happen if they were together—day and night—for much longer.

But she wouldn't *let* it happen, she told herself firmly. She simply couldn't. Not without knowing the truth about him.

ONCE A SLEEPY SUMMER resort town, Sam's adopted home of Port Credit had long ago been incorporated into Mississauga—the city Toronto's western boundary had, over the years, sprawled out to reach.

Port Credit, though, was unlike the rest of Mississauga. Signs on the main street proclaimed it to be Mississauga's Village on the Lake, and it truly had retained the flavor of a small town.

The houses near the water were mostly renovated old wooden cottages. Farther north were almost-as-old brick homes, while a working lighthouse stood guard at the mouth of the Credit River.

Sam loved the area. And usually the nearer he got to home, the more relaxed he felt. But today was an exception. By the time he reached the Mississauga Road exit and turned off the Queen Elizabeth Way, his stomach was in knots.

He glanced over at Carrie and, keeping his tone casual, said, "We'll stop by and check my house. Just make sure there's no sign that Leo or any of his friends have been there. Then we can head to your place and pick up what you need."

She nodded. Deciding to stay at his house, rather than hers, had been the logical choice. He'd told her he lived only a stone's throw from his boatyard; she could work regardless of where she was. She couldn't help wondering, though, how much work she'd be able to get done with him as a distraction.

Telling herself that was the least of her worries at the moment, she glanced out of the car as he turned onto Lakeshore Road.

A continuation of Toronto's Lake Shore Boulevard, Port Credit's main street paralleled the shoreline only a couple of blocks north of it. The street was lined with trendy little stores and restaurants, which she gazed out at as they drove.

Finally Sam swung down a side street and said, "We're almost there."

His words started her pulse beating rapidly.

What if Leo or one of his friends *was* at Sam's place waiting for them? What if, when he opened his door, someone was standing inside with a gun?

Reminding herself that logic said Leo wouldn't kill them—not just yet, anyway—she started silently repeating the words like a mantra. She was still saying them when Sam pulled into a driveway and announced, "This is it."

She took a moment to look at the few cars parked along the street.

Leo's Caddy wasn't among them. Nor was there a dark Probe or the four-by-four that had arrived at the Willenziks' cabin.

That didn't guarantee they weren't in for a nasty surprise, of course, but it made her feel a tiny bit less anxious.

"It looks...great," she said, finally letting herself focus on the house.

A two-story renovated cottage of board-and-batten construction, it was painted bluish gray and accented with white gingerbread trim. A pair of white wicker rocking chairs sat invitingly on the porch. The garden was a blaze of wildflowers.

She looked at Sam. "Did you do the renovating yourself?"

When he nodded, she said, "I'm impressed." And she truly was.

The board-and-batten was in such good condition it looked new, although she realized it couldn't be. The boards were too wide to have been milled in the last half century, so whatever damage they'd sustained over the years must have been carefully repaired.

The original windows had been replaced with modern ones, and she could see a couple of other areas where Sam had obviously updated and redesigned. But he'd maintained the building's integrity and original charm. She almost commented that he should have been an architect. Then she remembered that was what he'd started off intending to be.

When she glanced across at him once more, he'd retrieved his gun from beneath the seat and was tucking it into his belt.

Her pulse began racing again.

"Why don't you wait here," he said, opening his car door. "Everything seems fine, but I'll just have a look inside."

"No," she said so quickly she almost choked on the word. "I'll go with you."

Lord, even in the bright light of day she didn't want to be left on her own. Not that she was crazy about going in to check the house, either, but she'd feel safer being with Sam than staying in the car without him.

Reminding herself she'd better not start feeling so safe with him that she forgot about Jenny's warning, she climbed out of the air-conditioned Mustang into the gathering heat of the day.

It was going to be another scorcher. And she suspected that, if she tried, she'd actually be able to wring the humidity from the air. Not even the breeze off the lake was cool, but at least it was fresh. Taking a deep breath, she trailed Sam up the walk and onto the porch.

From there, when she looked down toward the end of the block, she could see a tiny patch of the lake, its surface shimmering diamonds in the sunlight.

Sam unlocked the door and pushed it open, but didn't step across the threshold. Instead, they stood where they were, listening to the twittering of birds and the silence of the house.

She found the silence reassuring, and obviously Sam did as well. "There's no sign I've had any company," he said. "But let's take a closer look."

Inside, the flooring was wide pine planks that had been polished to a satin sheen—over a period of decades, Carrie guessed.

The bottom halves of the living-dining room walls were paneled with burnished pine boards. The top halves were plaster, painted a deep shade of gray.

The decor plainly said this was a man's house, yet the room was warm and appealing. Exactly like the man himself, she thought. Unfortunately, when it came to the man himself, she knew that the "warm and appealing" might be only a facade.

Wishing yet again that Jenny had given her more details, she followed Sam into the kitchen, then along to a bathroom, and finally into a room he obviously used as a home office. There, the message light on his answering machine was blinking.

She nervously licked her lips as he pressed Play, expecting to hear Leo's voice. But there were two business-related messages before she finally did.

"Sam, it's Leo Castanza," his message said. "I don't know how you ended up at that cabin with Jenny last night, but I can't apologize enough for what happened.

"There was a total miscommunication between me and the fellow I sent to find my car. I just about had a stroke when he told me he'd tried to make you stop by firing warning shots—and I'll bet you did, too.

"At any rate, I'll explain everything when I'm talking to you in person. In the meantime, I want to touch base with Jenny, but all I'm getting at her place is her machine. So if she's still with you, or if you can get hold of her, ask her to phone me, huh? Otherwise, give me a call yourself."

It wasn't until Carrie heard the click of Leo hanging up that she realized she'd been staring intently at the answering machine.

"Well?" Sam said when she looked at him.

"It didn't take him long to learn who whisked her away, did it?"

Sam shook his head. "His 'fellow' would have written down my plate number and it's easy to run a check. But what about the rest of it?"

"I don't have a clue. He's going to explain everything? And he sounded as if he really expects Jenny to phone him. What do you think he's up to?"

"We know what he's up to. He's trying to get away with murder. The question is, how does he think he's going to manage it? But, look, maybe he left a message for you, too. And if he did, I'd like to hear what it says before either of us talks to him. So why don't you call and check?"

She took the phone from him and dialed her number. But when she punched in the code to retrieve her messages, her machine refused to cooperate.

"It does that sometimes," she explained, handing back the phone. "I think it has something to do with the humidity being so high."

"Well, it doesn't really matter. Just let me call the boatyard and tell them they might have to hold the fort without me today. Then we'll finish checking around in here. After that, we can go to your place.''

Once Sam had made his call, they headed up the burnished wooden staircase to the second floor—Carrie still trying to figure out what tricks Leo had up his sleeve. Given that message, he was obviously intending to play innocent with them. But what was the point? He had to know that Jenny would have filled them in.

Telling herself it was useless to speculate until they knew more than they did at the moment, she turned her attention to the upstairs rooms.

There were three of them, all bedrooms, one of which Sam was partway through replastering. A ladder stood in the middle of the room, surrounded by cans and tools, and a pile of drop sheets lay in one corner.

"This is the guest room," he told her when they looked into the smaller of the remaining two. "Think you'll be okay here?"

"Sure, but…"

"But what?"

She hesitated. While she'd been busily puzzling over what Leo might have in mind, she'd almost forgotten they'd decided she'd stay here. But now that Sam had reminded her, she was thinking she probably wouldn't be fine at all—that she'd be very uncomfortably aware he was sleeping in the room right next to hers.

"It just occurred to me," she said at last, "that if Leo's going to play things cool, there's no real reason for me to stay here."

He shook his head. "We can't be *sure* what he's got in mind. Besides, being in the same place will be more efficient. And it makes sense in case he *does* have our phones bugged."

"I guess you're right," she reluctantly admitted.

Giving her a quick smile, Sam turned and started for the stairs. Following him, she discovered that she couldn't force her eyes from his broad shoulders. Or stop herself from noticing the sexy way the bottom of his dark hair curled at the base of his neck.

Just looking at those tantalizing little curls started her fingers itching. But she was damned well going to keep her relationship with him platonic, even if she noticed a hundred and one sexy things about him.

She already had way more than enough to worry about. All she needed was to let herself get involved with a man Jenny had warned her off.

Trailing out of the house after him, she climbed into the car once more. That was when the irony of the situation struck her.

Jenny had been involved with Leo—a man who'd murdered one of his friends yesterday and then sent someone after Jenny to kill her. So wasn't she a fine one to be warning her sister about men.

On the way to Carrie's, Sam stopped at a pay phone to let her call Jenny's modeling agency and the restaurant where she waitressed. Then they continued on. When they reached her street, there was no sign of Leo or anyone he might have sent. Sam didn't figure that meant much, though.

Maybe someone had come around but left when

Carrie hadn't been home. Or maybe someone was still here, invisibly waiting for her to return.

Before they got out of the car, he stuck the Beretta beneath his belt again.

"Just in case," he said when he caught her eyeing him anxiously.

They went through the same routine they had at his place—opening the door, listening for sounds in the house, cautiously making their way through the entrance hall to the living room and then moving on to the kitchen.

There, her answering machine was blinking, just as his had been. This time, though, the very first message was from Leo.

"Carrie, this is Leo Castanza," he said. "I don't know if you've heard from Jenny, but we had a major argument yesterday and I'm kind of concerned about her.

"I haven't been getting any answer at her apartment, so I thought she might be with you. If she is, or if you've heard from her, give me a call, okay? I just want to be sure she's all right. My number's 555-1648."

"You know what?" Sam said when the message was done.

"What?"

"I don't think he knows you went to the cabin with me."

"How could he not?"

"Well, his guy didn't see us until we were taking off. And it was pretty damned dark, plus he was looking down from the second story. Maybe he couldn't tell there were three people in the car and not two.

"I mean, if Leo knew you were there, why wouldn't he have apologized for his guy shooting at you? The way he did to me?"

She nodded. "I guess he would have, wouldn't he."

Sam thought rapidly, feeling somewhat better about things. "You want to know what I'm thinking?" he finally asked.

"Of course."

"Okay, I'm thinking that if he doesn't know you were involved, why tell him? You could just call him and say you haven't heard anything from Jenny. End of story. You're out of danger."

Carrie simply looked at him for a long minute. "And where are you?" she said at last.

"Right where I've been all along. But instead of both of us playing detective, I can do it on my own, and—"

"Sam," she interrupted, "Jenny's my sister. And let's face facts. At this point, it's highly unlikely that Leo would still be having the slightest thought about trying to frame you. Whereas the odds that he wants Jenny dead are about a million to one. So can you really imagine me backing off and sitting on the sidelines?"

Of course he couldn't. Especially not when he was looking at the firm set of her lush mouth and the determination in her eyes. Her stubbornness made him half want to argue with her, half want to kiss her.

He quickly ruled out arguing. He already knew her

well enough to be certain it would get him nowhere. And when it came to kissing her... Hell, he'd been wanting to do that since sometime last night.

No, he could be more specific than "sometime." He remembered exactly when his initial awareness of her had blossomed into full-blown desire. It had been while they were driving to the cabin. She'd turned to him in the darkness of the car and said, "Thanks for what you're doing." And at that moment he'd known he was in deep trouble.

But he was going to have to give this whole situation a lot of thought before he seriously considered letting anything start up between them. Because that would mean he'd have to tell her about his past. And if he did it too soon, it would scare her off for sure.

On the other hand, if he waited too long, she'd figure he'd been intentionally holding out on her. And then...

Fleetingly, he thought about his one-time fiancée again. About the look on Valerie's face when he'd told her. And how much it had hurt when she'd left.

It wasn't a feeling he wanted to experience a second time. But there had to be some way of telling Carrie without frightening her away.

He glanced at her and caught her watching him once more. And his thoughts turned straight back to the idea of kissing her.

"So?" she said. "What do we do now?"

Exhaling slowly, he manufactured a smile. "Now we do a quick check of the rest of your house. After that, we pack whatever you want to take to my place."

The smile she gave him in return was extremely brief. "Very funny, but you know that's not what I meant."

"Yeah, I know."

Without being sure what Leo's game was, though, he just didn't know what they should do next.

"Okay," he said at last. "I guess it's time to pay Leo a visit. And if you're determined to hang in, we both go."

Carrie's face lost a shade of color.

"You're sure you don't want out?" he asked her.

"Positive. And you're right, going to see him is better than phoning. We want to see his reactions. But we can't forget he's a courtroom lawyer. He's probably been practicing his expressions in front of a mirror since he was a fifteen-year-old."

"Yeah...well, we'll keep that in mind."

CHAPTER EIGHT

SAM PROCRASTINATED ABOUT phoning Leo until after Carrie had gathered up what she figured she'd need over the next few days and they'd packed everything into his car. Then, doing his best to ignore his anxiety, he called Leo's office and set up an appointment for later in the day, telling him the situation with Jenny wasn't something they could discuss over the phone.

"I hope he spends from now until then worrying about what's going on with us," he told Carrie as he hung up. "In the meantime, let's try to figure out what he's up to at this point. If we put together those messages he left, what do we get?"

She hesitated for a few seconds, then said, "According to his version, he and Jenny had a fight. After that, she took off with his car and he sent someone looking for *it,* not her. Oh, and he almost had a *stroke* when he heard his hired hand had been shooting at us—or rather at you and Jenny."

"He probably almost had a stroke because the guy missed," Sam muttered.

She gave him a quick smile. Fleetingly, he thought that she had the most beautiful smile he'd ever seen.

"You know," she said, "he's going to ask how we ended up at the cabin. And his guy told Linda Willenzik not to let anyone know he'd been to see her, so if he hears that she told us…''

''We won't say anything about her. For all Leo knows, Jenny phoned and told you that's where she was going. But just to be safe, do you know where Linda works?''

''Yes.''

''Then we'd better hit another pay phone on our way downtown, let her know that if the guy shows up again she should just play innocent. That we won't have told anyone we talked to her.''

They headed out and stopped at the first phone booth Sam spotted. He was interested enough in what Linda had to say that he stood right outside the booth, where he could listen to Carrie's side of the conversation, but it didn't do him much good.

She'd barely identified herself before she lapsed into silence and simply listened. Then, after a few sympathetic words about whatever Linda had told her, she finally explained why she'd called.

''It would take a while to get into the details,'' she concluded. ''But trust me, we won't say we talked to you, so you shouldn't, either…. Right. Okay, thanks. Oh, by the way, I've got the keys you lent Jenny. Do you need them back right away, or—

''Oh, okay. Then I'll put them in the mail to you. And try not to worry. With any luck, you'll never see that guy again.''

''Well?'' Sam asked as they climbed back into the car and started off again. ''What was she telling you?''

''That her parents got a call from the provincial

police late last night. A neighbor *did* hear the shooting. But by the time the cops showed up at the cabin again, all they found was the door kicked in and the four-by-four—which, it turns out, was stolen in Toronto yesterday.''

"Stolen. Leo certainly has some nice friends, doesn't he."

"Charming. But do you think the police up there will contact you? I mean, when you phoned and asked them to go check out the cabin in the first place, you gave your name."

"Yeah, but there are a lot of Evanses in the book. They'd probably be more likely to run the Caddy's plates and contact Leo, but they might not even do that. I doubt they'll put much effort into a break-in when the only damage was to a door. So don't worry about them. Let's get back to Leo's version of what happened. We got to where he and Jenny'd had a fight, she took off in his car, he sent someone to find it and… What else do we know?"

"That his version doesn't have a word in it about a murder," Carrie said. "Even though he's got to know Jenny told us what happened. At least told *you* what happened. And—"

"Not necessarily."

"What?"

"He can't be certain she told me. I mean, I'm sure he figures she must have. But as long as there's a chance she didn't, he'd be crazy to say anything to us about it.

"Hell, come to think of it, he'd be crazy to, regardless. If he's trying to cover up a murder, he's not

going to admit the truth to anyone. Not even if he's
sure they know it already."

"But we're going to have to come right out and
tell him we know. Because we've got to tell him that
if any of us end up dead, his envelope will go to the
RCMP. If we don't make sure he's got that threat
hanging over his head…"

When Carrie's words trailed off, Sam simply nodded. Neither of them needed to elaborate further.

"But what if we *didn't* know about the murder?"
he said after he'd had time to think.

"What do you mean?"

"I mean, why not play Leo's own game? If he
wants to say that he and Jenny had an argument, why
don't we tell him that's what she said? And claim she
told us that's why she was running from him? Period."

Carrie shook her head. "I don't think he'd buy that
for a minute."

"Why not? If she'd decided not to tell us what
really happened—for whatever reason—the obvious
explanation for taking off would have been that they
had a fight. Hell, that's exactly why *he's* saying that's
what happened.

"And if we can make him believe we don't know
about the murder, then playing detective wouldn't be
as dangerous. He'd have no reason to suspect we were
poking around looking for evidence."

"But I doubt we can make him believe it."

"It's got to be worth a try. So let's figure out what
our entire story's going to be."

"But—"

"Carrie, it's our best shot. Let's just do it. And remember, the first rule for lying is to always keep things as close to the truth as possible. If you only change what's absolutely necessary, there's less chance of getting tripped up."

She looked at him speculatively. "How do you know what the rules for lying are?"

He gave her a casual shrug. "Misspent youth?"

"Really? I thought it might be because you have some horrible secret in your past."

His blood froze.

Then he told himself she was only teasing. But he wasn't entirely convinced of that.

WHILE THE MUSTANG CRAWLED along Queen Street West, trapped behind a streetcar, Carrie kept reminding herself that meeting Leo at his office this afternoon would be far safer than going to his house later. But despite the obvious truth of that, she'd rather have been heading almost anywhere else on earth.

As Sam stopped for a red light at the corner of University Avenue, she glanced over at him, glad that at least she wasn't on her way to face Mr. Castanza alone.

"You think we'll make it by three-thirty?" he asked, checking the dashboard clock.

She nodded, then looked out of the car again. They were getting close to Bay Street, home to many of Toronto's most prestigious law firms, including Leo's.

The light turned green and they started forward again—Carrie feeling more uneasy with each passing second. By the time Sam had found a space in the parking garage under City Hall, her mouth was so dry it felt as if someone had stuffed it with cotton balls.

"Hey," he said, glancing at her as he cut the engine. "This'll go just fine. We know exactly what we've got to do."

"Except for the parts we'll have to play by ear."

"Piece of cake. Haven't we done okay so far?"

She smiled, but it felt forced.

Sam reached across, took both her hands in his, and gave them an encouraging squeeze. "You want to go over the script one more time?"

"That's probably a good idea," she said, although they hadn't come up with much of a script.

"Okay. Basically, we just play dumb and dumber."

"Right," she said, very aware that he was still holding her hands. And that his mere touch was doing wicked things to her insides.

"Even when we give Leo the message about the envelope, we pretend we have no idea what it means. And we don't say a word that'll get him thinking we have any suspicions about *him*. As I said, piece of cake."

"Oh, Sam, you're making it sound so darned easy. But the entire time, he'll be trying to make us slip up and tell him what we really know. And what our real agenda is. It's going to be a game of cat and mouse, and we'll be the mice."

He shot her a grin. "Don't you just hate it when that happens? But we'll be careful mice."

After he'd said that, he simply sat looking at her.

The air in the car felt so charged that she was amazed it didn't start crackling. She couldn't force her gaze from his, and she knew that if she didn't, he was going to kiss her. She waited, barely able to breathe, telling herself she couldn't let him but afraid she would.

Then, without making even the slightest move toward her, he released her hands and said, "Okay, let's go get him."

His words were so far from what she'd been expecting that it took an instant for them to register. When they did, she didn't know whether she was relieved or disappointed.

Relieved, she firmly decided while they were getting out of the car. But she knew that was only partly true.

As she closed the door, her glance flickered to the easel they'd stuck in the back seat. Everything else she'd wanted to take to Sam's had fit into the trunk, but the easel hadn't. And seeing it reminded her that she was going to be alone with him in his house tonight.

It was a reminder she'd just as soon have done without, so she told herself not to think about tonight just yet. First, she'd see what Leo had to say for himself. Then she'd decide whether she still thought Sam's idea about staying together really made as much sense as he seemed to think.

They took the stairs up to ground level and stepped out into Bay Street's standard weekday crush of humanity.

Almost everyone, men and women alike, belonged to either the legal or financial establishments—easily identifiable by their power suits and purposeful strides. Only the bicycle couriers, zipping through the traffic like suicidal maniacs, were dressed for the heat.

"It's probably time to start psyching yourself up," Sam suggested as they walked.

She nodded, then tried to do exactly that. But before she'd begun feeling even marginally confident, they reached their destination—a marble-and-glass office tower at the corner of Bay and Adelaide.

Leo's office was on the twenty-seventh floor, and the law firm's reception area was the size of her town house. The receptionist, a gorgeous blonde, gave both of them a warm smile, then focused on Sam.

"Sam Evans and Carrie O'Reilly to see Leo Castanza," he told her.

She dialed a number and announced them. A couple of minutes later, another woman appeared.

Identifying herself as Mr. Castanza's secretary, she led the way through a maze of offices to the large corner one that Leo rated.

"Sam," he said, rising when she ushered them in. "And Carrie. It's good to see you again."

Liar, she whispered under her breath. He wasn't any happier to see her than she was to see him.

He gestured toward the visitors' seats, then eased back into his own leather swivel chair.

She kept her gaze on him as she sat down, searching for a clue that he was nervous, but she saw nothing except a forty-seven-year-old man with a prominent nose and a receding hairline. A man wearing a thousand-dollar custom-made suit who looked as if it would take a hurricane to ruffle him.

"I didn't realize you two knew each other," he told them.

"We only met yesterday," Sam said. Then he looked at Carrie with an expression so nakedly hungry it made her hot all over, even though she knew it was only part of their script.

Trying to look anywhere but at him, she glanced at Leo—just in time to catch the tiniest smirk on his face.

It was so short lived, she wasn't entirely sure it had been there. But her intuition told her it had. She hoped it meant he'd bought Sam's not-very-subtle display of his "motivation" for having gone chasing out into the countryside after her sister.

"Well," Leo said, focusing on her. "I imagine Sam told you about the fellow I sent to find my car? About how he got carried away? I have to apologize again for his firing off those shots," he added to Sam. "As I said in the message I left, he was acting strictly on his own initiative. I never dreamed he'd do anything like that."

"Nobody got hurt."

"Thank heavens. So Jenny's okay, then?"

"She was the last time we saw her."

"And when was that?"

"Late last night," Carrie said. "Leo, just so you've got all the facts, I should tell you that I went to the cabin with Sam."

"Oh? Then I owe you an apology, too. The shooting must have scared you half to death."

"Yes, it did."

He shook his head. "I should never have asked anyone to go looking for that damned car. I knew Jenny would eventually bring it back, but I was so angry at her for taking it...

"I guess I just didn't want her to think I'd put up with such infantile behavior. Getting back to the cabin, though, how did the two of you end up there?"

"That's not really much of a story," Sam said, neatly sidestepping the question. "But it wasn't long after we got there that your guy arrived. By the way, did he tell you that he broke in?"

"No, he didn't. I guess our miscommunication problem was even more serious than I realized." Leo paused, ruefully shaking his head. "I almost can't believe it," he continued at last. "All I asked him to do was find my car and bring it back. How could he have taken that to mean I expected him to bring Jenny along with it?"

As sincere as Leo was managing to look, Carrie was certain there'd been no miscommunication at all. She'd bet his actual instructions had been to find Jenny and kill her.

"Well, anyway," Sam was saying, "when he smashed in the cabin door, we decided he wasn't somebody we wanted to stick around and talk to. But it's what happened after we took off that's got Carrie and me so concerned."

Leo said nothing, simply waited for one of them to continue.

"Jenny was terribly upset," Carrie finally said. "And she told us she'd had a serious fight with you.

She didn't want to talk about the details, but I kind of pressed her. And that turned out to be a mistake, because she ditched us.''

"What?"

Leo clasped his hands on his desk and leaned forward. Only slightly, but it was enough to make Carrie's stomach muscles tense. He was a whole lot more interested in that little detail than he was letting his body language reveal.

"We'd stopped for coffee at one of those pull-off places on the way back to Toronto," Sam elaborated. "Jenny went to the washroom and just didn't come back."

"When I finally went looking for her, she was gone," Carrie added. "She must have hitched a ride with someone."

"Then you don't know where she is now?" Leo asked.

"No," Carrie said. "We've been by her apartment, but it didn't look as if she'd gone home at all."

"At any rate," Sam put in, "before she took off, she said she wanted us to give you a message."

"Why would she do that?" Leo asked. "She knows how to reach me twenty-four hours a day."

"She said she was never speaking to you again," Carrie told him.

He gave her a pained look.

"We've got no idea what this message is supposed to mean," Sam said, bringing them back to the topic. "But we thought that if you clued us in... Well, Carrie's going to be worried sick until we find Jenny, and she'd feel better if she at least knew what was going on.''

"And what's Jenny's message?" Leo asked.

Carrie held her breath. They'd reached the critical part of their script. If they were going to see an honest reaction from him, it would be now.

"Well," Sam said, "she told us to tell you—"

"Remind you," Carrie remembered to interrupt. "She specifically used the words *remind him,* not *tell him.*"

Sam nodded. They were doing pretty well so far. Carrie had delivered that line right on cue, and the longer they could draw out their explanation, the more unsettled they'd make Leo. That was their theory, at any rate.

Looking across the desk again, he started over. "She said to remind you that she has an envelope of yours. And to tell you that before she got the cabin keys from her friend, she mailed it to someone."

"Who?" Leo demanded.

"All she said was that it was a friend in another city," Carrie told him. "And that she sent it registered mail."

"But...now, here's the part we don't understand," Sam said, sounding puzzled. "She told us to tell you that if anything happens to any of us—and by *us,* she meant herself, Carrie or me—that the envelope would go to the RCMP."

As casually as he could, he leaned back in his chair and waited for Leo's reaction.

For a moment, none was visible. Then Leo slowly shook his head.

"I don't suppose you saw this envelope, did you?"

"No. As Carrie said, she mailed it before she went to the cabin. But what the hell is her message about?"

Leo shook his head again. "It's about the oldest game in the book. As William Congreve succinctly put it hundreds of years ago, 'Heaven has no rage like love to hatred turned, nor hell a fury like a woman scorned.'"

"What are you talking about?" Carrie said.

"Sam told you that he and I had a meeting at my house yesterday?"

She nodded.

"And that Jenny was there?"

"Yes."

"Well, after Sam left, I told Jenny we were through."

"What?"

"That was what our fight was about. And…" Leo paused, punctuating his words with an exaggerated shrug.

"She didn't take the news well, to put it mildly. She called me every name under the sun. And as we've already discussed, after she was through she took off in my car. It's because she was in such an agitated state that I left those messages for you two this morning. After I'd learned about my fellow firing off those shots, I wanted to touch base with her and make sure she was okay.

"I mean, she obviously had no way of knowing they were only warning shots—no more than you did. And given how upset she was, I figured if she thought someone had actually been shooting at her… At any rate, the bottom line is that I just wanted to be sure she was okay. I still do.''

Leo dug out his wallet and gave Carrie two cards. ''One of those has my office, home and cellular numbers. The other one I rarely give out, but it's the number for my personal answering service. If you hear from Jenny and can't reach me any other way, use it. They can always get in touch with me.''

The man was doing his best to sound as if he cared more about Jenny than anyone else on earth, Sam thought. It wasn't hard to see why he won the vast majority of his cases. Everything he'd told them hung together perfectly, and his delivery had been reasoned and totally sincere.

If they didn't know the real Leo, and hadn't heard Jenny's side of the story, they wouldn't doubt he'd been telling them the truth.

''I'm glad you've set things straight, Leo,'' he said. ''Knowing what the fight was about helps put things into perspective. But I'm still not clear on this message Jenny wanted us to give you. What's the story with the envelope? And the implication that some harm might come to one of us?''

''I don't have a clue what *harm* she has in mind, but it certainly wouldn't be coming from me. As for an envelope, there isn't one. Not one that I know anything about, at least.''

''What do you mean there isn't one?'' Carrie said. ''Are you saying Jenny made it up?''

''Look, I've got no idea, specifically, what your sister's playing at. But we both know she's a frustrated actress.''

Frustrated actress. The words lodged uncomfortably in Sam's mind, and a tiny doubt began whispering in his ear. He liked Jenny well enough. He hadn't lied to Carrie about that. But there *was* a sense of the theatric about her. He'd written it off as being part and parcel of her modeling career, but if it ran deeper than that...

He glanced at Carrie, telling himself Jenny would never have downright lied to them about what had happened. And that Leo must be lying through his teeth. But what if they hadn't gotten the entire, precise truth from Jenny?

"As I said," Leo continued, "this is the oldest game in the book. Hell, I see it all the time. Come to think of it, it's probably some of the stories I've told Jenny that gave her the idea. I mean, she's mad as hell. And she's obviously hatched some plan to get revenge—one that involves a fantasy about the three of you being in danger from me.

"But let's get serious. As much as she'd love to give me grief, she's deluding herself if she thinks I'm going to worry about whatever she's up to. For all I care, she can tell the entire world she's got some envelope the RCMP would be interested in. People would just figure she's nuts. And when it comes to the idea that I'm out to harm someone... Well, why on earth would I want anything to happen to either of you two?

"Especially you, Sam," he added. "After all the time we've spent refining the plans for my boat, do you think I'd want to be faced with finding myself another builder and starting over at square one?"

SAM WAS ABSOLUTELY DYING to talk to Carrie alone. Even though he didn't *really* believe any of Leo's explanation, he wanted to ask her a couple of questions.

But Leo had seen them out to the reception area, then proceeded to wait with them after they'd pushed the elevator button.

"Look, I'm sure Jenny will turn up when she's good and ready to," he was telling Carrie. "So you should try not to worry. As for you," he said, flashing a smile at Sam. "You told me you'd get started on my boat today, but I've got a feeling that didn't happen."

"'Fraid not."

"And I guess you're not planning on heading down to the boatyard tonight?" he added, glancing at his watch.

Sam shook his head. "Not a chance. By the time I drive all the way back to Port Credit in the rush hour, all I'll be good for is sitting out on the porch with a cold beer."

"But tomorrow you'll get things under way?"

"Definitely. I'll start my people on the preliminary work first thing in the morning."

Thankfully, the elevator arrived. Leo, though, rested his hand on the edge of the door, keeping it open after Sam and Carrie had gotten in, despite the fact that there were other passengers.

"You *will* give me a call when you hear from Jenny," he said to Carrie.

She nodded.

"Good. And if by any chance she gets in touch

with me first, I'll let you know.'' With that, he released the door and it slid closed.

Sam stared straight ahead as they started downward, growing more impatient with each stop the elevator made.

Eventually, they reached the lobby and headed for the exit.

"He dumped her," Carrie muttered once they were back on the street. "And she's just trying to get revenge. Do you believe he had the unmitigated gall to try feeding us that crap?

"Jenny had it figured exactly right. She told us if she went to the police that's what he'd tell them. And I guess he thought if it would be good enough for them, it was good enough for us."

Sam stopped dead, blocking Carrie's path, that little doubt still whispering in his ear.

"What?" she said, giving him a puzzled look.

"Let's grab a coffee." He took her arm and steered her through the traffic to a tiny deli across the street.

"You get a table," he told her. "I'll get the coffee."

He ordered it at the counter, thinking rapidly. Yesterday, everything Jenny had told him had seemed to add up perfectly. And the clincher, of course, hadn't even been anything she'd said.

It had been the fact that Leo knew there'd been trouble in Sam Evans's past—knew exactly what it had been and that it would make Toronto's finest only too happy to believe he'd killed someone in a drunken rage.

But yesterday, he'd been panicked about the idea

of Leo trying to pin a murder on him. Whereas, today, it was easier to see that bits of Jenny's story seemed kind of bizarre. Not that he was buying Leo's version, but—

"Three dollars, sir," the clerk told him, setting two mugs on the counter.

Digging a couple of two-dollar coins from his pocket, he told the fellow to keep the change and carried the coffee over to Carrie's table.

"Let me ask you something," he said, sitting down across from her. He realized he'd be smarter to ease into things, but he didn't have a clue how to do it. "What was the point of Leo's remark about Jenny being a frustrated actress?"

"It was just a cheap shot. I mean, at one point she thought she'd like to act. And whenever there was an open call, she'd try out. But she never got a part, not even a minor one, so she finally gave up. Why?" she added, eyeing him uncertainly.

"I'm just trying to make everything come together in my head, and..."

"And?"

"Carrie..." He paused again, swearing to himself.

She was clearly very upset, and he didn't want to make her more so. He also didn't want to make her mad as hell at him, and he had a horrible suspicion that was exactly what he was about to do.

But he hardly had any choice about pressing on. He had to figure out exactly what he should be believing.

"Just listen to me for a minute, okay?" he said, trying to sound like reason incarnate. "Maybe I'm way off base here, or maybe it's that Jenny's not my sister, so I don't have the emotional involvement you do, but a couple of things are bothering me a little.''

''What things?''

''Well...first, we didn't see a body. Then we didn't see an envelope. And Jenny flat out refused to tell us where it was so we *could* see it.''

''And?'' Carrie said again, her eyes flashing warning signs at him.

He swore to himself once more. ''Look, I know Leo's a son of a bitch. But he's also a rational, intelligent man. He does so well in the courtroom because he's able to maintain complete control over his emotions—and because he can stay on top of a situation even if somebody throws him a curve. Now, keeping that in mind, tell me if this rings entirely true. Yesterday, he loses complete control of his temper and kills someone.''

''Accidentally,'' Carrie said, a decided quaver in her voice. ''Jenny said he told her he was only defending himself.''

''Yeah, well, smashing someone over the head with a hunk of cast bronze strikes me as a little more than defending himself. Regardless of that, though, he kills a guy right in his own house—when he's perfectly aware that will make him the prime suspect.

''But he figures he can frame someone else for it. Even though, as a criminal lawyer, he knows how thorough the police are at crime scenes—that setting things up to convince them I was the killer will take not only skill but a lot of luck, as well.

''Then, even though Jenny herself told us he's not

normally a trusting man, he believes her when she
says she'll lie to the cops for him. And he also decides
to trust her with a couple of disks that are incredibly
important to him.'' Sam stopped right there and simply sat staring at Carrie.

She was silent for several seconds, then she said,
''What are you telling me? That you don't think there
was really a murder? Or that you don't think Jenny
ever really had the disks?

''Or are you telling me you believe Leo's entire
story? That you think he actually did break things off
with Jenny? That he only sent a man with a gun after
her because he wanted his car back? And that everything she's said and done since yesterday afternoon
has been part of some insane plot to get revenge?''

Sam swallowed uneasily. ''Look, I'm not forget-
ting that guy threatened Linda. Or that he shot at us.
And I'm sure he was acting on Leo's orders. I'm only
saying that…on the surface at least…there are things
that don't seem to make Jenny's version add up exactly right.''

Carrie caught her lower lip between her teeth, as if
she were biting back a hundred different things she
was tempted to say. Finally she murmured, ''Why
would she have phoned you if Leo wasn't going to
try to frame you?''

''I don't know,'' he said quietly.

''Maybe because it was part of a plan she hatched,
as Leo would put it?''

''Carrie, I just don't know. All I'm trying to say
is—''

''I know what you're trying to say!''

Tears spilling over, she pushed herself from her
chair and ran for the door.

CHAPTER NINE

STRIDING RAPIDLY ACROSS the crowded sidewalk, Sam caught up with Carrie just as the cab she'd hailed screeched to a halt at the curb.

"Look," he said, resting a firm hand on her arm. "I was only trying to figure out what the hell's going on. I wasn't calling Jenny a liar. I just—"

"You wanna cab or what?" the driver interrupted.

"Yes," Carrie told him, jerking her arm free and wiping tears from her face.

"No," Sam said, gesturing for him to take off.

The cabbie glanced at Carrie, and when she said nothing more, he hit the gas.

"Carrie, we've got to talk about this and figure out where we go from here."

"We? What *we?* Didn't you just tell me Jenny's not *your* sister? And that you don't have the emotional involvement I do?"

"That doesn't mean I—"

"Sam, I want to thank you for everything you've done. I'm not being facetious, I sincerely mean that. But feel free to take a hike."

"Dammit, I don't *want* to take a hike. Now, can we go back to my car? Please?"

She sniffed a couple of times. Then she wiped away the remaining tears and gave him a little shrug.

He sighed an enormous sigh of relief, aware just how desperately he didn't want to back off. Until they knew for certain who was zooming who, there was no guarantee she'd be safe on her own. And he was far more concerned about that than he had any right being.

There were too many people on the street to try carrying on a serious conversation, so they walked back to where he'd parked the car in silence. Then he spent the time it took to wind his way out of the underground garage and onto Queen Street, trying to come up with a line that wouldn't get him right back into trouble.

"It's a good thing I've got the contract for Leo's boat," he finally said, stopping for a red light. "It gives me a perfect reason for keeping in close contact with him—if we find we need to, I mean."

Carrie looked across the car. "Are you sure you don't want out?"

That was so far from what he wanted he couldn't help smiling. "What would you do if I said yes?" he teased.

She apparently wasn't up to smiling back, because she simply shook her head and said, "I don't know. But at the moment that's only one of a whole lot of things I don't know. When it comes to Jenny…well, I'll admit she's got what Aunt Liz calls a flair for the dramatic. She sometimes tends to exaggerate things way out of proportion. Even so, I can't believe she'd exaggerate something into a murder, then drag us into it.''

"She didn't drag you into it,'' he reminded her, starting across the intersection when the light turned green. "I did that, remember? And she didn't actually drag me into it, either. She only phoned to warn me. She didn't ask me to go looking for her.''

"Right,'' Carrie said slowly. "Whatever's going on, we only got involved because we chose to. But what *is* going on?'' She hesitated a moment, then added, "I guess I've also got to admit you were right. There are things about her version that don't add up. But when she's so scared of Leo that she'd run all the way to Costa Rica…''

Sam shook his head. "You know what I'm wondering?''

"What?''

"If there's something going on we know nothing about.''

"Like…?''

"I've got no idea. But it really bothers me that none of us saw a body. Not Jenny and not us. And that when we drove over to Leo's, his study looked so perfect.''

"But that's how he wanted it to look for the police. And we know the murder weapon was missing. And the area rug.''

"Even so, maybe we should be talking *alleged* murder weapon and *alleged* murder. Because everything Jenny told us was only what Leo had told her.''

"You think there *wasn't* any murder?'' Carrie's expression was so dubious that he shook his head again.

"I'm at the stage where I don't know what to think. But we've been totally focused on the idea that Leo's trying to either pin the murder on me or cover it up, when it's possible there wasn't a murder at all. Maybe the truth is that Leo and Bud have some master plan and Jenny's only a pawn in it. Or maybe reality is some combination of her story and Leo's, and she actually took off because... Oh, hell, I don't know, but what if this Bud just has some reason for wanting people to believe he's dead?"

"What sort of reason?"

"Maybe to defraud an insurance company? Or maybe he was in a bad marriage and wanted an easy out? It wouldn't be the first time someone tried to pull off one of those scams. Or what if he had a pile of debts and—"

"Sam, wait."

He glanced across the car again, not surprised that Carrie had stopped him. His train of thought seemed even crazier when he put it into words than when it had been playing around in his head.

"I'm sure those could all be possibilities," she said. "But they don't explain why Leo would tell Jenny he'd killed Bud if he hadn't. And what earthly reason could he have for wanting anyone to believe he's a murderer?"

"Yeah, you're right. There's no way that adds up. I wasn't really making sense, was I?"

Carrie shrugged. "Nothing seems to be making sense, so why should you be any different?"

They drove a block or more in silence, then he said, "Okay, there's no way we can be sure what the truth is. But I keep coming back to the question of why Jenny would have phoned me if Leo hadn't told her he was going to frame me. That's got me leaning toward the likelihood that he did murder Bud. Until we know for sure, though… Well, if Leo wants to go along pretending everything's normal, I guess that's the best thing for us to do, too.

"I mean, you and I will spend whatever time it takes trying to learn what really happened. But while we're doing that, I'll get my staff going on his boat. And you should at least look as if you're working on some boatyard-type illustrations—so your being there doesn't seem suspicious."

"I could tell people I'm illustrating a story called…how about *The Little Tug in Dry Dock?*"

"Perfect."

They drove for another minute, then he said, "I guess the bottom line is that we've got to keep assuming Leo wants to find Jenny. And act accordingly."

"But if he does… Sam, we simply can't let him."

"We won't," he said, wishing he could guarantee that.

CARRIE GLANCED OVER at Sam again, still trying to decide what she should do.

The radio reports had warned that the rush hour traffic on the Queen Elizabeth Way was even worse than usual, so he'd taken Lake Shore Boulevard, which meant they'd be passing within a few blocks of her town house. Ever since he'd chosen his route, she'd been wondering if there was an omen in it.

Finally, after she'd weighed the pros and cons a dozen times, she said, "Sam, I've been thinking that maybe I should just stay at my own place. At least for the time being."

"Oh?" he said slowly. "I thought we'd decided that your staying with me made a lot of sense."

"Well…"

Now what did she say? That she couldn't stop thinking back to earlier this afternoon—when she'd been certain he was going to kiss her? When, if she were deep-down honest with herself, she'd have to admit she'd desperately wanted him to?

And then did she go on to explain that Jenny had warned her not to get involved with him? And that the longer she spent with him, the less she could imagine herself managing not to?

Since she wasn't up to that level of honesty, she finally said, "I guess I'm thinking Leo would find out I was staying at your place and suspect we're up to something. And while we were talking to him, my intuition was telling me that we *definitely* aren't in any immediate danger from him, so—"

"Is your intuition always right?"

"It usually is." It had told her Sam wasn't a killer. "Besides, he's obviously decided to play the waiting game. He must assume that sooner or later Jenny will get in touch with me, that he'll be able to find her through me, if no other way. So I've got to be safe for the moment."

"He'll have someone keeping a close eye on you, though, because he'll want to know if she does get in touch."

She'd already realized that Leo would have someone checking up on her, but Sam's words still sent a
little shiver through her.

Trying to ignore it, she said, ''He'll be keeping an
eye on both of us, whether we're together or not. But
I don't think he'll do anything. Not in the short term,
at least.''

Sam was silent, focusing on the street ahead, but
she could see how tense his body was.

A minute later, without even glancing her way, he
said, ''Leo isn't a particularly patient man, so I don't
think we should be taking any chances.''

''Well...'' She sat gazing at his even profile, only
too aware of the chance she'd be taking if they followed their original plan.

The feelings Sam Evans had stirred up inside her
were so strong they were frightening. Just sitting here
looking at him had her heart humming and a sensuous
heat lazing around in her belly. And despite the fact
that the last thing in the world she wanted to do was
fall for the wrong man, a little voice inside her head
kept suggesting that Jenny might not have been right
about Sam. That maybe there was no real reason not
to get involved with him.

Carrie forced her eyes from him, telling herself it
was risky to listen to inner voices. In this case, for
example, she doubted it was the voice of common
sense talking to her. Rather, she suspected it was desire speaking.

''You're sure that's what you want, then?'' he
asked, stopping for the light at Park Lawn. ''You
want me to take you home?''

She made herself nod.

He didn't say another word, just drove across the bridge over Mimico Creek and made the turn that would take them to her cul-de-sac.

When they reached it, her heart skipped a dozen beats. Coming toward them, almost at the corner, was a dark blue Probe.

The driver quickly raised his hand to his face, doing a good job of hiding it from them while looking as if he were simply rubbing his cheek.

"Is that a neighbor?" Sam asked.

"No."

"Dammit," he muttered, glancing into the rearview mirror. "He's already made the turn. I can't see his plate number."

By the time Carrie'd shifted around so she could see behind them, the car had completely disappeared.

"And I think you've got more company," Sam said, nodding toward a nondescript sedan parked on the street in front of her house.

Her heart skipped several more beats. Two men were sitting in the front seat, and as Sam pulled into her driveway, they opened their doors and got out.

"Oh, Lord," she said. "Do you think they're friends of Leo's?"

"At first glance, I think they're cops."

That made her feel better—but not much. What did the police want with her?

By the time she and Sam climbed out of the car, the two men had practically reached it.

"Carrie O'Reilly?" one of them asked.

"Yes?"

He flashed a badge. "Detective James Dirk, Toronto Police Department. This is my partner, Gino Vecchiarelli. And you are...?" he asked Sam.

"A friend. My name's Sam Evans."

Dirk nodded, glanced into the back of the Mustang at Carrie's easel, then looked at her again. "We'd like to talk to you for a few minutes," he said, gesturing toward the house.

Silently, she led the way inside and into the living room—very glad that Sam simply followed along without asking the detectives whether he was welcome.

Once they were sitting down, Dirk leaned forward, his hands clasped between his knees. "Jennifer O'Reilly is your sister?"

She nodded, her heart in her throat. Were they here to tell her Jenny was dead?

"Do you know where she is?" Dirk asked.

"No." Okay. Not dead. But why on earth were they asking about her?

"Do you have any idea where she might be?" Dirk pressed.

She glanced at Sam. It was one thing to lie to Leo, another to lie to the police.

"Can you tell us why you're looking for her?" Sam said.

"I'm afraid not," Dirk told him. "But if you have any idea where she is... We only want to talk to her," he added, turning to Carrie once more.

"Well, she seems to have disappeared," Sam said.

Both detectives looked at him.

"We've been trying to figure out where she is ourselves," he told them. "As a matter of fact, we've just come from talking to the man she's been seeing recently. But none of us know where to begin looking for her."

"And this man's name is...?" Dirk asked.

"Leo Castanza."

Dirk and Vecchiarelli exchanged glances, then turned to Carrie again. "When did you last see your sister?" Dirk asked.

She thought rapidly. After what Sam had just said, the next person these two visited might be Leo. Which meant she'd better stick with exactly what they'd told him.

"We saw her last night," she said. "Sam and I picked her up from a friend's place and went to a restaurant for coffee. But then we...had a disagreement. And that was the last we saw of her."

"And the disagreement was about?"

She licked her lips anxiously, not certain how much she was obliged to tell them. "It was personal," she replied at last.

"I see," Dirk said. "And she didn't give you any idea where she was going?"

"No. I really can't be any help with that."

The detectives exchanged glances again, then Dirk dug a business card out of his pocket and handed it to Carrie.

"If you hear from her, I'd really appreciate you letting us know. As I said, we only want to talk to her."

THE INSTANT SAM CLOSED the door behind the two officers, Carrie whispered, "What's going on?"

She looked so frightened that he almost couldn't resist the urge to wrap his arms around her and pull her close. Instead, he forced himself to merely shake his head and say, "I'm not sure."

"Sam, do you think Leo's somehow trying to pin the murder on Jenny? Is that why those two want to talk to her?"

"No, I'm certain that isn't it. I'm still convinced the cops couldn't know about any murder in Rosedale without the media being all over it. Besides which, Jenny weighs...what? Maybe a hundred and ten pounds sopping wet? If she ever murdered someone, it wouldn't be by bashing his head in with a bronze sculpture. The cops would find the idea of that laughable."

"Then why are those guys looking for her? And why did you tell them we'd been to see Leo? Now that they know he and Jenny were an item, they'll pay him a visit."

"Right. That was the whole point."

"And you want them talking to him because...?"

"Because if he knows the cops are looking for Jenny, it might make him a little more careful about what he tries. Assuming they really are looking for her. And assuming they really are cops."

Carrie was silent, waiting for him to continue.

"Let me have that card Dirk gave you."

When she handed it to him, he headed for the kitchen and her phone.

She followed along, then silently stood beside him while he punched in the number.

"Sixty-nine Division," a man answered. "Constable Bennett speaking."

"Can I speak to detective James Dirk, please."

After a momentary silence, Bennett said, "I'm sorry, Detective Dirk's on days off. He'll be back Friday—evening shift. Could someone else help you?"

"How about Detective Vecchiarelli?"

"Sorry, he's not working today, either."

"Oh. Well, I'll call back. Thanks," he added, clicking off and putting down the phone. "Okay, they're not on duty, so I guess we can take our pick of explanations. One, they're really zealous guys who were working on their own time."

"We can rule that out, right?"

"I think it would be pretty safe. So let's move on to number two. Someone got them to come here and see if you'd tell the police where Jenny is."

"Gee, I wonder who that someone could be?" Carrie said wryly. "But could Leo really have set it up so fast?"

Sam shrugged. "I made our appointment with him before lunchtime. That would have given him loads of time to arrange for them to come here. Then he could have called them after our meeting to say exactly what he wanted them to ask about.

"And there's another possibility. Maybe our visitors weren't Dirk and Vecchiarelli at all. Maybe they were just a couple of guys Leo paid to impersonate the real item."

"Sam, you're standing there holding Dirk's card.

And when you called the station, whoever answered knew who you were talking about.''

"Yeah, but he didn't see the two men who came here. And I don't imagine it would be too hard to get hold of a cop's business card and a phony badge. Especially not for a guy like Leo.''

"Well, I think you're really reaching. What if I phoned Detective Dirk to tell him I'd heard from Jenny? He wouldn't know what on earth I was talking about if those guys were imposters and—''

"Carrie, what are the odds of you ever calling Detective Dirk to tell him you'd heard from Jenny?''

"Oh. Right. I guess that's a good point. So…do we phone the station again and ask whoever's in charge what those guys were doing here off duty?''

"No. If Jenny's right about how many cops Leo knows, we'd be taking a chance that he'd learn we called. And we don't want him thinking we're suspicious about anything.''

"You *do* think they were imposters, though.''

"I'm not sure. But whether they were or not, I think they were here because Leo asked them to be.''

Carrie simply stood gazing at him for a long moment, then her gray eyes filled with tears. ''Sam, we can't trust anyone, can we,'' she murmured.

"You can trust me,'' he said quietly.

"Can I?'' she whispered. ''Do you promise?''

This time, there was simply no way in the world he could resist. He took a step toward her and folded her into his arms.

"I promise,'' he whispered against her hair.

Just as she had when he'd comforted her at the

airport, she pressed her cheek to his chest—as if she wanted to be every bit as close to him as he wanted her to be.

He didn't need the smell of her perfume to start him thinking of sensuous kisses and slow sex, although its intoxicating scent definitely helped fuel his desire.

Mostly, though, what started his blood running hot was the soft warmth of her body and the way her slender curves molded perfectly to him. Her breasts were so soft against his chest, her hip so firm against his thigh that he was aching for her.

The ends of her long hair, cascading down her back, were tickling his fingers. And when he tangled its silky softness around them, he could feel the last of his willpower evaporating.

He wanted to make love to Carrie O'Reilly more than he could remember ever wanting anything else. But for the moment he merely held her.

"Carrie?" he said at last.

She eased out of the circle of his arms then, making him wish he hadn't spoken, and stood looking at him.

"I think you should change your mind about staying here on your own," he continued, trying to convince himself he was thinking solely of her safety. "Aside from anything else, the odds are awfully high that guy in the Probe was Leo's friend."

"But… Sam, if Leo sent those cops, why would he have someone else come around at the same time?"

He shook his head. "I don't know. Simple coincidence, maybe. Leo might have given the guy in the

Probe general instructions about keeping an eye on you. Which means you haven't seen the last of him.''

Carrie considered his words for a moment, then said, ''I don't want to be on my own the next time I see him.''

WHILE CARRIE AND SAM were unloading her things from the Mustang, she couldn't stop thinking that *butterflies in her stomach* perfectly described the way she was feeling.

She'd brought clothes on hangers, a suitcase with underwear and such in it, and her art supplies—which they couldn't leave in the car because, even this late in the day, it would get too hot sitting in the driveway. As they carried everything up to his guest room, those butterflies began multiplying like bunnies.

Before they'd left her place, she'd changed out of her dress into shorts and a sleeveless blouse. Even so, the upstairs of the house felt uncomfortably close. And that only made her queasiness worse.

Once they'd piled all her stuff on the bed, Sam saved her by opening the window. The moment he did, a breeze from the lake began acting as a natural air conditioner.

''I'll go open the other ones,'' he said, turning toward the doorway.

She watched him disappear from the room, only too aware of the crazy, insane, this-is-so-wonderful-I-can't-believe-it's-real feeling that kept growing stronger and stronger. It was terrifying the hell out of her, because unless Jenny had been wrong about him, it was bound to lead to disaster.

Her resistance to Mr. Samuel Evans had already worn awfully thin. And regardless of what her brain was still trying to tell her heart, she suspected that by coming to stay in his house, she might as well be waving a white flag of sexual surrender.

She'd just have to hope with all her heart that those *things* Jenny had been referring to weren't nearly as bad as she'd implied.

She was still thinking about that when he strode back into the room, saying, "Hey, you haven't even started getting organized."

He'd changed out of his meeting-with-Leo clothes as well, replacing his business suit with jeans and a gray T-shirt that clung tightly enough to emphasize his firm muscles. She couldn't stop her gaze from drifting across his broad shoulders, then down over his chest to his lean hips. And she couldn't stop herself from thinking that he was, as her great-aunt Bertha would have put it, a fine figure of a man.

"So," he said. "Do you want to get your things sorted out or would you rather take a break? There's a beer in the fridge with your name on it. Or…do you drink beer?"

"Yes. Beer's fine." But how could she possibly be falling in love with a man before he even knew what she drank?

She'd barely asked herself the question before the *falling in love* part began echoing in her head.

Was that *really* what was happening? Was what she was feeling a whole lot more than an incredibly strong sexual attraction? She exhaled slowly, considering the question.

She could barely think straight when he was around. And every time she looked at him, her knees felt weak and her pulse raced.

Lust, she told herself. That added up to pure and simple lust. And yet…deep down she knew there was more to it. Unlikely as it seemed, she knew she was precariously close to being in love with him—if she wasn't already.

And, given that, what on earth was she going to do if those *things* about Sam turned out to be as bad as Jenny had implied?

CHAPTER TEN

THEY SAT ON THE PORCH for over an hour, Carrie nursing a single beer, Sam stopping after two. Then he threw a couple of steaks on the barbecue while she began putting together a salad.

He considered opening a bottle of wine but decided he'd be a lot wiser to keep his head clear—because the time had come to tell her about what had happened.

"Sam?" she said through the kitchen window's screen.

He looked in at her, noticing again how the white shorts she was wearing accentuated her tan and left no doubt as to how gorgeous her legs were.

"Is oil and vinegar okay?" she asked.

"Sure. Fine."

"And do you like garlic?"

"Sure." As long as we're both having it, he added silently. Then he almost laughed at himself for letting his fantasies run wild.

But when she shot him a smile before turning to the fridge, all he could think about was holding her in his arms again. And once his thoughts started down that road, he couldn't stop imagining himself unbuttoning the buttons on her little yellow shirt.

Slowly. One by one. Kissing the skin beneath them as he went. Teasing her with his mouth and caressing her body until her craving matched his.

Without conscious thought, he smoothed his hand across the pocket of his jeans, feeling the condom package he'd stuck in it—just in case. Then he shook his head. That was undoubtedly the ultimate in wishful thinking.

Once he'd told her the truth about himself, she'd probably want nothing more to do with him. But he had no choice. He wanted her so badly it hurt, yet there was no way he could have her until she knew. And if she didn't believe things had happened the way he said, there wouldn't be a damned thing he could do about it.

Forcing his attention to the steaks, he almost didn't let himself think about her again until he took them inside.

Over dinner, they made small talk, but his mind kept drifting to the conversation they'd be having later—preventing him from enjoying the meal.

Once they'd finished eating, they carried their coffee out to the porch, his anxiety increasing by the minute.

Since daylight lingered forever in July, it was still twilight. But shadows were creeping stealthily across the garden as the moon rose above the lake.

They sat in companionable silence, sipping the coffee, until Carrie gave him a heart-melting look and said, "It's so peaceful here. With no high buildings to hide the stars, and the sound of the crickets, it's like being in the country."

He nodded. Under normal circumstances, he found evenings like this one peaceful, too. Tonight, though, his stomach was in knots. And no matter how hard he tried, he couldn't think of a good way to begin.

"I could sit out here for hours," she added. "But I'd better go up and sort out that mess on my bed."

"Right. Before you do, though," he made himself say, "there's something I want to talk to you about."

"Oh?" She smiled one of her heavenly smiles. "Please don't tell me it's that this countryish setting means the house has mice. I'm always drawing them for books, with no problems at all, but I have a totally irrational fear of real ones."

"No, I don't have mice," he told her, wishing to hell it was something as trivial as that. He could deal with her irrational fear. He just didn't know how well he'd be able to deal with her rejecting him.

"Then what is it?"

He took a deep breath, but as he was about to begin, the phone started ringing.

"Let your machine take it," she suggested. "Oh, no, don't," she said a second later. "It might be someone with a message from Jenny."

"Yeah, could be." He hadn't been thinking about that possibility, but *something* had been urging him to answer it.

Probably, he told himself, the *something* was his desire to avoid this conversation.

When he headed inside and picked up, it was Grace Chalmers on the line, one of his neighbors down the block.

"Sam, I just got back from walking Prince," she

said. "And…well, I didn't know if I should bother you or not, but when I told Robert, he said, 'Better safe than sorry,' so I decided to call."

"You're not bothering me in the slightest, Grace. What's up?"

"Well, we usually walk past your boatyard, and when we did tonight I thought I saw the beam of a flashlight inside the building."

His entire system went on red alert.

"I wondered if you'd hired a night watchman or something. But there was no car parked in the lot, and that made me think some kids might have broken in. So when Robert said it wouldn't hurt to give you a call…"

"No, I really appreciate it. I'll shoot right down and have a look. Thanks a lot."

Clicking off, he strode rapidly back across the living room.

"What's wrong?" Carrie asked when he reappeared.

"That was one of my neighbors. She thinks there could be someone snooping around at the boatyard. You wait here."

"What?" she said as he headed for the car.

By the time he had his door unlocked, she was hurrying after him.

"Wait, call the police. Don't go yourself."

"Carrie, there might not even be anyone there. Besides, the police could take forever arriving. I'll be okay," he added, opening his door. "My gun's in the car."

"Sam, I'm not staying here by myself!"

He hesitated for half a second. Then, deciding there was no time to argue, he flipped the switch to unlock the passenger's door.

"You'll have to wait in the car when we get there," he told her, starting the engine as she climbed in beside him. Backing rapidly out of the driveway, he sped down the street through the semidarkness.

At the end of the block, before he turned onto Shoreline Drive, he flicked off his headlights. When he made the turn, the boatyard was visible ahead of them—looking as deserted as it normally did at night. Reaching it mere moments later, he pulled into the small parking lot and cut the engine.

Beyond the fence, the building was in darkness. The yard itself was full of the shapes of boats in various stages of construction and repair. Near the water, his crane stood like a gigantic metal bird in the moonlight. Behind it, the moon cut a silver swathe across the lake.

"We're the only car," Carrie whispered.

He nodded. "Grace mentioned she didn't see one. But if there *is* someone, he'd have been smart to park on a side street. Or maybe it's just kids."

Or maybe, he silently added, it was a return of the trouble that had prompted him to get a gun in the first place.

"You're staying here," he reminded her, reaching beneath his seat for the Beretta.

"Oh, no I'm not," she said. "I'm not waiting out here alone like a sitting duck. I'm going with you."

"Dammit, Carrie—"

She abruptly ended the discussion by opening her door and getting out.

Swearing under his breath, he climbed out himself and quietly shut his door.

"Stay behind me," he ordered, starting for the gate.

The padlock was locked, so if anyone was inside, they'd gone over the fence. But a six-foot chain-link fence was hardly a serious obstacle. Tucking the Beretta into his belt, he unlocked the gate, then they headed for the building.

Adrenaline pumping, he tried the front door—and his anxiety level soared when it opened.

Unlocked. Did that mean they were dealing with a lock-picking pro? Or had someone gone in through a back window, then left through the door? Had they already missed whoever had been here?

"Are you sure we shouldn't just call the police?" Carrie whispered.

The fear in her voice almost made him decide that was exactly what they should do. But if someone was still here, he wanted to know who it was and what he was after. And if they left to call the cops, his intruder would undoubtedly seize the opportunity to take off.

"Stay tight to the wall," he whispered, flattening himself against it and then reaching over to push the door completely open.

That done, they waited, barely breathing. There wasn't a sound from inside, but it was a big building with hundreds of places someone could be hiding.

"Sam, we can't go in there," Carrie whispered. "You might not be the only one with a gun."

She was right, he realized. What the hell was he thinking? On his own, it might be okay to risk it. But not with her along.

He was just beginning to consider other options when he heard a faint scuffing noise from the yard.

"I think he's gone out the side door," he whispered. "Stay here," he added, starting to make his way along the front of the building.

Ignoring his words, Carrie edged along after him.

When they reached the end of the building, he had a good view of the boatyard. But there were as many potential hiding places outside as in.

They waited once more, Sam with his gun at the ready. Finally, thinking that they could be here all night, he decided a bluff might flush out his quarry.

"Where the hell are the cops?" he said. "It's been ages since we called them."

His voice carried through the night as loudly as he'd known it would, yet the yard remained silent and still. Then he spotted a figure moving between two boats.

Dressed in dark clothes, right down to a dark watch cap, he was only visible when he hit a moonlit patch. After watching him for a second, Sam shouted, "Stop or I'll shoot!"

At that, his intruder took off for the fence.

Sam started after him at a dead run. But once he got beyond the clear area next to the building, he had to slow down and make his way between boats—able to catch only an occasional glimpse of his quarry.

When he was halfway across the yard, he spotted the guy beginning to climb the fence.

"Stop right there!" he yelled.

The man flung himself over the top, dropped to the ground on the other side and raced off into the night.

Sam didn't even raise his gun. Regardless of what some people might think, he was no killer.

CARRIE'S HEARTBEAT WAS almost back to normal by the time Sam returned to where she was waiting in front of the building.

"I didn't even get a good-enough look to describe him," he muttered.

"But you didn't get killed, either."

That elicited a wry grin. "Yeah, I guess it's all a matter of perspective. Come on," he added. "Let's go inside and see what he was up to."

"You don't think there could be anyone else still in there, do you?" She doubted it was likely, but she wanted his reassurance.

"Uh-uh," he said. "If there'd been more than one, they'd have taken off at the same time."

He reached for her hand then, so naturally she knew he hadn't given it a moment's thought. But she was very aware of his touch—of how small her hand felt engulfed in his, how work-roughened his palms were and the way the warmth of his skin against hers was sending heat through her entire body.

Her heart racing once more, although this time not from fear, they walked into the building.

When Sam switched on the lights, nothing struck her as looking out of place. The reception area was relatively neat and seemed undisturbed.

Wordlessly, he led the way into a huge work area

that sided on the yard. It contained massive pieces of machinery, parts of boats and enough tools and workbenches that he could teach a night school shop class.

"Everything looks okay in here," he said, glancing slowly around.

"And when you had that trouble you mentioned?" she asked. "Did everything look okay then?"

"No. There was a lot of damage then."

"Do you know why?"

"Someone was giving me a message."

He didn't elaborate. He simply turned, her hand still in his, and headed back into the reception area.

After opening a few file drawers and looking inside the desk, he moved on to his office. As she followed him into the room, he flicked a wall switch.

"Wait a sec," he said when nothing happened. "We're just updating the wiring in here and they obviously didn't get finished today. But the lamp on my desk should be working."

There was light spilling in from the reception area, of course. And at the far end of the office a large window looked out over the moonlit water, so the room was nowhere near totally dark.

She could clearly see him making his way across it. And when he turned on his desk lamp, a pale yellow glow bathed that area of the office.

The room was enormous, just as he'd told her, stretching from behind the reception area all the way to the window at the back.

"Hopefully, they'll get the wiring wrapped up tomorrow," he said. "But if we put your easel by the window, you'll get lots of light regardless."

She nodded, although she doubted she'd be working much for the next while. She'd be spending most of her time trying to learn the truth about Bud's murder.

The office, she thought, turning her attention back to it, was decidedly masculine. The walls were paneled in mahogany and the few decorative items were nautical in nature.

A computer sat on Sam's big old wooden desk, but aside from it and a quietly ticking clock, the surface was relatively clear. In contrast, the long worktable near it was littered with rolled-up plans.

The remaining furniture consisted of a couple of bulky club chairs and a long couch. They were of the old-fashioned stuffed-leather variety that looked stiff rather than inviting. Curious about that, she tried out the couch while Sam checked around. It wasn't nearly as hard as it looked. In fact, it was actually quite comfortable.

"There doesn't seem to be anything out of place in here, either," he finally said.

"Do we call the police?"

He shrugged. "There's probably not a damn thing they could do to help, so I can't see the point of wasting their time."

He was about to say something more when the office door gave a little creak and began swinging slowly shut.

Carrie almost jumped out of her skin.

"It's okay." Sam grinned over at her. "It was just one of the cats pushing against it. They do it all the time—some sort of cat game."

"Aah," she said, only too happy to believe that was all it had been. "How many do you have?"

"Three at the moment. Without at least two or three, the boatyard would be overrun by rats."

"Rats," she repeated, unable to keep her gaze from sweeping across the floor.

"Sorry," he said quickly. "I forgot you're afraid of mice. But the rats aren't much of a problem. We see the odd one outside, but never in here. The cats do a good job."

She nodded, although she didn't feel entirely reassured. Her fear of mice might be irrational, but her fear of rats wasn't.

She'd learned all about the genus *Rattus* way back in Biology 101. Black rats were the primary host for bubonic plague, and small epidemics still occurred in North America, despite popular belief that modern science had eradicated it. And some species, like Norway rats, were both predatory and highly aggressive, hanging out in packs of sixty or more.

Just as she was starting to worry that three cats couldn't possibly be a match for a serious rat pack, Sam said, "Nothing out of place and nothing missing. You know, if Grace hadn't called, I'd have come in here tomorrow and not had the slightest suspicion that anyone had been poking around."

She forced her thoughts away from rats. "Why do you think he was poking around?"

"He must have been looking for something."

"What?"

"Well, except for sailboats in the America's Cup, boat designs aren't exactly state secrets, so we can probably rule them out. But do you remember Leo asking if there was any chance I'd be here tonight?''

"Oh, Lord. And you said there wasn't. I didn't think a thing about it at the time.''

"Neither did I. But now that I have, I'm thinking that he knows I work here in the evenings sometimes. So maybe it was more than a casual question.''

"You figure that guy was looking for the disks, then? That Leo thinks Jenny might have given them to us?''

"I figure he thinks it's worth checking into. And we might as well face facts. If he was behind this, he'll be sending someone to search our houses, too.''

As he spoke, Sam stepped around the side of his desk and switched off the lamp. With the door to the reception area closed by the cats, that left the room lit only by the moonlight drifting in through the window.

Carrie sat gazing toward that end of the office, unable to prevent a sense of hopelessness from welling up inside her.

"Carrie?'' Sam said, heading over to the couch. "What's wrong?''

She shook her head, not certain she could manage to speak.

"What is it?'' he asked, sitting down beside her. "You look like you're going to cry. Is that guy being in here the final straw?''

"I…Sam, I'm just feeling that we're in so far over our heads, we don't have a chance of getting out. I mean, we've got Jenny off hiding in a foreign country so she doesn't end up dead. And neither you nor I really have a clue about finding out what actually happened at Leo's. And in the meantime, he's holding all the aces.

"He's got cops in his pocket, a man who was ready to kill Jenny on sight, and someone happy to break in here for him.

"That makes us crazy, Sam. We're crazy to be mixed up in this. But as much as I wish we weren't, I can't even think about the idea of Jenny having no one to...

"I guess I'm trying to say that even though I'm going to do everything I can to help her, I know that realistically we're like Don Quixote and...and whatever his squire's name was."

"Sancho Panza. Don Quixote and Sancho Panza. Tilting at windmills."

"Exactly," she murmured.

"You want to be Don or Sancho?" he teased gently.

She did her best to smile. "You can be Don. I'll be Sancho."

For a moment longer, Sam simply sat there beside her. Then he wrapped his arm around her shoulders and pulled her close.

"We'll figure things out," he whispered, his breath fanning her cheek with its warmth.

Swallowing over the lump in her throat, she let herself breathe in the delicious woods-in-autumn scent that was uniquely his.

She loved that scent. And she loved him.

The fact was getting easier to admit to herself all the time. Because regardless of Jenny's warning, she'd never met another man she felt she could trust so completely. And as she'd told him earlier, her intuition was usually right.

Actually, at times she was absolutely positive she could rely on it—and this was one of those times.

Whatever Jenny had been referring to, either she'd been totally wrong about it or she'd been drastically exaggerating its seriousness. Carrie had come to know Sam well enough by now that she no longer had the slightest doubt about him.

"Sam?" she said, shifting a little so she could see his face.

"Yes?"

He caught her gaze, his eyes dark as coal in the moonlight, and whatever she'd been intending to ask him completely evaporated from her mind. Then her hand developed a will of its own and reached up to touch his cheek.

She brushed her fingers slowly over the day's growth of beard, then across the warm, sensuous softness of his lips. She'd never touched him like that before, and the intimacy of it started her heart beating so hard she could feel it.

Slipping her hand downward, she slowly slid it across the unyielding solidness of his chest.

"Carrie," he whispered. "Carrie, listen to me for a minute. I..."

She only had to lean forward a fraction of an inch to silence him, and the rest of his words were lost as his mouth met hers in a slow, sweet kiss.

Within seconds it turned into something else entirely, an explosion of passion that stole the breath from her body and replaced it with a frenzied heat of desire.

The heat spread through her like liquid fire, growing hotter each time his tongue tasted hers, hotter still when his hand settled on her breast. And when he began stroking her nipple with his thumb, shock waves of need surged through her.

She tangled her fingers in his hair, drawing his mouth impossibly closer to her own. His kiss, deep and hungry, made her dizzy. When he started to unbutton her blouse, the throbbing deep inside her grew so strong she could scarcely bear it.

Almost desperately, she reached down to his zipper. He groaned at her touch, and as she caressed his hard arousal through his jeans, he whispered her name so raggedly she barely knew what he was saying.

He unhooked her bra, slid the cups from her breasts and kissed their nakedness, his mouth hot and wet against her skin, his teeth teasing her nipples into aching hardness.

Then, slipping off her blouse and bra, he cupped both breasts in his hands and began kissing them once more, gradually easing her down onto the couch beside him.

Her breathing shallow and fast, she ran her hands up under his T-shirt, loving the feel of his skin. Then she reached down to his hips, fitting her lower body to his and arching against him, her need so intense she could barely keep from whimpering.

Abruptly, he stopped kissing her and cradled her face between his hands. "Carrie, listen," he said, his voice uneven. "I promised myself I wouldn't do this. There's something you don't know about me."

"I know," she whispered. "I know. Jenny told me. But it's all right. It's all right, Sam."

And it truly was. Nothing about this man could ever be too much for her to handle.

He simply gazed at her for a second, then pushed himself up from the couch and tugged off his clothes, revealing just how fully aroused he was.

She watched while he dug a condom from his pocket and put it on, her need growing stronger than she'd have believed possible. Then he eased her shorts and panties off and snuggled down beside her once more, pressing the length of his naked body against hers—skin against skin, heat against heat, longing against longing, his nearness making her want him inside her more than she'd ever wanted anything else.

"I was so worried," he whispered, slipping his hand between her legs, then smiling against her lips when he discovered how wet with longing she was.

"I wanted you so badly, but I was afraid you'd—"

"Shhh," she murmured, kissing him.

He stroked her until she did whimper, until she could barely catch her breath and the air burned in her throat, until she came with only his touch.

She cried out into the stillness of the room, her orgasm so fierce she could no longer breathe. She was falling through darkness while points of light exploded all around her—free-falling faster and faster.

And then, ever so gradually, she began to slow down. She could breathe a little once more. But she felt so liquid and languid, so fragile, that if Sam touched her the wrong way she'd disintegrate.

He didn't, though. He simply traced her face with his fingertips, gently following the lines of her nose and her jaw, then he buried his own face against the pulse in her throat and sent tiny aftershocks through her with soft kisses.

"You okay?" he whispered at last.

"Oh, Sam, *okay* doesn't begin to describe how I am."

She could feel him smiling again, and it made *her* smile. And then he was moving over her, sinking easily into her eager body and thrusting inside her.

Her breathing grew ragged once more, her heartbeat accelerating to match his. Their rhythm was instinctive and primordial, yet special and unique because she knew she'd never feel this way with any other man.

When he finally came, she felt like laughing and crying at the same time.

They lay together afterward, their bodies slick and motionless in the moonlit room—something so perfectly right about being with each other this way that she wished they could stay frozen in time forever. But eventually Sam propped himself up on one elbow and trailed his fingers possessively down her body.

"Have I ever told you how beautiful you are?"

"No," she said lazily. "But I'd be happy to listen."

"Will you settle for my telling you you're the most gorgeous woman I've ever seen?"

"That'll certainly do for starters."

She could see him smiling this time, and she couldn't have kept herself from smiling back for all the leprechauns' gold in the world. She'd never been as happy in her entire life.

"You knew all the time," he said softly.

"Knew what?"

He looked puzzled. "About me. You said Jenny told you. So you've known all along."

"Oh. Right. Yes, she told me at the airport."

After a moment's silence, he murmured, "You should have said something. Should have asked me about it or... Hell, there I was, falling in love with you, and the whole time I was so scared that you'd—"

"You were falling in love with me?" she whispered, her heart thudding against her ribs.

"You couldn't tell?"

"I...I guess I was afraid to read too much into things."

"You shouldn't have been. I realize it's happened incredibly fast, but that doesn't make the way I'm feeling any less real."

"Oh, Sam, I know. Because I feel the same way."

"Honestly?"

When she nodded, he smiled at her again—a smile so warm she could feel its glow.

"I love you, Carrie. More than I've ever loved anyone else."

"Oh, Sam." Her eyes filled with happy tears and she tangled a little of his chest hair around her finger. "I love you more than I ever *could* love anyone else."

"Is that how it's going to be?" he teased. "You always trying to top me?"

"Not always. Just now and then."

He cuddled her to him and she rested her cheek against his chest, listening to his heartbeat.

After a while, snippets of their earlier conversation drifted back into her mind and she said, "Okay, now tell me what it is that I don't know about you."

Easing away a little, he looked down at her, his expression uncertain. "Am I missing something here? You told me you *did* know. I heard you say those exact words. You said Jenny told you."

"Well, yes, but she didn't have time to go into the details. All she said was that there were things about you I didn't know. Things that meant I shouldn't let myself fall for you. You can see how well I listen to advice," she added with a smile.

Sam didn't smile back, and she was aware that his body had grown tense. As he shifted back another fraction of an inch, a chill of foreboding slithered into the space between them.

"Sam? What's the matter?" she made herself ask.

"Jenny didn't actually tell you at all," he said at last.

"Well...as I said, not the details."

"Oh, God," he whispered.

CHAPTER ELEVEN

"I THINK WE'D BETTER GET dressed before we talk about this," Sam said, reaching to the floor for his jeans and T-shirt.

Carrie's throat was already tight and his words made it tighter still. Something was very, very wrong.

With only moonlight in the room, she couldn't see his expression clearly, but from the tension in his voice she could tell how upset he was.

Suddenly embarrassed by her nudity, she scrambled into her shorts and was buttoning her blouse by the time he switched on the lamp.

He started back around the desk toward her, his bare feet thudding softly against the wooden floor. Then, apparently deciding it would be best to keep his distance, he stopped and stood with his hips resting against the front of the desk.

If he was trying for the casual look, he was failing miserably. His body was stiff and awkward, and he seemed to be wishing he were anywhere else but here.

He cleared his throat, then quietly said, "First, I want to say that everything I'm going to tell you is the absolute truth."

She swallowed uneasily. Uncle Ken used to warn

her that people who made a point of saying they were telling the truth were often liars.

But she knew Sam well enough to know he wasn't a liar. Unless, of course, falling in love with him had ruined her lie-detecting radar.

"And second," he continued, "I want you to know that I'd planned to tell you about this earlier tonight. The way things were developing between us, I knew I had to. But I was just about to begin when Grace Chalmers called and…and you know the rest."

She nodded, resisting the urge to tell him to get to the point. Whatever this was, it was obviously hard for him to discuss.

"Okay," he said, resting his palms on the surface of the desk. "Eight years ago, I was arrested and charged with a crime. I had nothing to do with it. I was simply in the wrong place at the wrong time. But I looked too much like the guilty party for my own good.

"I spent a few days in jail, then my lawyer got the charges dropped. Because I was innocent. Because the cops didn't really have any evidence against me.

"That didn't stop them from trying to put together a case, though. It was a perfect example of tunnel vision. Despite the lack of evidence, the detective in charge spent the next few months making my life a living hell—until he finally realized he was wasting his time and had to give up.

"My lawyer, by the way, was Leo. Slade Coburn hired him for me. That's how I initially came to know him."

Carrie nodded again, thinking that if the man he'd

worked for had gone out and hired a pricey lawyer for him, that said he'd believed in Sam's innocence.

"And I guess Jenny knew about what happened because Leo told her," he continued. "Although I've got to say I resent like hell his discussing my case with her."

"I don't blame you. It sounds highly unethical." She waited for him to go on, her anxiety gradually giving way to a feeling of relief. She wasn't sure exactly what she'd been expecting him to say, but it had been a lot worse than what he'd told her. And she'd been right in thinking that whatever he'd been involved in, she could handle it.

She was okay with this. There hadn't been enough evidence for the charges to stick, so he'd obviously been innocent.

"I guess it happens more than we'd like to think," she said when he remained silent. "The police arresting the wrong person for something. And...Sam, I don't really have a problem with it. I mean, I'm surprised, but... You look as if you think I *should* be having a problem with it," she added uncertainly.

"Some people do. Remember I mentioned that I'd been engaged?"

"Yes, of course."

"Well, when I told Valerie—that was her name— when I told her about it, she wasn't sure I was telling the truth. She couldn't quite convince herself that I was innocent."

"And that's why you broke up?"

Sam shrugged. "That's why she dumped me would be more accurate. She just wasn't prepared to take any chances because... Carrie, the crime I was charged with was murder.''

The word gave her such a jolt that she felt as if all the air had been sucked from the room. And suddenly, this *was* as bad as she'd been expecting.

She reminded herself that he hadn't been guilty, but it didn't help. The word *murder* had started mental lights flashing and sirens screaming. Because murder wasn't just a crime. Murder was...murder.

Doing her best to keep from looking shocked, she asked herself why Jenny hadn't found some way of telling her the details. Then she realized Sam was silently watching her, and tried reminding herself again that he hadn't been guilty.

This time it helped somewhat, and she began breathing a little more easily.

The only sound in the office was the quiet ticking of the clock on his desk, and as the seconds passed, she knew she should say something. But she couldn't think what.

"Do you want me to tell you about it?" he asked at last.

"Yes."

"All right. As I said, it was eight years ago, back when Slade still owned the company and I was just one of the guys who worked for him. One summer night, after we'd been working late, a few of us went to a pub up on the Lakeshore for a couple of beers.

"Well, there was a jerk who'd apparently been spoiling for a fight all evening. He tried to start one with me, but by that point the bartender'd had enough and turfed him.

"At any rate, my buddies and I stayed for maybe half an hour after that, then we left. I didn't have my car with me. I'd bought the house a few months earlier, and since then I'd been walking to work. It was a nice night, so I said I didn't need a ride, I'd just walk home. And sometime shortly after that, the guy who'd been looking for a fight got himself knifed to death."

"Oh, Lord," Carrie whispered.

She tried to meet Sam's gaze but couldn't. Instead, she sat staring at his bare feet. Convinced as she wanted to be of his innocence, she couldn't keep from wondering if there was even the slightest chance he'd killed the man.

"It happened in a lane behind Lakeshore Road," he finally continued. "I didn't walk down it on my way home, but I might have. And there were a couple of eyewitnesses who saw the murderer running away—still holding the knife. Their description of him fit me pretty well."

"But..." She shook her head once, again not knowing what to say.

"In any event," Sam said quietly, "I went to bed knowing nothing about what had happened. Then, in the middle of the night, there were cops at my door and I was under arrest."

"But if they had no evidence against you..."

Sam shrugged. "There was no murder weapon, no blood on any of my clothes. But as I said, they had a description that fit me pretty well. And when the killer ran off, he was carrying the knife in his left hand."

"And you're left-handed," she murmured.

"Uh-huh. So they had that, plus people in the pub had told the cops I'd had a run-in with the victim. And no one knew exactly where I was at the time of the stabbing."

"But even I know none of that was solid evidence."

"No, it wasn't. Hell, if you compare what little they had then to what Leo intended to trump up about Bud, it's... I was going to say it's funny, but that sure isn't the right word. *Ironic* would be better, I guess.

"So you see, when Jenny called to warn me, when she told me Leo was going to try to set me up, all I could think about was how hard a time the cops had given me when they had virtually nothing. And that now Leo was going to give them my fingerprints on the damned murder weapon.

"If I seemed a little crazy when I showed up at your place, it was because I kept thinking the same thing was happening to me all over again. Only this time Leo was going to make sure there was solid evidence.

"That's why I couldn't go to the police on my own, why I needed Jenny to back me up. And why I figured Leo actually might be able to convince them I'd killed Bud. When the cops have already suspected you of one murder... Hell, given Leo's influence, he might have gotten the detective who was convinced I was guilty the first time around put in charge of the case."

Carrie slowly nodded. Now that she knew what had

happened, it was easier to understand why Sam had been thinking the way he had.

"But who actually killed that guy in the lane?" she said. "Did they eventually find him?"

"No. They'd decided I was their man. So I figure they spent less time looking for the real killer than they did for evidence that would prove I'd done it."

"And the people who saw him running away? They didn't identify you as the guy they'd seen, did they?"

"Uh-uh. The cops did their line-up thing, but both witnesses said they weren't sure. That I looked like the man they'd seen, but that it had been too dark for them to swear I was him."

Carrie nervously pushed her hair back from her face. Sam wasn't a murderer. She just knew he wasn't. So why did she also know she'd feel a whole lot better if the police had caught the real killer?

SAM PULLED INTO HIS driveway and cut the ignition, feeling as if there was a hollow where his heart should be.

Neither he nor Carrie had said a word since they'd left the boatyard, and if one of them didn't say something before they went into the house... That was assuming she intended to *go* into the house.

When he glanced over at her, she was staring straight ahead through the windshield—not looking as if she was going anywhere.

The hollow in his chest began to expand. He was in love with this woman and he was going to lose her. Or maybe he had already.

"Look," he finally made himself say. "If you've changed your mind about wanting to stay here, I'll understand. We can go in and get your things and I'll drive you home."

She turned toward him then, heartbreakingly lovely in the moonlight. "Sam..."

He didn't breathe, just sat praying that her next words wouldn't be more than he could bear.

"Sam...I know you didn't kill anyone."

He let himself start breathing again.

"Rationally, I know you didn't. But...I want to be perfectly honest with you about this, but it's hard to explain how I'm feeling when I don't entirely understand it myself.

"I mean, I know what happened to you could have happened to anyone—including me. Logically, I know that. But there's still some sort of gut reaction that says if the police are convinced a person's guilty..."

"Not exactly the innocent-till-proven-guilty assumption," he pointed out as gently as he could.

"Sam, I know they make mistakes. But I guess thinking they're usually right is one of the things that got ingrained in me when I was a kid and...

"Do you understand what I'm trying to say? Consciously, I believe you, yet subconsciously there's this Pavlovian sort of response that says the police don't charge someone unless they have cause to. And even though I realize that's not always true, I can't deny having the reaction.

"But I think the main problem is that you really

took me by surprise, that this needs some time to sink in.''

He nodded. He knew only too well, though, that if her subconscious response didn't go away they'd be finished. If every time she looked at him she wondered whether he was a killer, there sure wouldn't be any chance of a future for them.

A future for them. Things had been so crazy since he'd met her that the future was the last thing he'd been thinking about.

But right this minute he was thinking that Carrie O'Reilly was the woman he'd been waiting for his entire life—without even knowing it.

"As for my staying here," she continued, "nothing has changed. For all I know, one of Leo's guys is rummaging around in my house right this minute. I don't want to be on my own any more than I did before.''

That was good, he told himself. At least she hadn't decided she was safer on her own than with him.

"And we've still got to figure out what really happened at Leo's," she added. "That hasn't changed, either. We still have to get to the bottom of it.''

"Okay," he said slowly. "Then we'll carry on as planned.''

"Right." She smiled at him, but it wasn't one of the heavenly smiles he'd come to adore. It looked artificial, and that stabbed at his heart.

He wasn't out of the woods yet. He wasn't even close. And if he lost her after he'd barely found her, he didn't know what he'd do.

They got out of the car and she followed him into

the house. Then, as he always did when he got home, he stuck his head into his office to check the answering machine.

"Just a sec," he said when he saw it was blinking. "I'd better listen to my messages."

He pressed Play and stood listening to the quiet whirr of the tape rewinding. When it started playing, a voice he didn't recognize said, "Hello, this is Susie-Q. I left a message for Carrie at her place, but I was told she might be there. If she is, would you ask her to call me, please."

Carrie stood behind Sam, her pulse beginning to race when she recognized the voice.

"That was a friend of Jenny's," she said when Susie's message finished. "Jenny must have contacted her."

"She didn't leave her number."

"No, and that was smart, wasn't it. Jenny must have told her to be careful, that our lines might be bugged. But even if Leo hears the name Susie-Q, it isn't going to tell him who she is.

"You don't think Jenny's ever mentioned her to him?"

"If she did, I'm sure she'd just have referred to her as Susie-Q. Her name's Susan Quentin, but Jenny wouldn't have bothered telling Leo that. They hung out with his friends—he had no interest in hers. Where's your phone book?" she added.

"We can't call her from here."

"I know. But the books at pay phones always have pages ripped out."

After Sam located his directory, Carrie looked up

the number, jotted it down on a scrap of paper and stuck it in her pocket.

"If Susie's got a number for Jenny in Costa Rica, I shouldn't use my calling card to phone, should I," she said, glancing at Sam once more. "We've got no way of knowing whether Leo can somehow tap into account records."

"Right, you're safer using coins. And there's a store near the top of the street that stays open till midnight. They'll give us change."

When Sam turned and started from the room, Carrie quickly followed along, her pulse still beating faster than normal. With any luck at all, Jenny *had* given Susie a number. And an opportunity to talk to her couldn't have come at a better time.

Because even though everything she'd said to Sam was true, even though she was pretty sure she just needed time to get her head around this murder thing, there was something bothering her that she hadn't mentioned to him.

He'd said there was absolutely no hard evidence linking him to the killing. But if Leo had told Jenny that, if he'd said there was no possible way Sam could have done it, then why had Jenny felt compelled to issue her warning about not getting involved with him?

CARRIE WROTE DOWN the number Susie-Q recited, then gave Sam a thumbs-up. He'd parked a few feet from the phone booth and was leaning against his car watching her.

"Jenny told me you already knew the area code," Susie added.

"Right," Carrie said, wondering if she'd have thought of that angle. This way, even if Leo learned who Susie was, she wouldn't be able to tell him much.

"Carrie, is Jenny in *serious* trouble?"

"Well, kind of. But…Susie, I know she'll tell you all about it once it's over. In the meantime, please don't say anything to anyone."

"No, of course not. And let me know if there's anything I can do to help."

"Thanks. I will. Bye."

She clicked off. Then, her fingers trembling just a little, she pressed zero and told the operator she wanted to call Costa Rica.

After depositing the money the woman asked for and waiting for what seemed like forever, she got a connection.

"Sol Playa Papagayo," a man answered. *"Sí?"*

"Do you speak English?" she asked, hoping against hope he would. She'd picked up a little Spanish on vacations, but not much.

"Sí señora," he assured her.

"Well, I'd like to speak to one of your guests. Señora O'Reilly?"

"Sí, Señora O'Reilly. Un momento, por favor."

After that, there was silence. Then the operator asking for more money. Then silence once again.

Just as Carrie was starting to worry that the man hadn't understood a word she'd said, Jenny came on the line.

"Carrie?" she said.

"Yes. Are you all right?"

"I'm fine. And I'm sorry it took so long, but there aren't phones in the rooms. They had to come and get me. But I wanted to let you know that I'm in a little town only a few miles from Playas del Coco. And to give you the number here. And to find out what's been happening there."

Carrie looked at Sam once more, tempted to say right off the top that what had been happening was she'd slept with him. And to ask Jenny why on earth she hadn't found some way of letting her know about that murder charge.

But instead of launching straight into the subject of her and Sam, she made herself begin by telling Jenny about their session with Leo.

When she was partway through, Jenny said, "That's a total crock. He didn't break up with me and... Carrie, the truth is exactly what I told you."

"All right. I knew he had to be lying. But the way things are looking, you'd better forget about calling him and trying to make a deal. For the time being, just let Sam and me see where we can get."

"Okay."

She took a deep breath. "There's something else I want to ask you about. Why didn't you tell me that Sam had been charged with murder?"

After a tiny silence, Jenny asked, "How did you find out?"

"He told me. But the question is, why didn't *you* tell me?"

"Carrie, I explained why at the airport. Because I

didn't have enough time. If I'd gotten into the details I'd have missed my flight. And the two of you were going to be trying to get to the bottom of this mess together. Since it was the only idea we'd come up with and there wasn't any alternative, you were stuck with him. So what would have happened if I'd said, 'Oh, by the way, Sam was once charged with murder'?

''There you'd have been, still having to work with him but totally terrified. It isn't as if I was putting you in any danger by not telling you. He would never hurt *you.* I mean, he's hardly a serial killer or anything. If he did kill that guy, I'm sure it must have been a question of Sam's life or his.''

''What!?'' Her legs suddenly felt so rubbery she was afraid they were going to give out.

''What do you mean if he *did* kill that guy?'' she said, resting her weight against the wall of the phone booth. ''Didn't Leo tell you he was innocent?''

''Well...no. But—''

''Deposit another six dollars for the next three minutes, please,'' the operator interrupted.

Swearing to herself, Carrie shoved the last of her change into the slots.

''But what?'' she demanded as the final coin dropped.

''Well, the only reason Leo told me *anything* was because I said I thought Sam was a major hunk. I was just teasing, just keeping Leo on his toes, but for some reason it really pushed his buttons. And he said, 'You think he's a major hunk, huh? Well guess what. Your hunk's a murderer.'''

"Oh, Lord," Carrie whispered.

There was another silence at Jenny's end, a longer one this time. Then she said, "You didn't listen to me, did you. You've gone and fallen for him, haven't you."

"Bingo. And now you're telling me that—"

"No, Carrie, wait. I honestly think Leo was lying to me. I mean, can you really imagine Sam killing someone? Unless it was totally in self-defense? And I don't think it was even that. I don't think Sam had the slightest thing to do with it.

"Leo told me he convinced the police it was a case of mistaken identity, but I'm sure there was no convincing involved. He was just trying to impress me, and to do that he had to make out that Sam wouldn't have gotten off without the great Leo Castanza's help.

"But if I believed everything Leo told me about his clients I'd think he'd never had an innocent one. Not a single one in his entire career. To hear him talk, they're all guilty as sin. But most of them get off regardless, because he's such a brilliant lawyer."

"Dammit, Jenny, I don't care about Leo's other clients. But do you really think he was lying when it came to Sam?"

"Yes."

She exhaled slowly. Knowing that her sister didn't believe Sam was a murderer made her feel a whole lot better. With the exception of Leo, Jenny had always been an excellent judge of people.

There was still something that needed explaining, though.

"Jenny, if you didn't think Sam actually killed that

guy, then why did you warn me not to get involved with him?''

"Because after Leo told me about the murder, he told me something I think *is* true.''

"What?'' she said, blood pounding in her head.

"He's mixed up in organized crime, Carrie. He uses his boat business to launder drug money for the mob.''

"WELL?'' SAM SAID AS Carrie stepped out of the phone booth. "Is Jenny okay?''

"Yes. She's fine.''

"And?''

She tried to put together a coherent sentence—but it was tough to do with her mind reeling. She had to ask Sam about what Jenny had told her. But the middle of Lakeshore Road wasn't the place.

Climbing into the car, she said, "She's in a tiny hotel in a town near the one I told her about.''

Sam got into the driver's seat and looked across at her. "And did you ask her about me? Ask what Leo told her about the murder charge?''

Anxiety was written all over his face, and she felt such a strong pang of sympathy that she almost reached for his hand. But she held back. Knowing the real reason Jenny had warned her off him had only given her something different to worry about.

"Carrie?'' Sam pressed. "Did you ask exactly what Leo told her?''

As much as she didn't want to get into a discussion about it here, Sam was the one with the car keys. And they obviously weren't going anywhere until he got an answer.

"She said that Leo told her you were guilty. But that she didn't believe it."

"That bastard!"

"Sam, I don't believe it, either. I told you that earlier."

"Except for your gut feeling."

"I didn't say I had a gut feeling that you'd done it. I never for a minute said that. And...Sam, can we go back to your place and talk there? Please?"

Without another word, he started the engine.

CHAPTER TWELVE

CARRIE DOUBTED IT HAD taken Sam more than twelve seconds to drive the two blocks from the Lakeshore to his house. And not more than another three to get a couple of beers from the fridge and bring them out to the porch for their little "talk."

Once he had, she'd desperately wanted to begin by asking him about the money-laundering thing. But he'd made her start by giving him a word-by-word replay of what Jenny'd had to say about Leo and the murder charge.

"So that's it?" he said when she finished. "Leo told her I'd killed that guy because she said she thought I was cute?"

"A 'major hunk' was how she put it. He must have figured that meant she was about to throw herself at you."

"He couldn't tell she was just pulling his chain?"

"Apparently not."

"So he said I was a murderer. To scare her off me. Dammit," Sam muttered. "I could kill him. I mean, I could if I was actually a killer," he added quickly.

"Carrie...you really are okay with that, aren't you? You're not going to be lying awake in the middle of the night, afraid I'll suddenly be coming at you with a knife?''

She shook her head, then took a sip of beer, thinking that if he really was mixed up with the mob, she wouldn't be under the same roof as him in the middle of the night.

"You don't know how terrific that makes me feel," he said, giving her a to-die-for smile.

"Yes...well." She hesitated. Now that the time had come, she was terrified to ask the question. Or, more precisely, terrified of what his answer would be.

She put down the glass and gathered up her courage. "Sam, I asked Jenny why she'd warned me about you if she didn't believe you were guilty."

"Good question. That hadn't occurred to me, but why did she?"

"Because Leo also told her that you launder drug money for the mob."

Sam gazed at her for a long moment, his expression unreadable. "And do you think that's true?" he said at last.

"Don't do that to me!" she snapped, feeling stretched almost to the breaking point. "This has been one hell of a day, I'm totally exhausted, I haven't slept since forever, and I don't want to play a guessing game with you. I just want you to tell me whether it's true or not."

"All right. It's not." He took a swig of beer, then simply sat watching her.

"So why did Leo tell Jenny it was?"

"How in blazes do I know? But if you want me to take a guess, the obvious one is that it was for the same reason he told her I was a murderer. He was giving her added incentive to steer clear of me—in case my being a killer wasn't enough to turn her off.''

He paused then, slowly shaking his head. ''Carrie, listen, it's been one hell of a day for both of us. But for Leo to say I launder money is so damned stupid I can hardly believe it.

''Just for starters, it wouldn't even be possible through a company like mine. And if Jenny'd known how the process works, she'd have realized that.''

''I don't know how it works, either,'' Carrie told him, praying his explanation would leave her totally convinced he couldn't be doing it. ''I don't even understand what it means really,'' she added.

''Well, okay, it means making money like drug money appear to have come from a legitimate source. And organized crime wants to do that because, otherwise, the cops can follow the money and get to the top guys.

''See, the government has access to a lot more information than your average citizen realizes. Banks and stockbrokers and whatever have to report all kinds of things to Revenue Canada. And if some supposedly legitimate guy has more money than can be reasonably accounted for, or if he's obviously living beyond his means, it's not long before either an auditor or some law enforcement type comes around asking questions. But 'laundering' makes extra money seem legit.''

''How?''

''Well...to give you a really small-scale example, say you own a burger joint. At the end of a day you've taken in five hundred dollars. If your expenses were three hundred, you've made two hundred dollars' profit."

She nodded.

"Okay, now say you sell drugs on the side and make a two-hundred-dollar profit on cocaine that same day. What you do is record your burger business income for the day as seven hundred dollars. Then, supposedly, your profit was four hundred. And what you've done is made that two hundred dollars of drug profits legitimate. You've 'laundered' it."

"You'd pay more taxes," she pointed out.

Sam simply looked at her, then shook his head. "How can an artist have a mind like a tax accountant's?"

She'd have smiled if she wasn't so upset.

"Yes, you'd pay more taxes," he continued. "But you'd still come out ahead of the game. And you wouldn't end up in jail for having drug money.

"At any rate, as I said, that was a small-scale example. Organized crime does it on a grand scale, but they can only make it work with businesses that take in a lot of cash. And my company takes in virtually none. Boats are big-ticket items. People pay me with checks or bank drafts. Never in cash. So I couldn't launder money if I wanted to."

Carrie exhaled slowly. His explanation sounded almost *too* simple. Besides, for all she knew there were a hundred other ways of laundering money. And how did she know how it was done, anyway?

When she asked that question out loud, he shrugged. "Did you think boat-building was the only subject I know anything about? I read. I watch 'Sixty Minutes.' If I'm curious about something, I find answers on the Internet.''

She thought about that for a minute. ''So when it comes to this 'mob connection' story of Leo's, you're saying he just pulled it of thin air?''

''Carrie...'' Sam paused, raking his fingers through his hair. ''I'd have figured that telling Jenny I was a murderer would be way more than enough to turn her off. But if he wanted to ice the cake, then the idea of telling her I was connected to the mob might have popped into his head because...

''Well, the trouble I told you I had at the boatyard, the reason I got a gun, was that some wise guy came around a few months back telling me I'd have to start paying protection money. I told him to go to hell— and the next night my boatyard got trashed.

''But the point is that I called and told Leo what had happened, hoping he could use his connections and put the word out to lay off me. And I think he actually did, because there was only the one incident. But the fact he knew about it could explain why he'd come up with a 'mob' story for Jenny.''

Carrie sat staring at her beer, desperately wanting to believe every word Sam had told her but afraid to.

The silence of the night stretched between them until at last he said, ''Carrie, it's impossible to prove a negative.''

''Meaning?'' she said, looking at him.

''Meaning I can't prove I didn't kill that guy in the lane and I can't prove I don't launder money for the mob. All I can do is tell you the truth—which is what

I've done. So it's up to you. You're going to have to decide whether to believe me or Leo."

She continued to gaze at him. Even though she knew Leo was a liar, she was still amazed that Sam had managed to make her choice sound so simple. To make it seem so obvious that she should believe him.

"You once told me your intuition's rarely wrong," he added quietly. "What's it telling you right now?"

She looked back at her beer, only too aware that her intuition was telling her Sam Evans was a man she could trust. A man she could commit to without fearing he'd betray that trust. A man she didn't have to hold back with.

And given that, wouldn't she be the world's biggest fool not to believe him?

Her heart pounding, she finally said, "Sam?"

"Yes?"

"It's awfully late, and I never did get around to organizing my stuff. It's still all in a heap on the guest room bed."

He gave her an uncertain smile. "You want me to help you clear it off?"

"Well...that wasn't exactly what I had in mind."

CARRIE WOKE TO MORNING light streaming in through Sam's bedroom window. His body was entwined with hers, and she could smell his scent on her skin and feel the warmth of his breath against her neck. She smiled with pure joy. It was the most wonderful awakening she'd had in her entire life, and she snuggled closer to him, resting her hand softly against his chest and willing him to wake up so she could tell him exactly that.

But just as he gave her a tired "Mmm" and nuzzled her throat with a sexy kiss, a thought began skimming around the edges of her mind, demanding her attention.

After they'd made love last night, and after she'd reached that warm and fuzzy almost-asleep stage, she'd thought of something important she had to tell him. But he'd already been asleep, so instead of waking him she'd told herself to be sure to remember what it was in the morning.

Now, though, she couldn't. She only knew it had something to do with Jenny.

"This is very nice," he murmured, trailing his hand down her nakedness and sending a rush of desire through her. "You must have the smoothest skin in the world."

"Sam, stop." If she let him get started, she wouldn't have a chance of recapturing that thought. She wouldn't be able to think about anything except how crazy he could make her with his mere touch.

"Stop? Really?" he teased, caressing her thigh.

"Well…" She'd just about decided that capturing the thought could wait till later, when the recollection of what it was crystallized.

"Leo's disks," she said.

"What about them?" Sam stopped midcaress, propped himself up on one elbow and looked at her.

"Now that I know you aren't connected to the mob, Jenny will tell us where they are."

"What? How do you figure that?"

"Because that was the real reason she wouldn't tell us. Because she thought you were. Connected, I mean. And that meant she'd be crazy to trust you too far. She said she was scared that if you got your hands on them, you might double-cross her and make your own deal with Leo."

"*What?*" He sat up straight in the bed, looking insulted as all get out.

"Sam, don't take it personally. She was just afraid to take any chances."

"When did she tell you this?"

"At the airport."

"Hell, she sure told you a lot in a minute or two, didn't she."

Ignoring the remark, Carrie scrambled out of bed. "We've got to go and phone her again."

He didn't move, just sat eyeing her naked body as if it were a mocha fudge sundae.

"We've got to go and phone her again *now,*" she said firmly. "You're the one who figured there'd be something on those disks that would help us. So we've got to talk to her before she heads to the beach or somewhere for the day."

With obvious reluctance, he rolled out of bed and reached for his jeans. Ten minutes later, they were back at the same phone booth on Lakeshore Road— Carrie inside it with a fresh stack of coins, Sam outside leaning against the hood of his car.

This time, whoever answered the hotel's phone responded to her with reasonable English.

"I'd like to talk to one of your guests, please," she told him. "Señora O'Reilly."

"Ah. No. The *señora,* she go. Early."

Carrie swore to herself. "Do you have any idea what time she'll be back?"

"No. She will not come back. She go with her suitcase."

Oh, Lord. Her heart started sinking fast. "You mean she checked out?"

"*Sí.* Yes. She checked out."

"But where was she going? Do you know?"

"No, *señora.* I am sorry. She just go."

"Well...*gracias.*" She hung up, her throat tight and her stomach doing flip-flops.

Gazing at Carrie through the Plexiglas of the phone booth, Sam could see something was dreadfully wrong. "What is it?" he asked the instant she stepped out onto the sidewalk.

"She's gone. Checked out of the hotel first thing this morning."

"Dammit," he muttered.

"Sam?"

When he looked at her again, there were tears in her eyes.

"Hey," he said, folding her into his arms. "Hey, she'll be all right."

"No. Something happened," she murmured against his shoulder. "Something scared her and made her run."

"Not necessarily. We told her not to stay in one place too long, remember?"

"Yes, but she hadn't decided she'd be leaving this morning when I spoke to her last night. If she had, she'd have told me. So something must have happened after that.''

"Carrie…" He stroked the silky softness of her hair, not knowing what else to say.

"She'll get in touch with us again," he finally said. "Once she's settled someplace else. And don't forget she's thousands of miles away. Whatever reason she had for moving on, I'm sure it wasn't because Leo's people tracked her down.''

"No?" Carrie eased back a little and looked up at him, her eyes still dark with tears.

"No. They couldn't possibly have done it that quickly," he told her, hoping he sounded a lot more certain than he felt.

WHEN SOMEONE FLICKED the library's lights off, then on, warning the patrons that it was almost closing time, Sam pushed the rewind button on his microfilm reader. Then he looked over at Carrie, who was still slowly scrolling through a film on the machine next to his.

Her skin was pale. And those tiny lines were apparent around her eyes again, the way they always were when she was tired.

He exhaled slowly, thinking she had to be far beyond merely tired by this point. She'd barely slept the past few nights. Instead, she'd lain awake in his arms, worrying about where Jenny could be and why she hadn't contacted them again.

He was worried, too, though he tried not to show it. He kept assuring Carrie that there could be a hundred and one different reasons why they hadn't heard

from her sister, but both of them feared the most obvious one—Leo's people had tracked her down.

But how could they have done it so fast? That *did*
seem almost impossible, which was the main hope
they were clinging to. And if she was okay, and if
she got in touch with them… Hell, all she had to do
was tell them where those disks were and they might
actually be able to make some progress.

And every bit as important, he thought, looking at
Carrie again, was that if she knew Jenny was safe,
she wouldn't be walking around close to tears all the
time.

Apparently sensing that he was watching her, she
glanced at him.

"Anything?" he asked, gesturing toward her
screen.

She shook her head and wearily rubbed her eyes.
"Is this only the third day we've spent sitting here
like this?"

"Yeah, I know what you mean. It feels like a
month."

"More like two. I'm starting to think we'll go blind
without figuring out who Bud is. But I just want to
finish looking through this one bit," she added, turning her attention back to her reader. "It'll only take
another minute or two."

Removing the little reel of old *Toronto Star* issues
from his machine, Sam stuck it into its box, wishing
yet again that they could have simply gone to people
Leo knew and asked who "Bud" might be.

But if they'd done that, Leo would have learned
what they were up to. So they'd had to go about their

task without anyone being aware of what they were doing.

They'd begun by using the computer at the boat-yard, and things had gone slowly at first, because Carrie had never used a computer before.

She'd caught on fast, though, and they'd eventually worked their way through every on-line database they thought might contain a mention of Leo Castanza—from legal sources to popular ones. Every time they came across his name, they'd checked the article or court report or whatever for any reference to a "Bud."

Whenever they'd found one, they'd followed up on the person. Unfortunately, none of the Buds they'd identified thus far had recently disappeared.

Most of them had been relatively easy to contact. A couple had proved to be deceased, but the deaths hadn't been recent. Now, having completely struck out with the most likely sources, they were reduced to checking the library's microfilm—copies of old newspapers and magazines and some local interest publications of various vintages.

"Sam, here's one," Carrie said.

As he turned toward her, she stuck a quarter into her machine and pressed the print button, adding, "It's from a law school alumni journal."

Even though he knew it was probably another false lead, he leaned over and watched the grainy print appear. She'd zoomed in on a photograph of several men seated at a round table in some restaurant or club.

The caption above it read, Friends from the Class of 1978 Reminisce.

The faces of the "friends" probably weren't clear enough for their own mothers to recognize them, but below the picture were the names of the individuals at the table. And one of them was Leo.

"Look," Carrie said, tapping her finger against the fellow sitting to his right. "This guy's name is Beauregard 'Bud' Racine."

"Beauregard? Gee, I wonder why he'd prefer Bud?"

"Never mind that," Carrie said. "We haven't come across his name before. But if he graduated with Leo, why didn't he turn up in the Law Society's membership list?"

"It probably listed him as Beauregard. That wouldn't have rung a bell."

The lights flicked off and on again—staying off for a few seconds longer this time.

"I'll rewind that for you," a woman said from behind them.

When they turned, she nodded toward Carrie's microfilm reader, then looked pointedly at the clock.

"Oh, sorry if we've kept you," Carrie said, tucking the print into her purse.

"That's all right. Did you get what you needed?"

"We hope so," Sam told her, thinking she couldn't possibly know how much he meant that.

CARRIE FOLLOWED SAM across his living room, praying they'd find another message from Susie-Q on his machine. Or one from some other friend of Jenny's. When they reached his office and she saw the message light blinking, her hopes started to rise.

But the message wasn't from any friend of Jenny's, to say the least. It was from Leo.

"Sam, it's Leo," he began. "I tried to reach you at the boatyard today, but they told me they weren't expecting you. I hope that doesn't mean nothing's getting done on my boat. I don't want there to be ice on the lake before she's finished. But what I was actually calling you about is Jenny. I haven't been getting any answer at Carrie's place, and I thought maybe she and Jenny had gone off together or something?

"She promised to phone me if she heard from Jen, let me know everything was okay with her, but maybe she forgot. At any rate, give me a call, will you. Tonight, preferably. I'll be up till after the eleven o'clock news—555-1648."

"I'd better get back to him," Sam said, punching in the number.

Carrie listened while he told Leo that they hadn't heard a word from Jenny. And that, yes, Carrie was very worried about her. And, no, Leo shouldn't be concerned about his boat—Sam had the project well in hand and his best craftsman was already doing the preliminary work on it.

"Report her as a missing person?" he said next. "Well…yeah. Carrie and I have talked about it. But she wants to hold off for a bit. As I said, she's worried, but she's pretty sure that Jenny's just trying to throw a scare into you and she'll turn up soon." Sam listened for a minute, then said, "I know. And I will. As soon as we hear from her."

He hung up and gave Carrie a shrug. "If I didn't

know better, I'd figure he was Mr. Sincerity. But you know what? I think that call tells us for sure that his people can't have caught up with Jenny. That he doesn't have a clue where she is.''

"Oh, Sam, I hope you're right.''

Draping his arms around her waist, he gave her a lingering kiss that turned her knees to jelly. "Let's hold that thought for a few minutes,'' he said at last. "Until we've checked out our latest 'Bud' lead.''

"I'll do it,'' she said, digging out the phone directory and turning to the *R*s. "Racine,'' she murmured, glancing quickly down the page.

"Here we are. Two listings. One's a residence number, the other an office one—for B. A. Racine and L. J. Kowalsky, Attorneys at Law.''

She read the home number to Sam, then held her breath while he punched it in.

"You know, there's something really absurd about this,'' he said when he'd finished. "Every time we call one of these Buds, we're hoping he won't answer his phone.

"A machine's picked up,'' he added after a minute.

Carrie waited, thinking this had happened several times before. Sam would leave a message, asking their latest Bud to return the call, and sooner or later he would. Alive and well. Not the Bud Leo had murdered.

Sam abruptly moved the receiver away from his ear; she could hear a faint screeching noise.

"Hear that?'' he said, his tone tinged with excitement.

She nodded.

"It's what I got after the beep, so his message tape must be full. That could mean something."

"Right." It could mean he hadn't been home for quite a while. Telling herself not to read too much into a full tape, she said, "Try the office number."

"It's almost ten at night."

"Try anyway."

He called it, waited, then said, "It's just ringing. We'll have to call again in the morning. Or maybe we should drop by," he added, hanging up. "Why don't you write down both of those addresses and phone numbers."

Once she'd finished and closed the book, he shot her such a sexy smile it almost melted her bones.

"So, what do you think?" he said. "You want to sit out on the porch for a while, or you just want to get to bed?"

Before she could answer, the phone began ringing.

"Sam Evans," he said, picking up. He listened for a few seconds, then replied, "I'll get back to you in five minutes."

Carrie watched him hang up, half certain that had been the call they'd been hoping for, half afraid it hadn't been.

"That was Susie-Q," he said, giving her a big hug. "She said she has a new number for us."

CHAPTER THIRTEEN

"IF WE USE THIS PHONE booth many more times we'll have to start paying rent on it," Sam joked, pulling up to the curb beside it.

Carrie smiled at him, aware her mood was about ten thousand times better than it had been before Susie-Q's call.

"You're sure Jenny will tell you?" he asked as they climbed out into the night.

"Yes," she said firmly. No matter what she had to say to make Jenny tell her where those disks were, she'd say it.

Her pockets loaded down with more coins from Sam's cooperative store, she phoned Susie and got the new number. Then she went through the process of calling Costa Rica again.

This time, Jenny had a room with a phone.

"Are you all right?" Carrie demanded when her sister picked up.

"Well, hello to you, too," Jenny said. "Now don't be mad at me," she went on quickly. "I know how worried you must have been but—"

"Worried? Try frantic." She gave Sam a little wave, even though, with the phone booth lit, he'd probably realized that she'd reached Jenny.

"Carrie, I know. I couldn't help it, though. Really."

"And you are okay."

"I'm fine."

"All right, then tell me what happened."

"Well, after I talked to you last time, I went for a walk and stopped for a drink at one of those little sodas. You know?"

"Yes," she said, mentally picturing the tiny holes-in-the-wall that sold soft drinks, beer and snacks.

"I'd barely sat down when another woman came in. A woman about my age, from California. There were only three tables, and the other two were full, so she sat with me.

"At any rate, she had a car, and she was leaving first thing in the morning for the Caribbean side of the country. We hit it off, so when she asked if I'd like to go with her, I said why not. You and Sam warned me not to stay in one place too long, remember? And I figured traveling with someone would be a good idea, because anyone looking for me would be looking for a woman on her own.

"So we started off, but she'd gotten directions for some back route. And you know what the roads are like down here."

"You ended up in a ditch or something," Carrie guessed. Aside from the main highways, most of the roads in Costa Rica didn't deserve to be called roads.

"Close. She drove into a hole and broke an axle."

"Oh, Lord."

"It was okay. I mean, neither of us was hurt. And even though we were pretty well in the middle of nowhere, we'd passed a house not long before it happened. So we walked back and... Well, to cut a long story short, the house belonged to this really nice family who insisted we stay with them until the car was fixed. I can't believe how friendly the people are here.

"Anyway, that's where I've been for the past few days. And they didn't have a phone or a car, so there was no way I could get a message to you. What's happening there, though? Have you and Sam gotten anywhere?"

"Not very far. But Leo was lying when he said Sam launders money."

"Oh? Who told you that?"

"Sam."

"Yeah. Right. Well, if he offers to sell you the Brooklyn Bridge, tell him you're not interested."

"Dammit, Jenny," she snapped, her sister's sarcasm sparking her temper. "Sam is not tied in with any criminals. And I trust him implicitly, so I want you to tell me what you did with those disks of Leo's. We've got to have a look at whatever's on them."

There was only silence at the other end of the line.

Carrie counted to ten, then said, "Jenny, are you listening?"

"Yes."

"Then listen good. Sam and I have been busting our butts trying to help you. But we don't have enough to go on and we've got Leo breathing down our necks."

"Really?"

"Yes. Really. So you tell me how we can lay our

hands on those disks. Otherwise, it'll only be a matter of time before it's too late.''

''But if you're wrong about Sam, he could—''

''I'm *not* wrong. Now tell me where they are.''

There was another silence. Then, in a very small voice, Jenny said, ''All right.''

''Thank heavens,'' Sam muttered to himself as Carrie gave him a thumbs-up. Then he stood watching while she put more coins in the phone, dug a pen and paper out of her purse and started writing something down—the name and number of whoever Jenny'd given Leo's disks to, he assumed.

If that was it, it was the first real break they'd gotten. Now they just had to hope there was something on the disks that would help them.

Finally, Carrie hung up and stepped out of the phone booth.

''Well?'' he said.

''Well, we'll have to take a drive in the morning. She had the disks in her suitcase when she went to Linda's cabin and buried them in the woods as soon as she got there.''

''So that message we gave Leo from her? About the RCMP getting them if anything happened to us? That was a total bluff?''

''Apparently.''

He swore under his breath. Since nothing awful *had* happened so far, maybe Leo had taken them seriously. But if he suspected Jenny's threat was only a ruse, he wouldn't hesitate to do anything he wanted.

''Pardon? Did you say something?'' Carrie asked.

"Just talking to myself. I hope Jenny didn't damage the disks while she was burying them."

"No, I'm sure she didn't. She can be infuriating at times, but she's not dumb. She said she sealed the envelope inside plastic bags, then put it in a cookie tin and sealed that. They should be fine."

"And she told you exactly where they are?"

"Yes. That's what I was making notes about."

"Then we'll head to the cabin first thing."

"Before we follow up on Beauregard 'Bud' Racine?"

"Good question. We'll have to give that some thought."

"Well, at any rate, I'll phone Linda right now and see if there's anyone staying at the cabin. When I called her the other day, she mentioned her parents would be up there for a bit—getting the door fixed and whatever."

Sam nodded. Calling to check made a lot of sense. He'd noticed a rifle hanging on a wall in the Willenziks' cabin, and after having their front door kicked in, unexpected visitors would make them very nervous.

SAM ROLLED OUT OF BED at seven, but he didn't have the heart to wake Carrie.

It had been the first good night's sleep she'd gotten since they'd lost contact with Jenny, and there was no reason for her to get up early. Beauregard Racine's office wouldn't likely be open before nine, and they'd decided last night that they'd stop by there before they headed to the cabin.

Linda had assured Carrie nobody would be there. Her parents had already finished fixing things up and come back to Toronto. And they were leaving on a trip to New York City this morning.

After he'd showered and dressed, Sam made a pot of coffee and took a mug out to the porch. He was on his first refill when Carrie appeared in the doorway.

She gave him one of her wonderful smiles. "Do I have time for some of that?"

"Sure."

She didn't turn away immediately, and he couldn't have taken his eyes from her if he'd tried.

Her hair was tousled, she was wearing nothing but her nightshirt, and she still looked half-asleep. She also looked so beautiful it made his heart ache.

They simply had to sort out this mess so they could get on with their lives. Safely. Without constantly worrying about what Leo might be up to.

"What do I wear?" she finally said, noting his dress pants and shirt. "Going-to-see-a-lawyer clothes and digging-in-the-dirt clothes aren't exactly the same."

"Yeah, I was thinking that, too. I figured I'd throw a pair of old jeans and whatever into the trunk. After we've been to Racine's, we could stop by your place and change. It wouldn't be much out of our way, and it wouldn't hurt to make sure everything's okay there."

"You think it might not be?" she asked uneasily.

He shook his head. "After our experience with that guy at the boatyard, I think that if someone's been looking around in there, or in here, we'll probably never know.''

She didn't look happy at that, but she merely nodded and headed for the kitchen. Sam went back to thinking about the two of them getting on with their lives. Together.

He was still thinking about it when they reached the offices of B. A. Racine and L. J. Kowalsky, Attorneys at Law.

''Not exactly a Bay Street law firm, is it,'' Carrie said as he parked the car.

''Not exactly.'' Racine might have graduated in the same class as Leo, but it was obvious he hadn't met with nearly as much professional success. The offices were in a dreary west end strip mall, right next door to a real estate agency—suggesting a practice heavy on agreements of sale and purchase. Sam didn't imagine that was the sort of stuff lawyers' dreams were made of.

They climbed out of the car and headed inside, where they were greeted by a receptionist who looked like somebody's favorite aunt.

''We'd like to see Mr. Racine,'' he told her.

''I'm sorry, he's out of town at the moment.''

Out of town? He glanced at Carrie.

''But perhaps Mr. Kowalsky could help you,'' the woman suggested. ''When one of them's away, the other one always looks after his clients.''

''No, it's a family matter,'' Carrie told her. ''I wonder…would it be okay if you told us where Bud is?''

''I'm afraid I can't.''

"It's urgent that we get in touch with him," Carrie pressed.

"If you'd like to leave your name and number, I'll be sure he gets the message."

"But… Oh, Lord, I don't want to get you in any trouble, but someone in the family is dying. And he wants to talk to Bud because… Oh, I'm sorry. If you're not allowed to tell me, I understand."

The woman eyed her for a long moment, then said, "Well, I guess it'll be okay under the circumstances. He's in Las Vegas."

While Carrie thanked her, then asked when he'd be back, Sam was wondering how much time Bud Racine spent in Vegas. If he enjoyed gambling more than lawyering, that would at least partly explain why he wasn't on Bay Street.

"When he left, he didn't say exactly when we should expect him home," the receptionist was saying. "Although, to be honest, I thought he'd have been back by now, because he's been gone almost two weeks. But he usually stays until the dice go cold, as he puts it."

Almost two weeks. Which meant he'd left town before the murder, Sam thought. But what if he'd come back without this woman knowing about it and paid Leo a visit?

It was a possibility. It was far more likely, though, that Bud Racine simply wasn't the man they were looking for. No more than the others had been. Bud Racine was probably still in Vegas with a hot pair of dice.

"Would you have a phone number for him there?" Carrie asked. "Or the name of the hotel?"

The receptionist nodded and reached for her Rolodex. "Sure. He always stays at the Mirage."

She jotted down the number and handed it to Carrie.

"Thanks. And could I ask you just one more question?"

"Sure."

"Well, you're going to think this is a strange one after I told you it's a family matter. But my branch of the family and Bud's have been estranged ever since I was a little kid. So I know how old he is and all, but would you mind telling me what he looks like?"

The receptionist did seem to think that was a strange question. Still, she simply shrugged and started in on a description.

With each word she spoke, Sam could feel his heart beating a little faster. That grainy photo Carrie had printed off the microfilm yesterday hadn't told them much. But this woman's description matched the one Jenny'd given them of the man Leo had killed.

Of course, it was still the sort of generic description that would fit thousands of middle-aged men. Even so, Sam couldn't keep his excitement level from rising.

When the woman was finished, Carrie said, "It sounds as if he looks a lot like my dad. And what's he done over all these years? Is he married? Do I have cousins I don't know about?"

Good question, Sam thought. As in, If he's gone

missing, how many people might be wondering where he is?

"He *was* married, but he's been divorced for years. And as far as I know he never had children."

"Oh." Carrie looked disappointed.

"Well, I hope you manage to get hold of him, dear, but you'll probably have to leave a message. I think he spends most of his time at the tables and not much in his room."

"Yes. Thanks. I'll do that."

They managed to make a reasonably sedate exit, then practically ran to the pay phone at the end of the plaza.

When it proved to be out of order, Sam swore to himself. He'd never had much inclination to get a cell phone, but he was starting to see how handy one could be.

"Come on," he said, taking Carrie's hand and heading for the car. "We can wait to phone till we get to your place."

"Or we can stop at the next phone booth we see."

"You're just a little eager, huh?" he teased.

"Well you think it's him, too, don't you?"

"I think it could be. But that's not the same as it *has* to be."

They drove a few blocks until Carrie spotted another phone booth, then they stopped and Sam called the Mirage from it.

"Mr. Racine's room, please," he said to the woman who answered.

"Just a moment, please.

"I'm sorry, sir," she said after a few seconds. "We have no Mr. Racine registered."

"Well...has he checked out?"

"I'm sorry. We're not allowed to give information about our guests."

But he wasn't where his receptionist figured he should be. And that just might mean they'd finally come up with a Bud who both knew Leo and had disappeared recently.

ACCORDING TO THE ADDRESS Carrie had copied from the phone directory last night, Beauregard Racine, LLB, lived on Wimbleton Road, which proved to be a pleasant residential street not far from his office.

"Do you think we're going to learn anything here?" she asked as Sam slowed the car, checking the house numbers.

He shrugged. "If Bud Racine answers his door, we'll learn he's not dead."

"He isn't going to answer his door. If he was back in Toronto and not dead, he'd have been at his office."

"Well, we'll just have to see what we find."

A couple of houses farther along, they swung into the driveway of a long brick bungalow. In the yard next to it, an elderly woman watering a flower bed shifted position so she could watch what they were up to.

"Morning," Sam said, giving her a smile once they'd gotten out of the car.

Following his lead, Carrie shot her a smile, as well. They'd taken about three steps toward the bungalow when the woman called, "If you're looking for Mr. Racine, he's not home."

As they stopped and turned, Sam whispered, "Do the long-lost relative thing again."

"Right," she whispered back.

Walking over to the property line, she said, "I'm Bud's…second cousin, I guess it is. He and my dad are first cousins."

The woman nodded, turning her hose off at the nozzle.

"At any rate, my husband and I are only in Toronto for a couple of days and I promised my dad I'd see Bud. I phoned, but his machine didn't seem to be working. So we decided to try just stopping by."

"Well, I'm afraid I can't even tell you when he'll be back."

"Oh. You mean he's out of town?"

"Uh-huh. And as I said, I'm not sure when he'll be home. He usually tells me—more or less, at least—because I take in his mail for him. But I'm not sure what's going on this time. He said about two weeks, then he popped back after just a few days, then he was gone again. Just flew in, then back out."

"Flew," Carrie repeated, glancing pointedly at Bud's driveway. Aside from Sam's Mustang, it was empty.

"He leaves his car at the airport when he travels," the neighbor explained.

Or he left it at Leo's, Carrie thought. And Leo got rid of it.

"Do you know where he went?" Sam asked. "When he left again, I mean?"

"Oh, yes, he went back to Las Vegas. He said he'd just come home to take care of some business, and then he'd be going back."

"When was that?" Sam said.

"I'm not exactly sure," she said slowly. "A week ago, maybe? Give or take a day or so."

"Well, it's too bad we missed him," Sam said.

"Yes, but I'll tell him you stopped by. What's your name, dear?" she added to Carrie.

"Marion," Carrie said. "His cousin Frank's daughter, Marion. And thanks so much for your help."

"You're very welcome." The woman turned her hose on again and went back to watering her flowers.

Carrie managed to keep quiet until she and Sam were inside the car—but just barely.

"It's him!" she said the instant she'd closed her door. "Sam, we've found him. He never went back to Vegas at all. He went to Leo's, and that was the last place he ever went."

"Maybe."

"Maybe? What do you mean, maybe? It's *got* to be him."

"Yeah, okay, let's go with probably rather than maybe. But we can't be positive."

"*I'm* positive. His receptionist said he always stays at the Mirage. So if he's back in Vegas, why isn't he registered there?"

"Well…"

"Because he's not back in Vegas," she said, answering her own question. "Because he's dead and his body's wherever Leo disposed of it. I'm certain he's *our* Bud.''

Sam shook his head. ''The problem is, being certain of something and being able to prove it are two different things.''

GETTING TO THE WILLENZIKS' cabin from the southwest end of the city took longer than it had from Linda's apartment, but Sam knew they were almost there when they passed the gas station he'd pulled in behind to lose Leo's Caddie the last time around.

''Only another couple of minutes,'' he told Carrie.

''Right,'' she said, glancing at Linda's map.

Fortunately, she hadn't thrown it away. He suspected that even in the bright light of day they'd have had a hard time finding the place without it.

''The driveway should be just up ahead now,'' she said.

There was barely time to nod before he spotted the almost hidden entrance. He made the sharp turn, his mouth suddenly dry and an unsettling sense of déjà vu seizing him. The last time they'd been here, they'd ended up getting shot at.

But this time, he told himself, things were going to end better. This time, they were going to get their hands on those disks. And with any luck at all, that would enable them to put all the pieces of the puzzle into place.

They reached the end of the zigzagging drive and the cabin stood before them in the clearing. Today, of course, there was no sign of Leo's Caddy—or any other car, for that matter.

It had to be ninety degrees out, but all the windows were closed up tight. Obviously, as Linda had told Carrie, there was nobody here.

"Oh, by the way," she said. "I never got around to mailing back the keys Jenny borrowed, so Linda said I should go in the back and leave them on the kitchen counter. The new front door lock will lock itself when we leave."

"Okay, we'll do that before we go."

He began to reach under his seat for his Beretta, then hesitated when Carrie nervously said, "You don't think we'll need that, do you?"

"No. I guess taking it with me's just becoming a reflex action."

Leaving the gun where it was, he climbed out of the car and retrieved the spade he'd brought along in the trunk, while Carrie dug Jenny's instructions from her purse.

"Okay, we walk straight in line with the back door to where the trees meet the clearing behind the cabin," she read as they started off.

When they neared the tree line, she glanced at her piece of paper again. "Now we take eleven paces straight into the woods, then look for a tree to our left with a dab of nail polish on it at eye level."

"A dab of nail polish?"

"Sam, whatever works, right?"

"Yeah, right," he said, starting forward out of the heat of the clearing and into the relative coolness of the woods.

After taking eleven of what he guessed to be Jenny-size paces, he stopped and checked around at what would be her eye level.

"Here," he said, finally spotting a little red dot.

"You see? You'd never have noticed that if you hadn't known exactly what you were looking for. Now, turn left just past the marked tree, walk eight paces, and stop.... No, I think you went a little too far. We're supposed to be standing directly between two pine trees, which I think must be right here."

He turned and looked back at her, certain that as a kid he'd played a game very much like this.

"There," she said, pointing off to the side of one of the trees she was standing between. "I think you want to try right beside that rock where all those leaves are."

"It doesn't look as if anyone's been digging there."

"She said she was careful to cover her tracks."

Not at all convinced that was the right spot, he strode over to it, knelt down and brushed away a bunch of the leaves. Sure enough, he exposed a small patch of earth that had recently been dug. So recently, in fact, that the smell of the loose soil mingling with the dry scent of the leaves was tickling his nostrils.

"She must have been a Girl Guide," he said, standing up again.

Carrie hovered anxiously beside him as he shoved his spade into the ground. He only had to dig a few inches before he hit metal, and when he did, she excitedly said, "That's it."

Kneeling again, he scooped away the rest of the

earth with his hands—exposing a red plaid shortbread tin.

Shoving the loose soil back into the hole, he quickly patted it down and re-covered the patch of ground with leaves. Then he started trying to get the tin open. Jenny had sealed it with clear packing tape, and she'd used several layers.

"Let's just get out of here," Carrie said.

"I want to make sure we've got what we came for."

"Sam, she didn't bury cookies. She said the disks are in there, so they are."

"Yeah, you're right."

He handed her the tin and picked up the spade. Then they started back in the direction of the cabin.

They were about halfway out of the woods when a man said, "Stop right where you are. And turn around nice and slow."

CHAPTER FOURTEEN

CARRIE HAD NEVER BEEN so terrified in her entire life.

The hulking figure who'd materialized behind them was straight out of a *Godfather* movie. Pockmarked face, scar running through one eyebrow, blue eyes so cold that looking at them made her shiver. But the scariest thing about him was the gun he was holding. It was big enough to make Sam's Beretta look like a starter's pistol.

"Sit down, then open that tin," he told her. "And you start diggin' a hole," he ordered Sam, training the gun on him once she was sitting on the ground.

"Anywhere in particular?" he asked.

Oh, Sam, she whispered to herself. She knew he'd been going for "relaxed and unconcerned," but the tension in his voice had given him away.

The man shrugged. "Wherever you want. It's your grave."

His words started her whole body trembling.

"That's a joke, right?" Sam said, plunging the spade into the ground.

"Yeah, sure, that's why you're laughin' so hard."

"You're going to kill us for a cookie tin?" Sam tossed aside a shovelful of dirt. "When you don't even know what's in it?"

"I heard your girlfriend say the disks are in it, and that's what I want. The boss said he was missing some computer disks—figured they might be hidden up here. Go back up and hang around, he said."

Go back up. Carrie realized this was the same guy who'd shown up last time. They'd never gotten a look at him, but the place was so hard to find it only made sense for Leo to send the same man again.

"I just follow orders," he was telling Sam. "And the boss said, see if anybody shows up to collect them. And if they do, get the disks and kill whoever came for them."

Sam tossed another shovelful of dirt to one side, then said, "The boss being Leo."

The man didn't reply to that. Instead, he looked over at Carrie. "Get that tin open," he ordered. "I wanna see for sure what's in it."

She was still so frightened she wasn't certain she'd be able to speak, but she managed to say, "The lid's taped on, I can't find the end of the tape, and there are about a dozen layers. I need a knife or something from the cabin."

There was a rifle in the cabin, and if she and Sam could just get inside, maybe...

But the man dashed her hopes by reaching into a pocket and producing a switchblade. His gun aimed at Sam's chest, he flicked the knife open, then edged closer to her.

"Put the tin on the ground and push it toward me with your foot," he told her. Once she'd done that, he said, "Okay, now shove back until you're leaning against that tree."

She scooted backward on her behind, not wanting to think about how cautious he was being. But if he kept that gun pointed at one of them every second until Sam had finished digging… Lord, she didn't want to think about that, either.

He slowly bent to pick up the tin, both his gaze and the gun still on Sam, who was lifting the shovel filled with earth. Then, faster than her mind could register it, Sam tossed the dirt toward his face and charged him with the spade.

They both went down, the tin flying past her head and the gun exploding with a deadly roar.

For an instant she was immobilized by pure terror. But she wasn't hurt. And both men were still in motion, struggling on the ground.

She pushed herself to her feet, frantically trying to figure out what she could do, and spotted the gun lying mere feet away. Her heart pounding, she rushed over and scooped it up with both hands.

Praying she didn't look as if she'd never shot a gun in her life, she pointed it in their direction and shouted, "Stop! Stop or I'll shoot!"

Both men froze. Then Sam started to shove himself up. But the other man lunged toward him like a striking snake.

Sam gave a sharp cry of pain and rolled to one side. His assailant leapt to his feet, the switchblade in his hand.

"It's just you and me now, baby," he said, taking a step toward her.

"Stop right there! And drop the knife!" she ordered, unable to keep her voice from quavering.

Even though she had the gun aimed straight at him, he took another slow step forward.

Her gaze flickered to Sam. He was trying to push himself up, but one of his legs was slashed. Around the cut, his jeans were dark with blood.

Her heart began pounding harder still. She might be the one with the gun now, but Sam could bleed to death!

Leo's guy edged forward another few inches, the blade of his knife glinting in a ray of sunshine filtering down through the trees.

"Don't take another step or I'll shoot," she said, her heart pounding. "And I told you to drop the knife."

He looked at it, then back at her, while she tried to recall everything she knew about guns. It wasn't much.

But this gun had gone off, which meant that if it had a safety, it wasn't on. All she had to do was pull the trigger.

And maybe kill him.

The thought sent a shudder through her. But if it was going to be him or Sam who died, there was no choice.

She waited, still holding the gun with both hands, its trigger hard as death against her finger. If he took one more step, she'd have to pull it.

A reptilian grin slowly spread across his face.

"You couldn't hit the broad side of a barn, let alone me," he said. "And if you was to pull the trigger on that baby, the recoil'd break your wrists."

"I'll take my chances if you don't throw down your knife."

He hesitated for another half second. Then, in a rush of motion, Sam hit him from behind. They went down again, Sam yowling with pain as they hit the ground.

But this time their attacker lost his knife. Carrie saw it flying through the air and followed it with her eyes until it landed in a pile of leaves and completely vanished from sight.

"Sam!" she shouted. "I've got the gun *and* the knife!"

INSIDE THE CABIN, using several lengths of rope from the storage shed, Sam tied Leo's guy securely to a kitchen chair. While he did, Carrie held the gun to the back of the man's head.

She kept her finger off the trigger, though. She was still shaking inside, and the last thing she wanted to do was accidentally take his head off at this stage of the game.

"All right," Sam said, grimacing with pain as he straightened up. "Search him. Take his wallet, car keys, whatever you find."

"Sam, shouldn't we have a look at your leg first?"

"In a minute."

Even with the man trussed up like a Thanksgiving turkey, she felt very nervous about searching him. But she made herself do it. Sam's face was so drawn and pale that he looked as if he'd pass out if he exerted himself much more.

Aside from keys and a wallet, she discovered a cell

phone zipped into a pocket of his pants and a second gun—a small one in an ankle holster.

Silently thanking the powers that be that he hadn't gotten to it, she put everything on the kitchen counter beside the cookie tin. While she was doing that, Sam asked the man where his car was parked.

He didn't answer.

"Look," Sam snapped. "We can make this—"

"Sam?" she interrupted. "I really think we'd better have a look at your leg."

He hesitated, then nodded and hobbled after her into the main room. There, he eased his jeans down to below his knees, wincing several times as he did. Then he cautiously lowered himself onto a wooden chair. His thigh was pretty much covered in blood, and more was still oozing from the wound.

Swallowing hard at the sight of it, Carrie knelt beside him and gingerly examined the slash. It was a good six or seven inches long, but when she looked closely she felt a touch of relief. It didn't seem terribly deep.

"It's not that bad," he said, peering at it himself. "It hurts like hell, but I think it'll be okay if we just wrap it up and get the bleeding stopped."

"I'll see what I can find."

She dashed into the bathroom, where there was a bottle of antiseptic and some adhesive tape in the cupboard. When it came to bandages, though, there was only the small plastic kind.

Grabbing the antiseptic, the roll of tape and a pair of nail scissors, she raced upstairs and rummaged through bureau drawers until she found one containing sheets and pillowcases.

After yanking out one of each, she hurried back down to Sam.

"Here," she said, handing him the sheet and scissors. "Start ripping that into strips while I clean the wound."

"No, we'll let a doctor worry about that later. As long as we stop the bleeding—"

"Sam, you were rolling around on the ground and your jeans are covered in dirt. If we don't get this clean you'll end up dying of tetanus. It's going to sting," she added, pouring antiseptic onto a corner of the pillowcase.

Sam steeled himself against the pain, but still cried out when Carrie dabbed at the gash. The antiseptic hurt worse than being slashed had.

"I'm sorry," she said, looking at him with tear-filled eyes. "I'm sorry. But I don't want you to die."

"I don't want to die, either," he told her. Then he gritted his teeth and started ripping the sheet apart for all he was worth—reminding himself how much he wanted a future with her. And telling himself he'd never have one if he were dead.

Each time she dabbed at his leg, pain shot through his entire body. After what seemed like hours, she murmured, "Okay, I think that's the best I can do."

"Good, then let's get it bandaged," he said quickly, before she could reconsider.

"I need your leg free so I can wrap it better. I'm just going to take off your sneakers and get your jeans the rest of the way off."

That done, she wound the strips around and around his thigh, securing each one with adhesive, until she must have used up half the sheet.

"My leg's so fat I won't be able to walk," he muttered when she was done.

"You shouldn't be walking, anyway. But I'll go see if I can find you another pair of pants."

"Wait," he said. "Before you do that, get the cookie tin and I'll open it."

She hurried into the kitchen and returned carrying the tin. As she started for the stairs, he attacked the tape with the nail scissors.

It took forever, but he got the lid unsealed. Then he just sat staring at the tin, afraid that, regardless of Carrie's assurance, the disks might not be inside.

Finally, he tugged off the lid—exposing a padded brown envelope. And sure enough, inside it were two computer disks, each safely ensconced in a clear protective jacket.

They were labeled "Disque Un" and "Disque Deux," and on the bottom left-hand corner of both labels were the words *LAC BAR*.

His high school French was rusty, but he knew *lac* was lake. He wasn't sure about *bar,* though he thought it might be the term for pub, just as it was in English. Making a mental note to ask his receptionist, who was from Montreal, about it, he glanced at the labels again.

As far as he knew, Leo spoke only English and Italian. So the French words struck him as strange. But he was much more curious about what was on the disks than about how they were labeled.

Just as he was wishing he had a laptop in the car so he could check out the data right away, Carrie came back downstairs.

"Look what I've got," he said, holding up the disks.

She gave him a wan smile. "I knew they'd be in there. And look what I've got," she added, holding up a pair of casual cotton pants with an elasticized waistband. "They should more or less fit you."

The less would be in the legs, Sam thought. He'd guess Linda Willenzik's father couldn't be more than about five foot six. But short pants were better than none at all.

Carrie helped him into them, cringing every time he sucked in his breath with pain. Then, as she started wiggling his sneakers back onto his feet, she said, "What do we do with our friend in the kitchen?"

"We leave him where he is."

"Sam, we can't do that. Can we?"

"I don't see that we've got a choice. We're sure not taking him with us. And if we call in the cops, they'd have to let him phone his lawyer."

"Leo," she said.

"Exactly."

"But…we can't leave him tied up here forever."

"No. Which means our time frame just got tight as hell. The minute he talks to Leo, the jig's up, as my father would say. When Leo hears it was us who came to collect the disks, he'll know we're involved in this up to our eyeballs."

"Oh, Lord," she whispered. "What on earth are we going to do?"

"First of all, we're going to get the Willenziks' rifle and the stuff you took off him and put everything in my car. Then we'll head back to Toronto, pop those disks into my computer and find out what's on them."

"And after that?"

"We'll have to see," he said. He had another idea, but he wasn't going to mention it yet. It was such a long shot that he didn't want to get her hopes up.

SINCE SAM'S LEG WAS throbbing so hard he couldn't drive, Carrie had car control, and she made good use of it.

Despite his protests, she drove straight to Peterborough to find a hospital. She didn't have much faith in her medical skills, and she wasn't taking any chances.

"This is going to make our time frame tighter yet," he complained as she pulled up at the emergency entrance. "We're liable to be here forever. People die of old age in emergency departments."

"I don't care. I'm not having you die of a knife wound."

She helped him inside, did her best to impress on the receptionist that he was a dire emergency, then went back out and parked the car in the lot.

When she came in again, he was nowhere in sight.

"He's with a doctor," the receptionist told her. "You were lucky. It's been a real slow day."

Thinking they'd never in a million years have gotten such quick attention in a Toronto hospital, she dug their attacker's cellular out of her purse.

She hadn't called Linda Willenzik's work number

often enough to remember it, but there was no difficulty getting it from Information. The difficult part, she thought, making herself punch in the number, was going to be explaining things to Linda.

As much as she didn't want to do that, she had to. If there was any change of plans and Linda or her parents arrived at the cabin and found Leo's guy there, they'd be at risk. Even without a gun he was probably dangerous as hell. And if somebody untied him...

Well, there was simply no way around telling Linda what had happened. But it didn't prove to be any easier than Carrie had anticipated. Every time she paused for breath, Linda said, "I just don't believe this."

Finally, though, Carrie reached the end of the story. "So we just need a little time," she concluded.

"Carrie, there's absolutely no way you can leave him there! Either you call the cops or I will."

"No, look, I realize this seems crazy, but it's the only thing we can do."

"Oh, no, it's not. I've already been having nightmares about the night he showed up at my apartment. And now he must be so pissed off that... What if he unties himself?"

"He won't. Sam was so thorough that Houdini wouldn't have been able to untie himself. Look, just give us twenty-four hours," she pleaded, pulling the number out of the air. "Make sure nobody goes near the cabin for twenty-four hours and...

"Linda, I can't go into any more details right now,

but if this guy gets a chance to talk to Leo too soon, Jenny, Sam and I will all end up dead.''

"But…this whole thing is insane!"

"I know it is. And if there was anything else we could do except leave him right where he is, we would. But there isn't.''

"Well…he's not going to die of thirst or anything overnight, is he?''

"No, people can go for days without water.''

"Then… Look, Carrie, I really want to help you. But if my parents ever found out I'd said you could leave him there, they'd disown me.''

"Then we never had this conversation. And there's no way you could know any of what I just told you, because the last you heard I was going to the cabin to get something Jenny left behind. Period.''

"Well…let's rework that a little. I'll give you your twenty-four hours. Then I'll call the police and say you just let me know what happened. That I called them as soon as we got off the phone.''

"Okay. It's a deal. And thanks *so* much.''

It was a little after two o'clock when she'd been talking to Linda, and a little later still when Sam slowly hobbled into the waiting room.

"You're okay?" she said, hurrying over and wrapping her arms around him.

"Fifteen stitches later, I'm just fine. But they gave me a local anesthetic, and I've got a hunch I won't feel this good after it wears off. By the way, the doctor said you did a great job.''

That made her smile. Then she thought about the

deal she'd agreed to with Linda and the smile vanished.

"I'll run and get the car," she said, "and pick you up at the door. We don't have any time to waste."

"I think we've got enough time for me to walk to the car."

"No, we haven't. We're at less than twenty-four hours and counting."

WHEN SAM LIMPED INTO the reception area of Port Credit Custom Boats, Monique, his receptionist, looked as if there were a hundred different questions she was dying to ask. But all she said was "Hi. I've got lots of messages for you."

He nodded. "And I've got a question for you. What does *bar* mean in French?"

"It would usually be referring to a kind of fish," she said, eyeing him curiously. "A bass, it would be in English."

"So Lac Bar would be Bass Lake."

"Right."

As he started toward his office, Monique's gaze followed him.

"A minor accident," Carrie told her.

"Ah."

"Very minor," he elaborated, knowing his entire staff had to be wondering what the hell was going on in his life. Normally, he put in long days at the boatyard, and six of them a week when things were busy. But not the last little while.

First he'd been conspicuously absent. Then he and

Carrie had spent a couple of days holed up in his office, searching the on-line databases—although he didn't imagine that's what his employees figured they'd been doing in there.

After that he'd been gone again, so they could check the stuff in the library. And today, of course, they'd been up in the boonies, practically getting themselves murdered.

To top things off, he'd shown up now with a bad limp and wearing a pair of pants that didn't even reach his ankles. Telling himself that, somewhere along the line, he should probably explain a little about what had been happening, he hobbled into his office and headed for his desk, leaving Carrie to close the door behind them.

Carefully stretching his throbbing leg straight out ahead of him as he sat down, he turned on the computer.

The doctor in emerg had given him a prescription for painkillers and told him to have it filled before the anesthetic wore off. But he hadn't mentioned that to Carrie any more than he'd told her he was supposed to stay off his feet.

That order would obviously be impossible to follow. As for the prescription, she'd have insisted on stopping to have it filled, and he hadn't wanted to waste any more time. By this point, though, he was starting to think it would have been a smart idea.

"Here they are," she said, carefully sliding the disks out of the padded envelope. "The keys to the vault, as Leo called them."

She hovered over Sam's shoulder while they waited for the computer to complete its warm-up. Then, his anticipation level soaring, he slipped Disque Un into drive A and typed in the command to copy it. He didn't want to risk playing around with the originals for even a minute. If he screwed them up, it would be game over.

"Here goes," he said, hitting the enter key.

All that got him was a message saying the disk was protected and couldn't be copied.

"Dammit," he muttered.

"Now what?" Carrie asked.

"I guess we try Disque Deux."

Not surprisingly, that got them the same message.

"If they can't be copied, the data's probably protected, too," he said. "I'll have a shot at getting it on screen, but I doubt that'll work."

As much as he didn't want to mess with the originals, his options were limited, so he tried to call up a directory for drive A.

The computer asked him for a password.

He tried *Leo*. When that didn't work, he tried *keys* and then *vault*.

"No dice," he told Carrie. "I'm just wasting time."

"Then what do we do?"

"We'll have to take the disks to someone who knows more about this sort of thing than I do."

"You've got someone in mind?"

He nodded. "I had this computer custom-built, because I needed some special features to run my design programs. And the guy who put it together's a high-tech genius. I guess we just have to hope he's genius enough to get us what we want.

"Dammit, it's almost five," he added, glancing at his watch. "He's only a few blocks along the Lake-shore, but if he closes at five, we're liable to miss him."

"Can you phone ahead? Tell him we're coming?"

"Good idea." He checked the number and called, feeling more than a little relieved when Wally an-swered. As it turned out, he wasn't closing until nine.

Sam shut down the computer, then painfully got to his feet and followed her out to the reception area.

"Sam?" Monique said, gesturing at the stack of messages still sitting on her desk. "Aren't you going to at least look through these?"

"I'll get to them tomorrow."

"Tomorrow's Saturday."

"Oh...well, I'll get to them eventually," he told her, thinking things were pretty bad when he didn't even know what day of the week it was.

He and Carrie made it out to the car and he gave her directions to Computers and Things. When they got there, Wally was sitting at a table littered with computer parts—minding the store and working on a job at the same time.

"Hey, Sam," he said, his glance flicking briefly to Carrie. "What happened?" he added when he noticed the limp.

"Nothing serious. But as I said on the phone, I need your help with something."

He introduced Carrie, then explained what they were after.

"Shouldn't be a problem," Wally said, taking the disks. "I've got software that's cracked all the security protection I've tried it with so far. How soon do you need results?"

"Yesterday would have been good," Sam told him. "But we only got hold of the disks today. We're really in a time crunch, and it's critical we get the information."

"I'll do what I can. But the software basically just tries every conceivable combination of letters and numbers that could be a password—one after another. And there are a zillion possible combinations, so how long it takes to break in is really a matter of luck."

"What's the longest it could take?" Carrie asked.

"Oh, the max so far is about twenty-four hours."

She gave Sam a worried look.

"We don't have that long," he told Wally.

"Well, I'll start the program running right now," he said, getting up and heading over to a computer. "And it can check both disks at the same time," he added, sticking them into two drives. "Beyond that, we'll just have to hope for the best.

"But give me a call later. A little before nine. And if I don't have anything for you by then, I'll leave it running all night and you can call again in the morning. It's the best I can do."

Sam nodded. They couldn't ask for more than his best. "There's one other thing. Do you have a really small but good tape recorder?"

"Hey, I've got a model you won't believe. You want to see it?"

"I want to buy it."

The recorder Wally produced was smaller than a TV remote and used an answering-machine-size tape. But he assured Sam its tiny mike would clearly pick up a conversation from across a room.

After they'd tried it out and Sam paid for it, he and Carrie started for the door, his leg almost killing him. As much as he hated to waste even another minute, he was going to have to give in and get that prescription filled.

When they stepped out onto the street, he gestured toward the drugstore a few doors down the block. "I just want to stop in there for a minute."

"Sure. But you *are* going to tell me what the tape recorder's for, aren't you?"

"For getting a taped confession from Leo," he said, trying to make it sound as if he did that sort of thing every day.

Carrie stopped dead and simply stared at him. "Have you lost your mind?" she said at last.

"Possibly," he admitted. "But our time's running out. And I'm hoping that whatever's on those disks will give us something to use as leverage."

"What if Wally's software doesn't find the passwords in time?" she asked as they started walking again. "Or what if whatever's on them isn't any help?"

"Well, I've got another idea."

"Which is?"

He opened the drugstore's door. "I thought that after we're finished in here, we could go looking for the murder weapon."

"What?"

He shrugged. "Or the next best thing."

CHAPTER FIFTEEN

DESPITE THE FACT that her curiosity was killing her, Carrie knew a busy drugstore wasn't the place to ask Sam to elaborate about looking for a murder weapon. So while they waited for the pharmacist to fill his prescription, she feigned interest in the magazines on display.

But as soon as he'd taken one of the pills and they headed back outside, she said, "Remember what Jenny thought Leo would have done to cover up the murder? She figured he'd have burned that area rug and the clothes he was wearing. And that he'd have dumped the sculpture in the middle of some lake."

"Which was probably a good guess."

"Then why would we even think about looking for it? It would take police divers a hundred years to search every lake near Toronto. So unless you haven't bothered telling me that you're psychic, that you know exactly where we should go looking..."

Since they'd reached the Mustang, she let that thought hang while she unlocked the car and climbed into the driver's seat.

"Where to?" she said while Sam eased himself in beside her. "Or should I ask which lake?"

"Nope. No lake. Head for Yorkville."

Yorkville? She glanced at the clock on the console. She hated driving in heavy traffic, especially to the center of the city at the height of rush hour.

"*Are* you psychic?" she asked, starting the car and pulling away from the curb.

"No. And I didn't mean we were going to go looking for the actual murder weapon. It was one of a limited edition, remember?"

She nodded.

"Well, when Leo was showing it to me, he mentioned he'd bought it at a gallery in Yorkville. And an artist would have all his work with one gallery, right?"

"Normally, yes."

"Then if we can find the gallery, we might be able to get our hands on one of the identical sculptures. And if we went strolling in on Leo with it, we'd panic the hell out of him.

"He'd think, oh my god, they know I killed Bud and they've got the murder weapon. And after that, all he'd be thinking about was how advanced the field of forensics has gotten. Because regardless of what he did with his sculpture, if the experts got their hands on it they'd be able to pull DNA evidence off it. And while he was in panic mode, we could press our advantage and try to talk a confession out of him."

"But..." Carrie paused. There were so many potential ways that scenario could go wrong that she didn't know which one to start with.

Their original plan had been to try to find evidence they could take to the police. This idea was something else entirely. An extremely frightening something else.

But as Sam had said earlier, their time was rapidly running out. Assuming they could find one of the other sculptures—and that was a major assumption—maybe trying his idea was the only choice they had.

Still, it made her very, very nervous.

"Leo isn't the panicky type," she said at last, deciding to start with one of the lesser problems they might encounter.

"But I think he is. Even though he doesn't normally show it, from everything Jenny told us he must have panicked after he killed Bud. Why else would he have believed she'd lie to the cops for him? She found that totally out of character, remember?

"And why else would he have trusted her enough to send her off with his precious disks? Same explanation. Because he was in panic mode. So if we could panic him again…"

"Sam…look, I've got serious concerns about this whole idea. If Leo *did* believe we had the actual murder weapon, he'd have nothing to lose by killing us right then and there.

"And tomorrow's Saturday. We wouldn't be walking into his office with it, where there'd be other people around. We'd have to go to his house. And walking in there would be like walking into a lion's den."

Sam shrugged. "I'm not exactly thrilled with that part of the plan, but we've got time to refine it. And don't forget we have three guns. Mine and the two we took from our friend back at the cottage. We'd hardly be defenseless."

"No," she said slowly. But neither would Leo. He wasn't the type who'd ever be defenseless, whether he was in panic mode or not.

She stared out at the cars crawling along ahead of them, barely able to imagine herself and Sam trying to best Leo Castanza.

"What if he had his sculpture melted down?" she said when that thought occurred to her. "Then he'd realize we suspected him, but he'd know we couldn't possibly have the real evidence. That we were only trying a bluff, and—"

"Uh-uh," Sam interrupted. "He'd have wanted to get rid of the murder weapon as fast as possible, not mess around with it. Besides, melting it down isn't something he could have done himself. He'd have needed someone with a blast furnace. Or a serious welding torch, at the very least. And he wouldn't want anyone knowing what he was up to."

"No...I guess he wouldn't."

Glancing at the clock again, she wondered exactly how many galleries there were in the Yorkville area. Off the top of her head, she'd guess somewhere around thirty. And even if most of them didn't close till nine o'clock on a Friday evening, it would be pretty hard for her and Sam to hit all of them.

Telling herself not to be pessimistic, she looked over at Sam. "Okay, if we actually manage to get our hands on another one of the sculptures, how do we make Leo believe it's the real McCoy? His was number one of the edition. The others will all be marked with different numbers. So if he asks to see—"

"We won't be able to let him."

"But that would tell him it wasn't his."

"Well, we'll have to figure some way of—"

"Sam, that's not the plan's only serious flaw. Once he's over his initial panic, he'll realize that to get our hands on the actual murder weapon we had to know exactly where to go fishing, or digging, or whatever. And how do we make him believe we did?"

"I don't know. I guess you're right. There are a few flaws. But first let's worry about finding the sculpture, then we'll figure what to do about everything else."

BACK IN THE EARLY 1800s, when Toronto was still a town named York, Yorkville had been the village at the Yonge Street tollgate into the city.

Now that Toronto had grown into a major metropolis, Yorkville was right at the heart of it—a fashionable district made up of streets lined with carefully renovated nineteenth-century homes and a hub of trendy shops and restaurants.

Most of the businesses were housed in historic buildings, but Carrie parked under the modern complex of Hazelton Lanes, a low-rise enclave of pricey condominium apartments and exclusive shops. It had to be as good a place to start as any, because it contained a few galleries as well as an art-antique shop on the lower level.

She and Sam headed for that first, hoping against hope Leo hadn't bought his sculpture there. If he'd purchased it resale, the gallery that represented the artist could be anywhere in the world.

When they asked the owner about a cast bronze sculpture of a polar bear, he shook his head.

"Sorry, he didn't get it here. But I do handle that sort of thing occasionally. I could put you on my mailing list if you like."

"No, thank you. We were just interested in that particular piece," Carrie told him.

"One down, only thirty-something to go," Sam said as they left the shop.

She forced a smile. But thirty-something was an awfully large number. And despite the painkillers, it was obvious his leg was going to slow their progress.

"Maybe we'd better split up," she suggested. "Why don't you take Cumberland, while I check the other places in here and then do Yorkville Avenue."

"And we'll meet up where and when?" he asked, glancing at his watch.

When she checked hers, her heart sank. The traffic on their way downtown had been horrendous, and it was almost six-thirty.

"We should be able to cover those two streets by eight," she said. "So let's touch base then, at the corner of Yorkville and Hazelton. That way, if neither of us has turned up anything, we'll still have time to try the galleries on Scollard."

Sam nodded and limped off without another word. She watched him for a moment, thinking that getting into most of the galleries involved climbing stairs. Then, telling herself there was nothing she could do about it, she started for the upper levels of Hazelton Lanes.

When she struck out there, she began making her

way along Yorkville Avenue, growing more discouraged with each place she tried.

At this point, she and Sam had virtually nothing. Oh, they were almost certain the victim had been Beauregard ''Bud'' Racine. But they couldn't even be a hundred percent sure of that. As for the rest, they didn't know what was on those disks and they had no sculpture to even attempt a bluff with.

If that was where things stood by tomorrow afternoon, they were going to be in big, big trouble.

She reached the last gallery on the street and climbed its stairs. Her legs were aching; she could only imagine how Sam was feeling.

Inside, the sole sales assistant was in the midst of a conversation with an elderly couple. While Carrie waited, in her mind's eye a cosmic clock was ticking away the last hours of her life. Sam's too, of course. It was a most unsettling image.

Impossible as it seemed, each day she woke up more in love with Sam than she'd been the day before. She wanted to live the rest of her life with him, not die with him before their time.

And even though he hadn't come right out and said he wanted to spend forever with her, he *had* said he loved her—enough times that she'd lost count by now. And she loved him so very much.

What better basis could there be to build a future on?

Telling herself they had to do whatever it took to ensure they were going to *have* a future, she eased closer to the sales assistant as the couple finally turned away.

But when she asked him about the sculpture, he simply said, "Sorry, it's not one of our artists."

Barely remembering to thank him, she hurried back outside, a fresh worry beginning to nag at her.

Jenny had told her that Leo was always trying to impress people. Which meant he might not have bought the sculpture in Yorkville at all. Maybe he'd just said he had to imply he'd paid top dollar. If that was the case, she and Sam were wasting precious time.

She hurried down the street toward the corner they'd agreed to meet at, hoping he'd had more luck than she had. The instant she spotted him, though, the dejected slope of his shoulders told her he hadn't.

When he glanced her way, she tried to look optimistic, but apparently she didn't do a very good job of it. As she reached him he said, "Nothing, eh?"

She shook her head.

"Well, let's head for Scollard Street."

He was limping more than he had been earlier, and she wished she could tell him to just sit down someplace and wait for her. But with less than an hour until nine o'clock, she might not be able to cover the remaining galleries by herself.

They split up again to try the first two on Scollard, then rejoined forces outside the third. It had a handwritten sign taped on the inside of the door reading, Back in Ten Minutes.

"Sure," Sam muttered. "Whoever's on night shift probably went home early."

"Well, we can try the rest and come back to this

one," she said. Then, just as she was turning away, something inside caught her eye.

She focused on it, afraid she was hallucinating. Or that it wasn't the right one.

"Sam?" she said, pointing at it.

"Hallelujah!" he cried. "That's it!" He wrapped his arms around her and hugged her tightly.

"Now we just have to pray the night shift *didn't* go home early," he said, releasing her. "But while we're waiting, give me the phone and I'll see if Wally's found anything."

She dug the cellular out of her purse and waited while he made the call, desperately hoping Wally would have something for them.

But after Sam asked, he shook his head, dashing her hopes.

"Sure," he said. "Probably by morning you will. But if you do get anything before you close up, give me a call, would you?" He rattled off the cellular's number, then said goodbye.

They waited anxiously as ten minutes passed. Then another five.

Finally, a young woman came hurrying along the street and apologized all over herself for having kept them waiting.

"It's all right," Carrie told her. "But we saw something through the window that might be just perfect in our living room."

The woman unlocked the door and trailed them over to the sculpture.

"It's wonderful, isn't it," she said as Carrie ran her fingers over the cast sculpture of a polar bear.

"The artist is really establishing a reputation for himself, and this is number seven of a limited edition of only ten. It's the sort of piece that will appreciate significantly in value. I think your wife loves it," she added, smiling at Sam.

He nodded. "How much is it?"

"Twelve thousand dollars."

"Ah. Well, for that kind of money, I'd want to see how it looks at home before we make a final decision."

The woman nodded. "Of course. Many of our clients feel that way. I can take a twenty percent deposit, fully refundable if you decide the piece isn't right for you, and let you have it until…would Monday give you enough time to decide?"

Sam nodded again, already digging out a credit card.

WHEN THEY STOPPED at a restaurant on their way home, Sam told Carrie to park the Mustang where they could keep an eye on it from inside. He wouldn't want to have his car stolen under any circumstances, but especially not when the sculpture was in the trunk.

Now that they had it, even if they didn't learn what was on those disks, there was at least a chance they'd be able to trick Leo. Of course, it would be better if they did know what was on the disks. And a whole lot better still if they could devise a plan for exactly how to bluff Mr. Castanza.

So far they were way too short on specifics. And they didn't manage to come up with the perfect approach over dinner, even though it was their sole topic of conversation.

As they rose to leave, Sam looked across the table at Carrie, wondering if he should try to convince her it would be better if he went to see Leo alone tomorrow. But he knew there wasn't a hope in hell she'd go for the idea.

The prospect of having her with him, though, made him awfully uneasy. She was a gutsy lady, which was one of the things he loved about her. But he had no illusions about how dangerous trying to get a murder confession out of Leo was going to be. And if anything happened to her...

If anything happened to her, he'd kill Leo with his bare hands. It was as simple as that.

He stared silently out into the night as she drove, until they were nearing ''their'' telephone booth and she said, ''Do you think I should stop and call Jenny?''

''No, we've got nothing definitive to tell her, so why not wait until tomorrow.''

''Until after we've seen Leo.''

''Right,'' he said. Then, trying to ignore the thought that after they'd seen Leo they might both be dead, he reached across and rested his hand on her thigh.

The warmth of her body heat filtering through the thin fabric of her dress made him want her almost desperately, even though he knew he couldn't make love to her with his leg the way it was.

''What are you thinking about?'' she asked, glancing at him.

"About how much I love you."

That made her smile.

"I'm glad," she said. "Because I'd hate to love you as much as I do and not have you love me back."

"There'll never be any chance of that."

"Never?" she teased.

He shook his head, wanting to say more but not letting himself. He had a horrible feeling that if he told her how very much he loved her, he'd be tempting fate.

She turned down his street and a minute later they were pulling into the driveway.

"What do we do with the sculpture?" she said, cutting the engine. "Sleep with it under our pillow?"

"That might be a bit uncomfortable, but we'll take it inside and lock up very carefully."

Once that was done, they headed upstairs, pain shooting through Sam's leg with each step he took.

"I should sleep in the guest room tonight," Carrie said when they reached the top of the stairs. "With your leg the way—"

"Not on your life." He pulled her into his arms and simply held her, breathing in her scent.

As always, it made him think of a lush spring night in the country. It was a scent he'd love for the rest of his life.

He kissed her forehead, her nose and finally her mouth. She responded with a passion that almost made him forget the pain in his leg. And almost made him forget the rest of his life might consist of mere hours.

SIMPLY WAKENING to the warmth of Sam's body against hers was enough to make Carrie smile. Then reality began seeping into her drowsy mind and the smile vanished.

Checking the clock radio, she saw it was a few minutes past seven. A few minutes past seven on the day they had to confront Leo—and somehow make him admit he'd murdered Bud Racine.

She lay there, silently telling herself they were going to do it, trying to convince herself they really could. Then she climbed out of bed, grabbed her robe and went downstairs to start coffee and hit the shower.

When she came back up to the bedroom—two mugs of coffee, a glass of water and Sam's painkillers on a tray—he was awake but pretending not to be.

Putting the tray on the bedside table, she leaned over and kissed his shoulder, ever so careful not to touch his injured leg.

"Mmm, that's nice," he said sleepily.

"How does your leg feel?"

"Stiff as a board. And it still hurts like hell. But one of those pills will help."

He gave her a lingering kiss that left her longing for more, then cautiously eased his legs over the side of the bed and reached for the water and pills.

"Good coffee," he said, moving on to that.

She merely nodded, then sat down beside him. If he could play it cool, so could she. Finally, though, she couldn't stop herself from saying, "Today's the day, huh?"

Reaching over, he rested his hand on hers. "We'll make out okay."

She nodded again, wishing she could honestly believe they would.

"The doctor said to keep my leg out of the shower. But I'll get cleaned up as well as I can. After that, it should be almost time to call Wally."

"And if his software still hasn't hit on the passwords?"

"Let's not worry about that unless we have to."

Draining the last of his coffee, Sam tentatively pushed himself up off the bed and tugged on his robe.

"You'll be okay on the stairs?"

"Sure."

Resisting the urge to hover and make certain he negotiated them all right, she stayed where she was and drank more of her coffee. Finally, the faint sound of him turning on the shower told her he'd made it to the bathroom safely.

Assured of that, she headed into the guest room and was just about to start drying her hair when the phone rang, making her jump a foot. Thinking her nerves were in even worse shape than she'd realized, she hurried back into Sam's bedroom to answer it.

When she said hello, there was a moment's silence. Then a man said, "Is this Sam Evans's number?"

She recognized the voice and her heart skipped three beats. "Wally?" she said. "It's Carrie. I was with Sam yesterday."

"Oh. Right. Is he around?"

"Yes, but he's in the shower. Are you calling about the disks?"

"Uh-huh."

"I'll take a message," she said, then held her breath.

"Okay, just tell him my program did its thing during the night. I came in early, so anytime he wants to stop by I can get at the data for him."

"Oh, that's fantastic. Absolutely fantastic. Thanks, Wally, and we'll be there just as soon as we can." Hanging up, she hugged herself.

Even though she was still frightened half to death about the prospect of confronting Leo, there was no denying things were looking better.

Last night they'd located the sculpture. And this morning they were going to learn what was on those disks.

Clearly, they were on a roll. And didn't good things always happen in threes?

Or was that only bad things?

CHAPTER SIXTEEN

SAM SAT STARING at Wally's computer screen, trying to make sense of what he was seeing and feeling more discouraged by the second. He'd been counting on the disks being a major help, but it didn't look as if they were even a minor one.

"You're certain that's it," he said to Wally.

"Uh-huh. Only one file per disk. With a fifteen-digit number in one and a single word in the other. The rest is empty space."

"Okefenokee." Carrie read the single word aloud again. "What on earth's the significance?"

"Unless Leo's been peddling swampland in Florida," Sam said, "I don't have a clue."

"I'll bet it doesn't have any real significance," Wally told them. "But don't worry about it, because I think I know what you've got here."

Sam looked at him, hoping to hell he wasn't just trying to be funny. "You mean you know and you've been holding out on us?"

He grinned. "I wasn't holding out. Only waiting for the right moment. But I'd say you've got the account number and password for a Swiss bank account—the keys you need to access it from anywhere in the world."

"A Swiss bank account?" Carrie said. "You mean you think *that's* why the labels are in French? I was assuming the disks came from Quebec."

Wally shook his head. "I figured I knew what they were yesterday, the minute I saw the labels. But I didn't want to say anything until I'd seen the data."

"Just out of curiosity," Sam said, "how do you know about Swiss bank accounts?"

"I used to have a customer with one. He died a year or so ago, and his wife was like you. She had his disks but didn't know how to access the data on them. And when she contacted the Swiss bank, they were going to make her jump through a bunch of lengthy legal hoops. So she came in to see if I could help her."

"And you did," Carrie said.

"Uh-huh. And once I got what she needed, we were able to simply log in and transfer money from Switzerland to her local bank."

"It's as easy as that?" Sam asked.

"Basically, yeah. When you open a Swiss account, you specify which local account you want linked to it. Then you just transfer funds via computer and make your physical deposits or withdrawals down the street."

When Sam turned to Carrie, her face was mirroring his own excitement. "'The keys to the vault' suddenly makes sense," he said.

She nodded, then looked at Wally once more. "But why are two tiny bits of information like that on separate disks?"

"Security. Account holders are supposed to store

the disks in separate locations to minimize the risk of some crook accessing the account.''

''And what about the Bass Lake bit?'' Sam asked. ''Do you know what that refers to?''

''Bass Lake?''

''Yeah, at the bottom of the labels. Lac Bar. Bass Lake.''

Wally grinned again. ''Sam, I don't know about any Bass Lake, but on the other disks it was the account holder's initials printed there.

''Just give me a second, though. I'd better see what those guys want,'' he said, starting toward a couple of teenagers who'd wandered in.

''LAC BAR is initials?'' Sam said to Carrie.

''Oh, Lord,'' she whispered. ''Leonardo something Castanza and Beauregard A. Racine. B.A. were the initials on his office window.''

''You're right.'' His mind racing, he tried to recall Leo's middle name. He'd seen it only weeks ago on the contract Leo had signed for his boat. But what was it?

''Antonio,'' he said as it popped into his head. ''Leo's middle name is Antonio. So this has got to be a joint account. And, hell, I'll bet these disks were *really* stored in two separate places—that Leo had one and Bud had the other, so neither of them could access the account on his own.''

''And on the day of the murder,'' Carrie said, ''Bud turned up at Leo's with his disk. And... But why would he bring it along? Wouldn't he have memorized the password? Or the number? Whichever he had?''

"Memorized a fifteen-digit number? I doubt it. But why he brought it along isn't important. The point is *that's* why Leo's computer got turned on while Bud was there. The two of them must have been accessing the account when they got into their argument. Then, in his panic, Leo just didn't think about turning it off."

"Oh, Sam! Everything's starting to add up! Bud goes to Vegas, then reappears after only a few days—but tells his neighbor he's going right back."

"Which probably means he'd been losing at the tables and needed money," Sam added, picking up her train of thought. "So he came home to get some from that account."

As he finished speaking, Wally turned away from his other customers and headed back across the shop. When he reached them, Sam said, "Can you give us a couple of blank disks? With Disque Un and Disque Deux labels that look like those? With LAC BAR on them?"

"Labels that *look like* those? Hey, we're talking modern technology here. I can make you identical copies."

"Terrific. And while you're doing that, I'm going to write out some notes I want to leave with you—along with the real disks. If you haven't heard from us again by closing time tonight, you've got to get everything we've left here to the RCMP. To someone as high up as possible."

"Hey, are you serious?"

"Deadly."

THE CELLULAR THAT CARRIE and Sam had taken from Leo's hired gun had lost its charge, so they went back to Sam's to phone Leo. Carrie just didn't feel up to doing it from a pay phone.

Actually, she barely felt up to it when she was sitting on the living room couch—Sam on one side of her and the phone on the other.

"You'll be fine," he said as she dug Leo's cards out of her wallet.

"I sure hope so, because if I don't sound normal it'll make him suspicious."

"No it won't. He'll just think you're worried."

"And boy, will he be right," she said, forcing a smile.

"Carrie, we're almost there. Once we've been to see him, it'll be over. Jenny will be able to come home. And you and I won't find ourselves looking over our shoulders every ten seconds. We'll be normal people again."

She managed another smile, thinking how wonderful that would be. But they weren't there yet, and she was very afraid they never would be. Not with an obstacle like Leo Castanza still standing in their way.

Her fingers trembling a little, she punched in his home number. When his machine answered, she hung up without leaving a message.

"Jenny's mentioned that he often goes into the office on Saturday mornings," she said, trying that number.

She got another machine, then hit voice mail when she tried his cellular. "He's either talking on his cell or he has it turned off," she told Sam, punching in the number for the answering service.

Finally, she got a real person. "Mr. Castanza's line," a woman answered. "May I take a message?"

"Yes. My name is Carrie O'Reilly. Would you please tell Mr. Castanza that I have to speak to him urgently. Tell him it's about my sister, Jenny. And that it's extremely important."

"And your number, Ms. O'Reilly?"

"Oh, yes." She gave the woman Sam's number, then hung up.

"Did I sound desperate enough?" she asked him.

"You should have been an actress," he said, wrapping his arm around her shoulders and pulling her close.

She rested her head against his chest, breathing in his autumn scent and trying not to think about what might happen when they saw Leo.

But that was precisely what she had to think about. What the two of them had to think about.

"Sam?" she made herself ask. "Exactly how are we going to play this scene with Leo? And if you say we're going to play it by ear, I'll smack your sliced-up leg."

He kissed her nose. "I think we've figured out enough of the story to convince him we know everything. Our major problem's going to be getting him to admit the truth."

"And there's no way around having to do that, is there."

"Uh-uh. Between the disks and what we know, the police might have enough to put together a case. But building one takes time, whereas if we can tape Leo confessing to murder, they'd arrest him so fast he wouldn't know what hit him.''

''Before he could arrange to have us killed,'' she said. Since the thought was constantly hovering in a corner of her mind, she figured she might as well voice it.

Sam kissed her again, on the lips this time, then said, ''Leo's not going to have us killed. We won't let him. Once we've got him on tape, we'll be handing the police their case on a silver platter.''

''You're saying police, but you mean RCMP, right? That's who you told Wally to contact.''

''Yes, but if we really do end up with a confession, we won't have to worry about Leo's friends on the force. We'd be talking about one of the city's top criminal lawyers being charged with murder. That would be such a high-profile case it would be too risky for anyone to try tampering with.''

''*If* we end up with a confession.''

''I know,'' Sam said quietly. ''It's a big if. But Leo's the kind of guy who always wants everyone to think he's brilliant. And he screwed up here. So if we can get him trying to explain that away…

''Well, if he thought there was no risk, that it didn't matter what he said because he was going to kill us anyhow, he just might say enough to incriminate himself. And I've thought of a way to make him figure he's in complete control.''

As Sam outlined his idea, Carrie kept telling herself it *could* work. But only if things fell into place perfectly. And she couldn't help thinking the odds were against that.

They had to try something, though, before Linda Willenzik called the cops. Once she told them there was a lowlife tied up in her cabin, they'd go and collect him. Then he'd get his opportunity to phone Leo. And if Leo learned it was Carrie and Sam who'd shown up to get the disks, he wouldn't open his mouth in front of them, let alone say enough to incriminate himself.

Telling herself that line of thought was totally counterproductive, she forced every ounce of her attention to the last of what Sam was saying.

"So what do you think?" he concluded.

Before she could begin to tell him, the phone rang. Nervously, she picked up.

"Leo!" she said when it proved to be him. "Thank heavens you called. I really need your help. I've heard from Jenny and she's in big trouble."

"Where is she?" he demanded.

"I've got to talk to you in person."

"Well, that would be a little tricky at the moment. I'm at the golf course and I'm just about to tee off. You do know where Jenny is, though?"

"Yes, but I just can't get into what's happening over the phone. Look, I hate to interrupt your game, but I've got to see you as soon as possible."

There was a moment's silence before he said, "Okay. Can you go to my house?"

"I can go anywhere you'd like."

"Okay. Be at my house in an hour."

"YOU KNOW, IF I WAS wearing boots I'd be shaking in them," Carrie said, pulling into Leo's driveway and parking behind his Caddy.

"Then it's just as well you're wearing sandals," Sam told her. "Ready?" he added, giving her a forced-looking smile.

"*Terrified* would be more accurate."

"We're going to do it, Carrie. It's two against one. How can we lose?"

Even though she could think of a hundred different ways, she merely dredged up a smile of her own, then reached into her purse and turned on the tape recorder.

After checking that its tiny mike, attached to the handle of her purse, was virtually invisible, she popped the trunk and got out into the heat of the day, positive that Leo was watching from inside the house.

Heart hammering, she took the carton the sculpture was packed in from the trunk and set it on the driveway. That done, she opened Sam's door and gave him her arm to lean on as he eased himself out of the car.

"Do I look helpless enough?" he whispered.

"You look as if you're dying," she whispered back. And he really did look sick. Perspiration was beading on his forehead—compliments, no doubt, of the jacket he was wearing to conceal his Beretta.

"You okay with that weight?" he asked when she picked up the carton.

"As long as I only have to carry it into the house."

They'd barely reached the steps when Leo opened the front door.

"I wasn't expecting you, Sam," he said. "But what the hell happened to your leg?"

"A little accident at the boatyard."

"Little," Carrie repeated. "He practically passed out on the way over here. He should be in the hospital."

Leo nodded. "Looks as if he should be. So what are you doing here?"

"Oh, this thing with Jenny," Sam said vaguely.

"Yes...well, come inside where it's cool." Leo gestured at the carton as Sam dragged himself up the front steps. "What have you got there?" he asked Carrie.

"Something for you," she told him.

"Oh?" He stepped back out of the doorway to let them in, then closed the door and turned toward the living room.

"Let's go into your study," Sam said. "This thing we've brought is for in there."

"Oh. Sure."

As Leo started off, Carrie shot Sam a so-far-so-good look, but she wasn't feeling any less frightened.

Once in the study, she set the carton on the coffee table in the conversation area. Then she sat down on the chair next to Sam's, while Leo sank into one of the two on the other side of the table.

"Open it," Sam said, nodding toward the carton.

Leo glanced from one of them to the other. "What's this got to do with Jenny?"

"You'll see," Sam assured him.

Shrugging, he pulled open the carton's flaps and

started taking out the packing material. A second later he stopped, his face losing three shades of tan.

"What the hell...?" He glanced up at them again, and when he did, he turned even paler. Sam had produced his Beretta and was pointing it at him.

"We were here poking around after the murder," Sam said. "And I noticed your sculpture was gone."

"What murder?"

"Was there more than one?" Sam produced the phony disks and set them on the table, their labels facing Leo. "I was referring to Bud Racine's murder. You know, the fellow you used to share this bank account with.

"But as I was saying, I noticed the sculpture was gone. And I figured the forensic folks would appreciate us finding it for them. So I... Oh..."

"Sam!" Carrie cried as he slumped forward.

Before she could move, Leo lunged across the coffee table, seizing the Beretta and rapidly stepped away from them.

"You two are fools, just like Bud was," he muttered, training the gun in their direction.

"And you're not?" Sam asked, his voice little more than a wheeze. "If you were partners with Bud, I'd say—"

"We weren't partners."

Sam took a slow, deep breath. When he spoke again, he sounded more like himself. "Those disks tell us you were. You were teamed up with a third-rate lawyer who—"

"I was *not* teamed up with him." Leo gave them a cold smile. "But we won't worry about that. This gun puts me in charge now, and I want a few answers. Did you access that account?''

When Sam didn't reply, Leo leveled the gun at Carrie. ''Did you?''

Her heart pounding, she said, ''I don't know what he did. I wasn't there.''

Leo eyed her for another second, then aimed the gun at Sam.

''Go ahead, Leo. If you're going to kill us anyway, it may as well be now.''

''Dammit, Sam, tell me whether you've taken money out of that account or not.''

''You know I couldn't actually take money out. All I could do was transfer it into another account.''

Leo's face turned purple. ''Damn you to hell! You moved some of it into Bud's account, didn't you?''

''No. I moved *all* of it.''

Leo looked at the disks.

''They're not going to help you,'' Sam said. ''There's nothing on them about how to get money out of Bud's personal account. But I know how to do it. And luckily for you, I'm willing to make a deal.''

''Oh?''

''Yeah, because Carrie and I would rather not get shot. So A, you don't kill us. And B, you tell me where the money came from in the first place. Do those two things and I'll give you back your share.''

''Why do you care where it came from?''

Sam shrugged. ''Simple curiosity. Or maybe I'd just like the satisfaction of forcing you to tell me something you don't want to.''

''You're not forcing me! I'll tell you, but only because it makes no difference. Breaking into that account puts you in such deep shit you'll never be able to say a word about any of this.''

Leo paused, as if reassuring himself that telling really wouln't make any difference, then said, ''All right. What happened was that Bud had a friend on the Ontario Securities Commission who figured out a perfect scam. He didn't want to be involved in pulling it off, but he was willing to turn a blind eye. Only he wanted to be paid for that. And for the idea, of course. Paid up front. And Bud didn't have enough money.''

''So he came to you,'' Sam said.

''Right. And since they were talking ten million bucks, I figured it was an ideal way to top up my retirement fund. It still will be,'' he added, ''once I've got my share back. And you're sure you can get it out of Bud's account?''

Sam nodded. ''But I've got one more question. Why did you kill him?''

Leo glanced at the Beretta he was still pointing in Sam's direction, then looked back at Sam. ''I'm going to give you a free piece of legal advice. You knew Bud was dead, yet you withheld the information from the police. Then you stole ten million dollars. Under the law, that's what moving money out of someone else's account amounts to.

''I just want to be sure you realize that if you ever open your mouth about my being involved with Bud's death, you'll wind up spending a very long time in jail.''

Sam shrugged.

''You *do* understand what I'm telling you.''

"Yeah, I understand."

Leo looked at Carrie. "You're in the same boat. And you'd better make sure your sister's clued in, too."

"I will," she said, her heart pounding harder than ever.

"We *both* know where things stand, Leo," Sam said. "So now tell us why you killed him."

It was so long before Leo spoke again that Carrie didn't think he had any intention of telling them. Then, at last, he said, "Because we'd agreed not to touch the money until the time was right, but he wanted at it."

"Oh?" Sam said. When Leo didn't continue, he added, "Then you didn't really have a perfect plan at all, did you. Not if Bud—"

"It *was* perfect! We got the money without a hitch. All we had to do was let it sit, because there's always a paper trail with securities. And if Bud had suddenly started spending money like crazy—which is exactly what he'd have done if he'd had it—people would have asked questions. Ones with answers that could have implicated me.

"So part of our deal was to leave the account untouched until after his father died. Once he'd come into an inheritance, nobody would have wondered about him having a lot of money.

"But he decided he couldn't wait for however many years the old man had left. He showed up here insisting he wanted his entire share right then and there."

"And you told him no," Sam said.

"Of course."

"And he didn't like that, so you killed him."

"No. I killed him because I had no choice. Because he pulled a gun and made me start processing a transfer to his account. But that's enough about what happened. Let's talk about how long it's going to take you to get at the money. When do I get my half back?"

Sam shook his head. "That's not going to happen. I lied. I'm not giving it back."

"Really." Leo stood staring at Sam, his eyes cold as steel. Then I'll just have to figure out how to get at it myself," he said at last. "But first I'm going to make sure neither of you can interfere."

He pointed the gun at Carrie.

She could see his finger tightening on the trigger. She watched while he pulled it.

A dead click filled the study.

"Sorry, Leo," Sam said, the gun from the ankle holster already in his hand. "That one's not loaded. But this one is."

"WELL, I'D SAY THAT'S IT for the moment." Detective Rice closed his notebook. "And I guess you'll be darned happy to get out of here. Police headquarters is hardly a fun place to spend your Saturday afternoon."

Carrie glanced at Sam, thinking they were finally going to get the chance to talk to just each other. They hadn't had a second alone together since they'd arrived at Leo's.

"I'm glad we were able to get in touch with your

sister," Rice added to Carrie. "Even if it did take us a while."

She nodded. She was glad, too. Rice had let her talk to Jenny, and just recalling the conversation made her smile. They'd both ended up in tears. But they'd been tears of relief that Jenny would be on her way home just as soon as she could get a flight.

"I guess all that's left to say is thanks again." Rice pushed himself up from behind his desk. "For a couple of civilians, you two did one heck of a job. Or maybe I should say it was a heck of a job for *anyone* to have done."

He saw Carrie and Sam to the elevator, saying goodbye once more when it arrived.

There were half a dozen other people in the car, so they rode down to the main floor in silence. But the minute they walked out of the building into the late afternoon sunlight, Sam draped his arms around her waist and drew her to him.

"We *did* do one heck of a job, didn't we," she whispered.

"Yeah, we sure did."

"But you know, when Leo asked if you'd taken money out of that account, I was absolutely terrified."

"*You* were terrified? How do you think I was feeling?" He smiled down at her. "I didn't know what the hell to say. It had never even crossed my mind he'd ask something like that. And all I could think about was that if I said the wrong thing, he'd realize I was winging it. And Lord only knows how things would have turned out then."

"But you didn't say the wrong thing. And everything turned out fine.'' She rested her cheek against his chest, the solid thudding of his heart reinforcing the fact that their nightmare was over and they'd really made it through alive.

''The only good thing about all this,'' he said against her hair, ''is that if it hadn't happened, you and I would probably never have met.''

''Probably not,'' she agreed, willing him to go on.

He didn't, and that started an uneasy feeling snaking around inside her.

When he'd told her he loved her, she'd never doubted him. But what if her definition of love and his were entirely different? Maybe his love for her was a drift-away kind of love. And if it was, now that they no longer had a life-or-death crisis in common, he'd gradually drift right out of her world.

He continued to hold her in his arms, apparently as oblivious as she was to everyone else on the street. But the silence between them lengthened. And as desperately as she wanted to ask what he saw happening to them from here on in, she couldn't.

So instead, she finally said, ''Sam and Carrie's big adventure.''

''What?''

She looked up and met his gaze. ''It's already starting to seem as if this all must have happened to someone else. Like in a movie—*Sam and Carrie's Big Adventure*.''

That made him laugh. And his laughter made her think how much she loved hearing it. And how wonderful it would be to hear it every day for the rest of her life.

"So now that the adventure's over?" he said. "Are you going to be able to live without so much excitement?"

"Excitement? Oh, Sam, that wasn't excitement. Excitement is a roller coaster ride, or a trip to an exotic destination, or—"

"Or a wedding?"

"A wedding," she repeated slowly, even though his words had started her heart racing. "I guess some weddings are exciting. Maybe that depends on the people involved."

"Well, why don't I tell you about the ones I've got in mind. The groom's such a tough guy that people are always slashing him up or pointing guns at him. And the bride's an absolutely gorgeous illustrator who moonlights as a private eye."

A feeling as warm as the sunshine began bubbling inside her.

"And after they get married," Sam continued, "they spend their honeymoon in some really exotic destination."

"That sounds pretty exciting to me," she murmured.

"Good," he said softly. "I was praying it would."

HARLEQUIN SUPERROMANCE®

From April to June 1999,
read about three women whose
New Millennium resolution is

By the Year 2000: *Revenge?*

The Wrong Bride by **Judith Arnold.**
Available in April 1999.
Cassie Webster loves Phillip Keene and expected to marry
him—but it turns out he's marrying someone else. So
Cassie shows up at his wedding...to prove he's got
The Wrong Bride.

Don't Mess with Texans by **Peggy Nicholson.**
Available in May 1999.
Susannah Mack Colton is out to get revenge on her
wealthy—and nasty—ex-husband. But in the process
she gets entangled with a handsome veterinarian,
complicating *his* life, too. Because that's what happens
when you *"Mess with Texans"!*

If He Could See Me Now by **Rebecca Winters.**
Available in June 1999.
The Rachel Maynard of today isn't the Rachel of ten
years ago. Now a lovely and accomplished woman,
she's looking for sweet revenge—and a chance to win
the love of the man who'd once rejected her.
If He Could See Me Now...

Available at your favorite retail outlet.

HARLEQUIN®
Makes any time special ™

Look for a new and exciting series from Harlequin!

HARLEQUIN
Duets ™

Two __new__ full-length novels in one book, from some of your favorite authors!

Starting in May, each month we'll be bringing you two new books, each book containing two brand-new stories about the lighter side of love! Double the pleasure, double the romance, for less than the cost of two regular romance titles!

Look for these two new Harlequin Duets™ titles in May 1999:

Book 1:
WITH A STETSON AND A SMILE
by Vicki Lewis Thompson
THE BRIDESMAID'S BET
by Christie Ridgway

Book 2:
KIDNAPPED? by Jacqueline Diamond
I GOT YOU, BABE by Bonnie Tucker

2 GREAT STORIES BY 2 GREAT AUTHORS FOR 1 LOW PRICE!

Don't miss it! Available May 1999 at your favorite retail outlet.

HARLEQUIN®
Makes any time special.™

IN UNIFORM

There's something special about a man in uniform. Maybe because he's a man who takes charge, a man you can count on, and yes, maybe even love....

Superromance presents *In Uniform*, an occasional series that features men who live up to your every fantasy—and then some!

Look for:

Mad About the Major
by Roz Denny Fox
Superromance #821
Coming in January 1999

An Officer and a Gentleman
by Elizabeth Ashtree
Superromance #828
Coming in March 1999

SEAL It with a Kiss
by Rogenna Brewer
Superromance #833
Coming in April 1999

Available wherever Harlequin books are sold.

HARLEQUIN®
Makes any time special ™

HSRIU

COMING NEXT MONTH

#830 THE WRONG BRIDE • Judith Arnold
By the Year 2000: Revenge?
One year ago in Boston, Cassie and Phillip fell in love.
Phillip had to return home to Ohio for family reasons, but he
promised Cassie he'd come back, that they'd get married. He
broke his promise—and Cassie's heart—because she never
heard from him again. *Until now.* Her best friend, Diane, has
just received an invitation to his wedding…and he's marrying
another woman. The *wrong* woman!

#831 A MAN I USED TO KNOW • Margot Dalton
Love That Man
Some things don't change. Dr. Lila Marsden is on duty when
Tom Bennet is brought into Emergency. She recognizes him
at once—as a national rodeo champion *and* the man she used
to love. He's still living the dangerous life of the rodeo
circuit—one of the reasons they split up—and even though
he's a single father now, he's not ready to settle down.
Unfortunately, he still takes Lila's breath away.

#832 TEMPORARY WIFE • Joan Kilby
Marriage of Inconvenience
Veronique Dutot and Burton O'Rourke—each has something
the other needs. Veronique is a talented chef, while Burton
happens to need a chef for the new cooking show he's
producing. Veronique, who's from Tahiti, needs to stay in
Canada…and Burton offers to marry her. But a temporary
marriage of convenience soon leads to feelings that are
neither temporary nor convenient!

#833 SEAL IT WITH A KISS • Rogenna Brewer
In Uniform
A woman in the SEALs? Not in Mark Miller's navy. And he
can keep it that way by making life as tough as possible for
Lieutenant Tabitha Chapel—the first female recruit. But
Tabby's woman enough to take everything he doles out
and more.…